Colin + P

THINKING OF YOU
BOTH

DEADLY
Inheritance

Richard
Ann
x

Richard Allen

RICHARD ALLEN

Richard Allen is a retired police Superintendent who, in addition to uniformed duties, saw service with the CID, the Vice Squad, the Drug Squad and Special Branch.
Richard is the author of two best-selling works dealing with police management and leadership,
which were listed as recommended reading by both the US Department of Justice and the Police Staff College.

'DEADLY Inheritance' is the fifth in the
Mark Faraday Collection.

By the same author:

Non-Fiction:

Effective Supervision in the Police Service

Leading from the Middle

Fiction:

DIRTY Business

DIE Back

DARKER than Death

In the DARKEST of Shadows

Published by MARS Associates

ISBN 9781976852558

www.richard-allen-author.com

Member: Crime Writers Association (UK)
Member: International Thriller Writers (USA)

to:

Dr Rachel Hall MRCP MRCPath
Clinical Director
and
the doctors, nurses, reception staff
and volunteers
Oncology and Haematology Department
Royal Bournemouth Hospital
England
for their professionalism and exceptional care

-   all good people

'Revenge, at first though sweet
bitter ere long back on itself recoils.'

Paradise Lost
John Milton 1608-1674

Prologue

Thursday 11th May 1895

Boston, Massachusetts, United States.

THEY BOTH ENTERED. The two brothers. Herbert and Isaac. She was still there. *'Dirty Nell'*. Not her real name, of course. A cheap name coined by a drunkard and it had stuck. A name that did nothing to describe her beauty and grace that enhanced the dinginess and mean surroundings of this drinkers' den in Court Street. But they paid for her with as much dignity as they could, quietly and discretely, as agreed with the tavern keeper. They didn't rush or cause a stir. They drank their ale patiently with apparent expert attention to each sup as the premises became rowdier and more crowded, then, they slipped out, leaving the crude and raucous laughter behind, through the dank rear passage into the late evening shadows of the rear courtyard with *'Dirty Nell'*, across the wet cobbles of Congress Street, behind the Old State House, onto State Street and towards Long Warf and the *SS Mobile*. They walked carefully with their charge across the slippery cobbles, but purposefully with an air of authority, necessary as they approached the gangplank guarded by clay pipe-smoking seamen who acted as the sentries. The brothers nodded at the seamen who nodded in recognition, seamen who could barely contain their lecherous grins, as the little party reached the companionway that led to their cabin a mid-ships.

The *SS Mobile* was a 5,780 ton, single-screw freighter powered by triple expansion steam engines. She was equipped for a range of cargo including four hundred horses in stalls, but she also carried twenty-six passengers in luxury cabins. By 1898, the *Mobile* would be owned by the US War Department and have become the US Auxiliary Transport *Sherman* with accommodation for eighty officers, one thousand other ranks and one thousand mounts. But today, there were only twenty-six passengers including the redoubtable Colonel and Mrs R Drury-Lowe; the Reverend H G Martin; the Reverend and Mrs I C Sturgis; Doctor Francis Sercombe; Mr and Mrs J D Nasmith and their daughters, Miss Elizabeth, Miss Edith and Miss Louisa; together with the two brothers, Herbert and Isaac Smith, and their veterinary surgeon.

The two brothers were respected horse dealers, horses that were destined for Bristol, England. Some had already been allocated to the Bristol Fire Brigade and the Bristol Omnibus Company. By 1918 the brothers would have supplied the British Army with more than a third of a million mounts.

Meanwhile, on the bridge was the ship's master, Captain Sydney Sayland, pouring over the Admiralty charts as he made his final preparations to sail on the early morning tide. A storm was anticipated and the crossing would be hard. But Captain Sayland would sail across Massachusetts Bay, onwards to England. Sayland had met the two brothers on the outward journey. He had been impressed that they had been accompanied by their own veterinarian. Clearly, he concluded, these brothers were resourceful, prudent and caring business men who would take all reasonable steps to ensure that their valuable investment was safe.

The captain had not met *'Dirty Nell'*, but *'Dirty Nell'* was safe too.

Chapter One

Thursday, 20th March – more than 120 years later.

Bristol, England.

IT WAS DUSK, BLUSTERY, WET AND COLD when she landed at Bristol International Airport. The wind had ruffled her luxuriant and carefully styled hair but, otherwise, she looked good after her journey. She always looked good. Really good. And much younger than most admiring men would have thought. She was remarkably trim and fit with the most elegant of walks. One amongst one hundred and twenty-three passengers. Inside the Arrivals terminal, she waited for what seemed like an age amongst the milling crowd until the siren sounded, a yellow light flashed and the black conveyor belt jolted, then grumbled its way around a great oblong loop laden with suitcases, small and large, battered and pristine, colourful and dull. Her case wasn't dull. She didn't do dull. Her case was large, white and pristine. As soon as the suitcases appeared, fellow passengers pushed forwarded as if urgency was everything. But she was in no hurry and stood back, as well as she could, from the bustle and jostling with an air of disinterested dignity. There was no need for her to rush. She knew he would be waiting for her.

Once she had retrieved her suitcase, she passed care-free and elegantly through HM Customs and Immigration with the others, most of whom hurried by. Then she was in the bright and airy concourse. And he was there with his beaming smile and carrying a box-like present under his arm. He always had a present for her. But this present was very special and for a very special occasion. As always, the present had been carefully and beautifully wrapped with a large purple-coloured silken bow. They stepped towards each other and embraced and kissed. They spoke for a short moment, engrossed in each other's words like deadly conspirators — which, of course, they were. They hugged again before he picked up her white Samsonite suitcase, adjusted the handle and towed it effortlessly towards the taxi rank.

Chapter Two

Thursday, 10th April.

Bristol, England.

IT SHOULD HAVE BEEN LIKE ANY OTHER EVENING. It was not. Normally, Christopher Miller would arrive home between 6.30pm and 7pm. He was a wealthy, seriously-minded entrepreneur and corporate lawyer, but, he could also be fun, a fun released by Maria. As he approached his home he would convert to fun mode. He would stand under the portico at their elegant, glazed front door. He would ring the bell and call out: 'Special delivery, ma'am,' or 'Electricity company to read your meter,' or he would open the letter box and blow a tune on an Indian tuk-tuk horn or imitate angel signals, waving his arms up and down. And Maria would open the door and welcome her lover and soul mate home.

Today, at 6.13pm, the bell rang and the ornate, brass door knocker rattled. He spread himself over the vertical bevelled glass of the front door like Batman. Maria skipped along the hallway and opened the door. As she released the catch, his weight propelled the door inwards toward her. Blood spurted from the neck wound and cascaded from his mouth, accompanied simultaneously by a terrible, animal-like rattle of fearful choking. Arterial blood continued to pump, pumping now across the block-printed silk wallpaper in the hall to her left, from the single stab wound in his neck, as his heart raced in a vain effort to maintain pressure and, in so doing, accelerated the victim towards his inevitable death.

***

She had driven. Driven fast. Along Saville Road and Rockleaze, skirting Durdham Down, a city gem larger than Hyde Park, and now partially occupied for another six days by festive crowds, Patterson's Circus and the magnificent red, candy-striped big top. She turned right and right again, along oak-lined roads in this most exclusive of suburbs. She slowed her dark-grey Volkswagen Golf GTi and parked a hundred yards from the gates which provided her with an opportunity to get a feel for the location. She stood alongside her car for a short while sensing her surroundings, then walked to the main entrance gates. At the gates she produced her ID. The uniformed constable recorded the time: 18:49 – exactly one hour before sun set - wrote her name on his clipboard and ushered Detective Superintendent Kay Yin through the smaller, single wooden door in the brick wall that was alongside the large wooden double gates that gave access to Grange Lodge.

A Bath stone gravel drive swept from the double gates towards the house. Another officer, a detective, waited to escort her along the blue and white police-taped route towards the front door and the police gazebo, avoiding the driveway itself or the possible entry and exit routes of the killer, but Kay stood there quietly and sharply focused. Looking. Absorbing. Assessing.

It was a good-looking house. Grange Lodge. Modern. Large. Red brick. No ground floor extensions. No bolt-on conservatories or gawky loft additions. Not ostentatious. Not a lottery winner's house. Just quietly impressive and architecturally designed. The grounds with their neat lawns and discrete stone urns on pedestals, the carefully tended beds of shrubs and the tall pines casting their long evening shadows, were marred by a white police tent, the lighting rigs and two crime scene vans parked a little to the right. Police officers, mostly in white forensic coveralls, were milling about purposely, some huddled together, others pointing, some removing samples or taking photographs, others kneeling on the grass and gravel where the killer had more than likely been. She glanced about her again, making her own personal crime scene assessment. But time was passing.

'Okay, John,' she said. 'Brief me, please.'

'The deceased, ma'am,' said twenty-nine year old Detective Inspector John Harding, 'is Guy Hernandez, thirty-seven years, employed as a sales executive by Young and Sons, the Maserati dealership at Cribbs Causeway. He was returning a Maserati Gran Turismo S to its owner, Mr Christopher Miller, thirty-nine years, the owner of Grange Lodge, after its bi-annual servicing. It appears that Hernandez drove the car through the main gates, up the drive to the front door, got out, rang the door bell, was stabbed once in the neck from behind, fell forward and apparently grabbed the door knocker for support. As Mrs Maria Miller, Miller's Italian wife, opened the door,

Hernandez fell into the hallway and bled out within minutes of the door opening.'

'Police and medics arrived within four minutes, I understand?'

'Yes, ma'am,' replied Harding, slightly taken aback that the superintendent should already be aware of exact timings. 'The house alarm system has integral panic buttons. Mrs Miller hit the hallway button and the call was instantly routed to Force HQ.'

'But she made no phone call for an ambulance?'

'No, ma'am. Mrs Miller acted quickly and, apparently, calmly. She grabbed a thick scarf, Llama wool I believe, and tried to stop the bleeding. I think Mrs Miller has consoled herself that she tried all she could but, the truth is, he was dead by the time the medics arrived. I haven't disabused her of that thought, well, not at the moment. She's still pretty shaken up.'

Kay thought that Hernandez would have died well before the medics arrived, but let the opinion rest. 'And she wasn't alarmed or forewarned in any way by the deceased being up against the glass of the front door?'

'No, ma'am. Apparently Mr Miller is a bit of a joker when he arrives home. Mrs Miller thought it was him larking about.'

'And the man in the street?' she asked of the man whom she had seen being questioned by a detective in the back of an unmarked police car.

'That would be Paul Waterworth, a colleague of the deceased. He was following Hernandez in his own car. Once Hernandez had dropped off Mr Miller's car, Waterworth, who lives in Longwell Green, was going to drop Hernandez at his home in Hanham.' Kay thought that that sounded reasonable enough, with Hanham situated to the east of the city and on a direct route towards Longwell Green.

'Did he witness the attack?'

'No, ma'am. Waterworth and Hernandez left the garage at the same time, but Waterworth was delayed for a few minutes by a traffic accident at the White Tree roundabout. When he arrived the gates were closed and he just parked outside and waited. He says that the first he knew about the attack was when our units arrived with blues and twos.'

'Where was Christopher Miller?'

'He's a lawyer and broker, amongst other things, and was at his office in Queen Square. He arrived home at 6.42.'

'What other things?' she probed, her questions flowing relentlessly.

'He's a broker in stocks and shares, bonds and financial services; property development here and in Gibraltar and is the non-executive director of an investment banking division.'

'And how did Miller travel from his office to his home?'

'He was given a lift by a Miss Sarah Withers, his personal assistant.'

'Well, we seem to have lots of examples of the law of unexpected consequences – or do we?' She paused for a long moment. 'Where is Miller now?'

'In the kitchen, at the rear, with his wife.'

With most murders there is very often a friend or family connection somewhere. Preservation and integrity of evidence is vital. Kay posed the question. 'And no cross-contamination?'

'Mrs Miller has changed into a forensic suit and they have been kept apart,' then added: 'He's not very pleased, quoting various Acts of Parliament to me and emphasised the fact that he knows the Deputy Chief Constable.'

'Oh, that's good. I know the DCC as well, so we will have something in common,' she replied unimpressed at the reference to the austere and humourless Anita Winters, then thought for a few more moments. 'Describe the deceased?'

Harding was uncomfortable and hesitated before answering. He wasn't sure whether it was Kay Yin's petite

Oriental beauty or her probing questions. He found her difficult to assess. She was focused but alluring. She was serious, but when she smiled her smile was magnetic and disarming. But it was her dark, almost black, fawn-like eyes that unnerved Harding which were, at the same time, penetrating and captivating. 'Six-two; about one hundred and eighty, ninety pounds; black hair; an Italian with a Mediterranean complexion, wearing a dark grey rain coat.'

'And how long have Mr and Mrs Miller been married?'

'Just under two years.'

Kay looked towards the two-door Gran Turismo S. A beautiful car but, maybe not a family car. 'Any children?' she asked.

'No, ma'am.'

'And is Mrs Miller a lawyer and broker too?'

Harding was feeling the pressure. Kay's questions were reasonable but they seemed endless. 'No, I mean, yes … she's a lawyer. Works out of the same Queen Square premises. Miller owns the building, the top floor of which is his personal suite of offices, the other four floors Miller rents out as barristers' chambers. That's how he met his wife who worked for Stockley, Kray and Burgess, specialising in European trade law.'

'Any high profile cases, do you know of?'

'At the moment, I'm not aware of any, ma'am,' Detective Inspector Harding replied, but he felt as if he was appearing on the television show, *Mastermind,* with the inquisitor looking at him, awaiting his answers – or his errors. His answer was defensive and he replied with a slight edge to his voice. 'I will chase that up.'

Kay tried reassurance. 'It's okay, John, I've just arrived. And so relax. You've had a lot to do and you have already gathered some very useful background information.'

But his response was again defensive. 'I already have *actions* logged in respect of Mr and Mrs Miller, Waterworth, Hernandez, Miss Withers, Young & Son, Stockley, Kray & Burgess and the White Tree accident.'

'John, this is your first murder, isn't it?' she asked calmly.

'Yes, ma'am.'

'Okay, let's establish some ground rules, John, from here on in. My policy is to allow officers to use their brains, their initiative. I can't do everything myself, but I need to probe and ask my officers questions. But there should be no need for you to be on your guard with me,' she said. Kay looked directly at the detective with those eyes which were both captivating and penetrating. Whichever, they held John Harding's attention. 'This is your first murder and I only took up post at HQ CID seven months ago. Things are new for both of us. As is so often the case, we are confronted with what appears to be a clear, yet confusing, picture with some hard facts but little explanation. There's clarity where there is no clarity; patterns where there are no patterns and what appear to be hard facts, we know from experience, can so easily turn to dust. And so, I ask questions, John, not to catch you out, but to provide context so that I don't go blundering about. Also to provide an investigative focus, objective clarity and a fresh pair of eyes so as to make sure we are exploring all avenues. I'm here to get a job done – that's all.'

'Yes, ma'am,' he replied, although still wary of this thirty-three year old detective with an already formidable reputation.

'And so,' she asked lightly, 'how many bedrooms?'

'Five, two en-suite, and one bathroom, and a separate self-contained suite.'

'The self-contained suite is for a live-in relative or a staff member?'

'There is a live-in housekeeper, Mrs Mia Vickers, aged fifty-two, who occupies a pleasant two-room, self-contained suite at the rear, top floor.'

'And a gardener-handyman?'

'Not sure, ma'am,' he replied, frustrated that he was unaware.

'There will be one somewhere,' she mused to herself. 'Last thing, I think. The entrance gates are operated by way of a key pad and intercom. The victim, Hernandez, must have known the code or he used the intercom?'

'No, ma'am. The car is fitted with an integral dashboard switch. It seems that the victim simply activated it.'

'Would you know at this stage,' she asked gently, 'who has the entrance code?'

'The code for the entrance gates is the same as the house and I am told that it is only known to Mr and Mrs Miller and Mrs Vickers.'

'And have we any idea how the killer entered and exited?'

'I am pretty sure he came firstly to the rear of the house from the direction of The Downs and the circus,' he said, pointing in the direction of more blue and white police tape. 'The brick boundary wall that finishes at the front entrance gates, doesn't continue completely around the approximately one acre of the grounds. It joins a much older stone wall by some bushes and this stone wall is lower and not in the best state of repair. Some of the stones are missing on the exterior and would provide for an easy foothold. Any reasonably agile man could climb the wall. Some muddy, although indistinct, foot prints near the front door are consistent with the wet, soft earth near the stone wall. We've taken samples and the scene is being examined now. For the moment, I am working on the premise that the killer entered and exited at that point.'

Kay Yin thought for another few moments and concluded that there were no further questions she needed to ask at this stage. 'Okay. Thank you. A nice summary. One other thing, John. When we are in company with others, it's "Ma'am" or "Superintendent". It helps to remind our subordinates who is wearing the bigger hat and has a tendency to reassure the public that there isn't a sloppy chain of command. Otherwise, like now, it's "Kay". I'm comfortable with "Kay" – because that's the name my parents gave me.'

'Yes, ma'am.'

Kay didn't correct him. 'Okay, let's call in at the tent and then we can speak with Mr and Mrs Miller.'

***

The kitchen of Grange Lodge led out through large glazed doors to the rear patio and the setting sun. It was large and superbly equipped reflecting an Italian influence: the handmade Tuscany tiles, the Bertazzoni cooking range and Premio pizza oven. There was a central island, a collection of fragrant herbs hanging immediately above, together with bright copper pans, yet it was a kitchen-breakfast room dominated by a very English pine, farmhouse-like table surrounded by comfortable pine chairs with arms. Christopher Miller was seated in one of these comfortable chairs to the right wearing an expensive business suit, although he didn't look very comfortable at all. He adopted a critical evaluation posture with a right hand-to-face gesture, his index finger pointing up his cheek while another finger covered his mouth, the thumb supporting his chin. His legs were tightly crossed with his left arm across his stomach, head and chin angled slightly downwards. Kay had anticipated that he would have exuded concern for Maria, but no, there was an over-riding and smouldering resentment, maybe due to the attack in his home, the distress caused to his wife, the police intrusion and presence, the questions already posed by DI Harding or his loss of control. Whatever. Resentment, nevertheless.

Two crime scene officers were finalising their examination of a distressed and anxious, yet very composed, but clearly extraordinarily attractive Mrs Miller to the left between the table and cooking range. Detective Sergeant Sarah Bailey acknowledged Kay who raised her right hand as if to say 'Don't let me disturb you, Sergeant'. Miller merely glared. He didn't stand.

'Are you the officer in charge?' Miller's voice was cultured but frosty and demanding.

'You must be Mr Miller. I'm Detective Superintendent Yin, the Senior Investigating Officer.' Miller remained seated. Glaring.

'And about time too,' he said brusquely, making an exaggerated examination of his Patek Philippe wrist watch. 'You have only just arrived! Why the delay?'

'There is much to do, Mr Miller, before I enter your home,' she replied calmly.

'Well, I have already spoken with your Deputy Chief Constable who is expecting you to call her immediately.'

'Oh,' she asked enquiringly, 'does the DCC have information that will lead me to the man who murdered Mr Hernandez?'

Miller had assumed that the mention of Miss Anita Winters, the Deputy Chief Constable, would have resulted in some sort of sycophantic response, but Kay Yin wasn't into sycophancy, nor was her husband, Chief Superintendent Mark Faraday. For a short moment Miller was flustered, only to respond dismissively: 'I wouldn't know,' adding, 'I believe she wishes to talk to you about the way this investigation is being conducted and the unnecessary and intrusive behaviour of Inspector Harding here,' adding, as if his final comment would have a dramatic impact: 'I'm not reassured at all.'

Kay knew that families often reacted in very unexpected and varied ways. Sympathy and empathy were important, but Kay was determined to establish a professional working relationship with Mr Miller and had no intention of being distracted nor bullied. 'As far as I am aware, DI Harding has conducted himself in strict compliance with the established protocols, and so, the DCC is not my first priority. Let me tell you what *my* priorities are which I hope will reassure you, Mr Miller.'

Miller was taken aback. He had expected compliance. 'You don't consider ringing your DCC a priority?' he countered.

Kay didn't answer the question directly. '*Actions* have already been identified and enquiry teams are already active. Those activities were my first priority, Mr Miller. My second priority is your continuing safety and that of your wife.'

'Our safety?' he questioned, although the aggression in his tone had begun to lessen.

'One option that we will need to explore is that Mr Hernandez was not the intended victim, but *you* were. He was driving *your* car. His age and appearance is not dissimilar to your own. It could be that the killer thought that Hernandez was in fact *you*. That is a very *reasonable* option we must consider, along, of course, with others.' She paused but Miller remained silent, the enormity of what was being said registering. 'It was fast approaching dusk, Mr Miller, and the sun sets at the rear of your home. Mr Hernandez's arrival time at your home was not that far removed from your own routine. It follows that I must assume that the killer may return.' Kay continued in a matter-of-fact, no-nonsense way. 'My forensic team are very likely to be here for another three hours. Meanwhile, two armed uniformed officer will be outside your home until further notice. Another will be on duty discreetly in the road, outside your entrance gates, and an armed response unit will be ... well, very close indeed.'

'My third priority will be to visit Mrs Hernandez and her two young children. I will seek to reassure *her* that we are doing all we can to find her husband's killer and, hopefully, comfort her with the knowledge that he didn't die alone and that your wife and the medics did all they could to save his life. And then, and *only* then, will I call the DCC.'

The thought of the victim's wife and children, their suffering, seemed to shift Miller's self-absorbed focus. For a few moments he remained utterly quiet, the arrogance of his posture had gone. He had uncrossed his legs, leaned forward, elbows on knees, head in hands. Then he looked up, thoughtfully. Some long moments passed before he spoke again. Tears stung his eyes and the sharpness in his voice had lessened. He was hesitant but seemed determined to say what he knew he needed to say. 'I'm sorry, Superintendent. I have been rude to you both. It has been a shock. I just needed to comfort Maria and I wasn't allowed to hold her. That's all I needed to do ... I felt ... helpless.' A tear, a single tear, rolled down his left cheek. He made no effort to wipe it away. He knew it was there for all to see, but he didn't appear to be ashamed for it to be seen.

'There is no need to apologise to us,' she said gently. 'This is a difficult time, Mr Miller, but we need your help now, sir.'

'Of course, of course,' he replied eagerly, at the same time looking across to Maria, the thought of her vulnerability clearly distressing him. 'How can I help you?'

'You are a lawyer and a broker?'

'Yes, a little corporate law from time to time, although my main focus is stocks, bonds, but also properties.'

'As a broker, would you normally bring sellers to the table or buyers?'

'Oh, sellers,' he replied as if the choice was an obvious one.

'And do you own properties, develop them yourself?'

'Yes, large houses or small office blocks converted to apartments, that sort of thing. And I'm involved in some negotiations regarding the Bristol Port Company's expansion plans.'

Kay wanted to keep on track. 'In respect of acquisitions and brokerage, you obviously try and secure the best deals for your clients and your company?'

'Of course.'

'And so, there will be winners and losers?'

He thought of his recent enterprises, all of which had proved to be sound investments. All good. Some spectacularly so. 'There always are, of course.'

'And when representing clients, you fight for their interests against a competitor to secure the very best outcome for them?'

'Yes, but that is what I have to do.'

'Of course, sir. No criticism was implied. I understand that completely and, therefore, it would be helpful if we could have details of your clients - winners and losers - over the last three years.'

'Oh. That might be difficult,' he replied thoughtfully. 'Client confidentiality might get in the way.'

'I understand that too, Mr Miller, but I'm thinking here of details that would already be in the public domain, particularly those cases that were possibly acrimonious. It would be helpful if you could tell me of anyone that immediately comes to mind.'

He pondered the question, searching his memory, trying to identify possibilities amongst complicated cases involving numerous players. Kay glanced towards Mrs Miller, concern, or was it anxiety, etched into her smile, she wondered. Mr Miller answered. 'No one comes immediately to mind. But you have me concerned now. Negotiations are often tense, of course, finger pointing and table top thumping, but in the end we arrive at an agreement and shake hands. Now I'm wondering what would have been said later, after the handshakes, in the car parks following these meetings, or when the participants have returned to their offices and have had an opportunity to reflect on the numbers again.'

'One thing whilst it's in my mind,' asked Kay. 'My technicians have accessed your alarm panel. Who has the code?'

'Only Maria, Mia and myself,' replied Mr Miller.

'No one else would ever be given the number?'

'No, we are quite anal about giving out the number,' he replied with a smile towards his wife, acknowledging that it was he who was cautious about releasing the number. 'It's my number, the one I use for banking. I know you should have different numbers for your cards, your mobile phone, iPad, and everything else, but sometimes I get the numbers jumbled and we are very, very careful. Even Mia, whom we have no reason to mistrust at all, believes that the number is for the alarm and gates only and nothing else.'

The officers began to gather up their kit and the evidence bags as they finished with Mrs Miller who approached Kay and shook her hand. 'Thank you for taking the time to speak to us, Superintendent,' she said with a radiant smile, her luxuriant black hair flowing around her shoulders as she walked. 'I apologise for Christopher's abruptness. It was not intended. We worry about each other so.' She turned to him. They hugged unashamedly.

Tears filled his eyes as he spoke quietly to Maria, completely absorbed in what he was saying. 'I wasn't here. I couldn't protect you. I felt so bloody helpless.' He turned to Kay, bit his lower lip, collected himself and cleared his throat. 'I am usually so in control, but I lost it ... I lost it. I'm sorry about that.' He turned toward DI Harding. 'You didn't deserve that Inspector. I was angry with you ... not you, the situation, and rang Anita.' He looked at his watch. 'It's too

late now but I shall ring her in the morning and apologise …
'. His thoughts drifted back to the attack. 'I kept thinking
that if Maria had opened the door just a few seconds earlier
then she could have been stabbed.' Mrs Miller wiped the
tears from his cheeks. They both appeared to be needy
people concluded Kay, maybe needy in differing ways, but
needy nevertheless – and not a bad thing to be – an
assessment to be tucked away in the back of her mind. It
was a good moment for Kay Yin to ask more questions.

'Mrs Miller, European trade law is your area of expertise, I
believe?'

'Yes, that is my specialty but I work primarily for the EU
Procurement and Recoveries Unit,' she replied as she
leaned back onto the kitchen table as the forensic team
continued to pack away their exhibits and kit.

'You will need to help me here, Mrs Miller, what does that
unit actually do?'

'It's part of the EU Legal Services and deals with the
recovery of debts owed to the Commission.'

Kay pondered the answer and its implication. 'You are
based in Bristol, I understand?'

'I have an office here but I spend most of my working week
in Brussels.'

'I see. And your working week, is that Monday to Friday?'

'I fly into Brussel-Nationaal, usually at a little after 9am on Mondays and a car takes me to my office. I usually fly out on the 16:40 on Fridays. Every fourth week I have a long weekend, flying home at about 4pm on Thursday and back to Brussels on the first flight Tuesday morning.'

'What are you suggesting?' bridled a now concerned Mr Miller. 'Is my wife a suspect?'

'Oh, no,' she replied. There was a pause as she considered a further response. Now was as good a time as any. 'If we are going to find Mr Hernandez's killer and, maybe, more significantly prevent him from killing again, we, that is you and the police, need to establish a trust. And so, let me say this to you. I will not compromise this investigation, but I will be as open as I can with you both. In that spirit, if you are asking me if you are both, along with your housekeeper, *persons of interest*, then the answer is clearly yes.' Christopher Miller seemed stunned by her openness. 'Why?' she posed rhetorically. 'Because at the moment I am interested to understand why the killer of Mr Hernandez was so reckless, or unconcerned, that your home was occupied? Did he believe that your wife or housekeeper were not at home and therefore would not open the door? Yet the killer appeared to be aware of your routine? Was his intention simply to murder and leave the scene or was he frightened away by your wife answering the door so promptly? At the moment, it seems unlikely that this was a vehicle theft that went tragically wrong. There are plenty of other ways to steal cars, even an expensive Maserati. It seems unlikely that this was a bungled burglary. We will be investigating these possibilities, of course, but my gut reaction is that this was a deliberate, premeditated murder – of the wrong man.' Mr Miller held his wife's hands, all arrogance gone, replaced by deep concern. 'Are there any questions you have for me?'

'Yes, a lot,' replied Christopher Miller, anxiety muddling his thoughts, 'but I can't think of any at the moment. I have been so wrapped up in what could have happened to Maria that I haven't concentrated on the implications.'

'That's absolutely understandable,' she said tactfully. 'Let me leave you with my contact details and then I can introduce you to one of the uniformed officers, Constable John Clapp, who will be guarding your home tonight.'

***

Detective Superintendent Kay Yin programmed her satnav for Mrs Hernandez's address and drove along The Avenue, then left into Ivywell Road and up towards its junction with Rockleaze. But she didn't have to reach the brow to realise what it was that was ahead of her, like a dying orange sunset under dark, heavy, foreboding clouds. In front of her on Durdham Down itself were neat rows of parked vehicles, mostly cars, interspersed with SUVs and a few camper vans. She pulled her vehicle over the kerb to her right and parked on the grass. She got out and pulled herself up and stood on the bonnet, her black Italian-styled jacket and denim blue jeans stark against the horizon. Across the roofs of the vehicles she saw its heart, like a torch spluttering in the darkness. This spluttering torch rapidly developed into a large, ugly, voracious flame of bright fluorescent yellow and crimson-orange licking at the black, billowing smoke. She spoke into her police radio.

'Hotel Charlie Three to Control, over.'

'Go ahead, Hotel Charlie Three,' replied the Communication Centre's operator.

'Hotel Charlie Three, I am at the junction of Ivywell Road and Rockleaze. One-hundred yards in front of me is a vehicle in circus Car Park D well ablaze. Request fire brigade attendance. I will remain at scene, over.'

'Roger, Hotel Charlie Three. Wait one.' It was less than one minute before the operator spoke again. 'Hotel Charlie Three, fire brigade en route, ETA eleven minutes.'

'Roger that. I am now approaching the scene. Unless there is a senior uniform officer present, I will make myself prominent and require all uniformed officers to report on me most immediate, over.'

The Communication Centre called all uniformed personnel and directed them towards the fire and Kay Yin. She donned her yellow police tabard, secured her VW and sprinted towards the now blazing vehicle. Flames were leaping higher and the yellow and orange flames, now streaked with blue, mixed with the billowing black acrid smoke.

She clambered onto the bonnet of a parked car which gave her a panoramic view of the scene and so as to make herself a clear RV point. From this vantage point she was able to see the seven constables converge towards her from various directions. But she was also able to see the body in the blazing vehicle. By now the blazing vehicle's windows had blown. Against the intense yellow-white heat of the vehicle's interior, the front, side and rear pillars holding the car's roof in place gave the appearance of a black Gothic arch, in the middle of which was the silhouette of an erect, inert, monk-like body.

'Ma'am,' called out Constable Ann Giffen, 'there's a body.'

'Noted,' replied the superintendent as she jumped down from the car. She pointed her finger at each officer. 'Now listen in. Circle the fire and keep the public clear. Push outwards for thirty yards and secure the site the best you can and await the fire brigade. Your number one priority is public safety. Are we all clear?'

'Yes, ma'am,' replied the constables pleased to be able to respond to direct and clear instructions.

'But the body,' called out a defiant Constable Giffen.

'Concern yourself with the living, officer, not the dead,' Kay ordered sharply, noting the circus' little Austin Gypsy fire engine arriving. She also noted the remark made by Constable Giffen as the officer left to secure the perimeter.

***

Nicholas was a strikingly handsome man of Mediterranean, film star appearance, endowed with effortless charm. With heavy eyebrows, dark eyes and an engaging smile, he would easily attract attention. Nicholas was therefore noticeable. And so, Nicholas had not made the mistake of hailing a taxi. The use of taxis would form part of any investigation by the police, he speculated. And so he walked along the Circular Road overlooking the Avon Gorge, then into Ladies Mile, across Bridge Valley Road, past the stately Lord Mayor's Mansion House to his left, and up through the tree-lined Promenade, into Bridge Road and onwards towards Sion Hill. As he walked his gait became more confident, his countenance smug as he reflected upon his success. At last he felt free of the years of nagging resentment, stoked by a bitterness skilfully and mischievously generated by his mother and her mother before her, a bitterness that had become ingrained and had always been hard to suppress. Now the future was clear. He would be wealthy, not only with an inheritance secured but also a handsome bonus – he had not had to pay that sad drunkard, Victor. He reflected upon how clever he had been to dupe Victor. He had unobtrusively approached Victor's car and slid like a snake into the front passenger seat. They had chatted like old friends, during which Victor confirmed that he had wandered around the circus stalls making himself conspicuous. Nicholas had shown Victor the gun as if confiding in an old friend. He had shown Victor the 'hammerless' feature of the small, compact weapon. And Victor had been fascinated and intrigued as Nicholas knew he would be. Then Nicholas thrust the weapon into Victor's ribs and pulled the trigger. There had been a muffled crack and the muzzle flash had been completely obscured by Victor's clothing. If Victor sensed anything, it was very short lived. He had had no time at all to reflect upon Nicholas' duplicity.

Nicholas had already contemptuously cleared Victor's pokey and scruffy little one-bedroomed flat of anything that could connect him with murder. It was small; the fittings, fixtures and furniture rudimentary and took little time to search. He had searched every drawer, every cupboard, behind the mirror and a solitary picture hanging over the bed, and had removed two framed photographs from the wall. He had searched the dirty floor under the bed and in and under every kitchen and bathroom unit. He had found the diary – that was good - and odd notes screwed-up in a waste bin. These he had placed in a non-descript overnight bag. The search took little time and so he carefully searched the flat again until completely satisfied.

Now he continued to walk back towards the hotel taking the gentle, tree-lined gradient until he reached the little winding pathway on his right. He slowed his pace and pretended to search his pockets whilst, at the same time, checking that there were no other pedestrians about. Satisfied, he rid himself of the Forehand and Wadsworth .38 revolver, lobbing it, like a hand grenade, into the Avon Gorge near the suspension bridge. Now, all evidence had been disposed of, other than his jacket, but, of course, he had a plan for dealing with the jacket and trousers that would have undoubtedly been contaminated by gun-shot residue.

On his return to the Avon Gorge Hotel, Nicholas had gone to his room. Once he had entered and locked the door, he selected a small bottle of red wine from the mini-bar cabinet, then removed the laundry bag from the wardrobe before entering the en-suite and, removing his shoes and socks. He stood in the bath, then carefully removed his jacket, spilt red wine on the sleeve and a trouser leg, then placed them in the laundry bag, along with his socks. He stepped out of the bath and swilled away any possible residue with the shower and wiped over the tiled floor with a towel. The possibility of the police searching his room, he reasoned, before Housekeeping had cleaned in the morning, and discovering any residue on the bedroom carpeting or in the bathroom itself, was remote. Satisfied, Nicholas changed into a double-breasted blazer and clean trousers, left his room and handed the laundry bag to Reception for an overnight dry-clean. He was calm, confident and relieved as he made his way to the hotel's Bridge Café Restaurant. He thought of the romantic interludes in this very hotel over the years as he sipped a pre-dinner Prosecco, and reflected upon his night's work, his own careful planning, the search of the flat and then the eventual meeting with Victor.

Timing had been everything. And everything had worked to perfection. His flight into Bristol and his schedules placed him fortuitously in the city but not at the scene of the Grange Lodge murder. His visit had been a pre-planned business trip, arranged many months in advance with a member of the prestigious Society of Merchant Venturers who, since 1552, had included the most prominent and talented citizens of Bristol, one of whom was Desmond

Green of Greaves, Scutt and Pinnock, wine merchants of Denmark Street. These wine importers had been more than enthusiastically disposed towards the proposals made by Nicholas. There were trade obstacles to overcome because of the EU, of course, but their companies had the advantage of a centuries-old reputation and, as throughout history, trade would always be trade. And the meeting provided the perfect cover for his murderous plan, so brilliantly executed – he liked the expression 'executed' – and that is what Nicholas considered it to be, a legitimate and justifiable execution. For nearly one hundred years his family had been the victims, humiliated and disadvantaged because one old fool could not keep his trouser flies buttoned up. But soon he would not only have wealth assured but also unassailable social status and then high rank. As he thought of his future, his smug smile dwindled to be replaced by tight-lipped bitterness. Nicholas knew that his life, and that of his father, had not been uncomfortable, far from it, but he believed that their lives could have been much more comfortable and secure. It was that insecurity and a perceived favouritism, constantly confirmed by his mother, that embittered down the years and grew to infect his family like a contagious disease. And perception was everything. But, he needed to show respect. He had ordered flowers. Now, he glanced at the menu as an attentive waiter hovered.

After an exaggerated delay, he spoke to the waiter without looking at the man. He did not consider the waiter worthy of his attention. 'I will skip the starter and have the Ribeye,' adding, 'not well done, with salad and sweet potatoes, and a bottle of Cabanernet Franc Serbal,' he ordered, tapping his index finger on the key card to his room, a superior room, giving him a picture-perfect view of Brunel's masterpiece, the graceful Clifton Suspension Bridge, its twin supporting towers, massive wrought-iron chains and seven-hundred and two foot span, all beautifully illuminated.

'Of course, sir.'

Nicholas relaxed into the arms of his chair. He glanced about the restaurant, its pleasant décor and care-free diners. Life - and death - were good. He smiled a satisfied smile at the thought of his wit. The wine waiter appeared and poured and waited. Nicholas sipped the bright, pale red wine with its pronounced perfume as if a connoisseur, although he did not have a discerning pallet. He nodded approvingly to the wine waiter as the first waiter returned. The first waiter removed a knife, replacing it with a steak knife. At first Nicholas was irritated by the apparently slothful attention of the waiter, but then stared at the razor-sharp knife. Nicholas' self-satisfaction and composure seemed to suddenly desert him. He seemed to be afflicted by some sort of rigor mortis. He leaned into the table. He held the table in front of him, both hands flat on the white linen, his thumbs pressed painfully to the underside of the table top. He seemed transfixed by either someone in the far distance or by a monumental, all-consuming thought. There was no one in the far distance. There was a monumental, all-consuming thought.

'Are you alright, sir?' enquired a concerned waiter. Nicholas didn't reply. 'Sir. Are you alright?' the waiter asked again, anxiety in his voice, concerned that Nicholas might be experiencing a seizure.

Nicholas leaned back into his chair. He licked his dry lips. He offered a cadaverous-like grin to the waiter. 'Everything is fine, thank you,' he said, his voice strained and harsh. But now he thought that he was a victim yet again.

The waiter moved away.

But everything certainly wasn't fine at all for Nicholas Milano.

Nicholas had left Victor's killing knife in the blazing car.

***

Chief Superintendent Mark Faraday was in attendance. Durdham Down was part of his division – the Bristol City Division. The Bristol Constabulary had been formed in 1836. It had originally consisted of four territorial divisions. In 1974 the city force had amalgamated with the Somerset and Bath force, together with the southern division of the Gloucestershire police. During early 2006, the force amalgamated again with the remainder of Gloucestershire Constabulary to form the Severnside Police. It was a cost-cutting and efficiency-saving exercise and further reorganisation took place. Bristol City was divided into districts, then reverted to three divisions, becoming one mega-division in a force of only six divisions.

But the reorganisation had not been without controversy. Faraday's appointment to command the premier division that provided policing services for a population of over four-hundred thousand, and with more than seven-hundred staff under his command, was resented by some who saw this relatively junior, thirty-eight year old chief superintendent, gaining precedence over his longer-serving peers. In the working parties and negotiations that preceded the reorganisation, Faraday had been realistic. He had been prepared to accept the primacy of HQ Traffic for the policing of the main arterial roads within the forty square miles of Bristol. Whilst retaining elements of Divisional CID, he accepted that many of his detectives had transferred to Major Crime at HQ CID as part of 'rationalisation'. Kay was now part of Major Crime. But, in one area, Faraday was adamant. He had fought hard to retain command of Divisional Operational Support units, mobile units that would be deployed, along with a variety of other duties, in response to public disorder. He was adamant that he did not want units drafted into the city who had a superficial understanding of local issues and little empathy with the local population, a population who could view these units as something akin to the feared CRS of France, the Compagnies Républicaines de Sécurite.

***

Three fire engines from the local brigade arrived on The Downs within twelve minutes and promptly and efficiently went to work. The fire had spread, of course, before being brought under control. A total of twenty-four vehicles were damaged, eleven beyond repair. Then followed damping-down. Statistically, accidental car fires in the UK are declining, whereas arson is on the increase. It was prudent for Kay to assume that this particular fire was deliberate. Arson then. Arson and murder. More police officers arrived and the scene of the incident, now designated by Superintendent Yin to be a crime scene, was secured. But the detailed examination of the vehicle and its macabre occupant would have to wait many hours because of the residual heat of the vehicle itself and the ground upon which it lay. Meanwhile, a much wider area was screened off by a blue, seven-foot high police fence, photographs of the whole scene were taken, and the make and index numbers of every vehicle, damaged or otherwise, were logged in an area approximately fifty yards by one-hundred and twenty yards and interviews undertaken. Whilst damaged vehicles were confined to a much smaller area, the owners of other vehicles parked near the fire could, potentially, provide information leading to the identification and movement of, or anyone associated with, the deceased and the burnt-out vehicle.

Two detectives from Major Crime arrived and reported to Kay. Once her briefing and management of the scene were completed, Kay spoke on 'talk-through'. 'Hotel Charlie Three to four-nine-seven, over.'

Constable Giffen replied. 'This is four-nine-seven. Go ahead, over.'

'From Hotel Charlie Three. My private vehicle, a grey Golf GTi, is parked on the verge at the junction of Ivywell Road with Rockleaze. Report to me there please, over.'

'From four-nine-seven. Roger that. Five minutes.'

A little over eight minutes later, Constable Giffen, in a less than enthusiastic pace, approached Kay Yin who was standing against the front passenger door of her car. 'Constable Giffen, ma'am.' She looked sullen and apprehensive.

'Thank you. Nasty business,' said Superintendent Yin. Giffen wasn't sure whether the comment was a question or observation. She remained silent. 'Have you attended an incident like this before?' enquired Kay lightly.

'No,' she replied warily.

'Maybe a house fire with a fatality?' Kay probed reasonably.

'No,' she replied, a reply that was followed by silence, which the constable found unsettling, before asking: 'Why do you ask, ma'am?'

'I am wondering what you may have learned from this evening?'

PC Giffen seemed confused at the question. Her response was hesitant. 'There … there was a loss of life … a lot of damage … there was the potential for more fatalities … I suppose.'

'And, initially, with such a small number of officers we were able to protect the public, facilitate the fire brigade to do their work and preserve any forensic evidence. Do you agree?'

'Yes,' she replied hesitantly.

'Why do you think that was?'

'I don't understand.'

'Okay, let me pose another question to you. What powers did you and that small number of officers exercise in order to be successful in your task this evening?'

PC Giffen thought for only a short moment as if the answer to the question was self-evident. 'The public were told what to do and did it.'

'Yes, but why did they comply and what actual powers did the officers use to ensure that happened?'

The question seemed to confuse the officer. 'I don't know, ma'am.'

'I know', offered Kay, allowing the full answer to linger in the air before continuing. 'The powers that the officers used are those which capable officers use on a daily basis, details of which cannot be found in any law book nor are they contained in any Act of Parliament.' She paused. 'They are the powers of personality and persuasion.'

'I'm sorry, ma'am. I'm having some difficulty in following this and why you have singled me out.'

'Well, let me explain it to you, Constable Giffen. The population of France is the same as the UK, yet they have twice as many police officers as we do. Italy, population the same, but with four times as many police officers. Not only are the British police small in number, they are not regularly armed nor do they carry long batons. Our methods are based upon long-held traditions, mostly observed, where the public and the police realise that it is in their common interest to accommodate and co-operate with each other. The public are prepared, by and large, to play by the rules, and the police are, by and large, prepared not to abuse the rules. One Lord Chancellor referred to it as "the great confidence trick" that works to the mutual benefit of all. Part of that "confidence trick" is the image of capable and disciplined officers going about their duties diligently, responding to the guidance and directions of their more senior officers. Such an image gives reassurance and confidence to the public that their welfare is in good hands, that the police are well led and managed, and subordinate officers carry out the orders they are given. And so, the question is this.' Kay paused before continuing. 'Do you really believe, Constable Giffen, that referring to me as … what was it … oh, yes, a "callous Chinese bitch" would engender confidence amongst the public?'

Constable Giffen's jaw seemed to tighten under the unblinking and uncompromising glare of Superintendent Yin. 'I think … I think you misunderheard, I mean, you misunderstood … misheard me, ma'am.'

'No. No, Officer,' Kay replied emphatically, 'I heard you *very* clearly. So let me make something *equally* clear to you. From a personal perspective I don't care what you think of me. What I do care about is the effect that your comments could have had upon the public and your colleagues, where your colleagues may have been emboldened to have endangered themselves by attempting some sort of half-cocked rescue bid of a carbonised *corpse*.'

There was a silence as PC Giffen attempted to calculate her options. She opted for Option Two. Option One was to argue. Not a wise course. Option Two was better. 'Are you disciplining me?'

'I'm exercising my prerogative and giving you advice, Miss Giffen, on the assumption that you understand the disrespectful, racist and imprudent nature of your comment. If that should prove to be the case, then the matter is closed – unless by your future conduct you remind me of it - and I shall make my notes accordingly. Do you understand your position?'

'Yes, ma'am.'

'Then carry on.'

Chapter Three

Friday, 11th April.

Bristol, England.

HIS DAY DID NOT START WELL. During a fretful night and whilst eating his breakfast in the hotel's Bridge Café Restaurant, Nicholas had come to terms with his carelessness in leaving Victor's knife in the car, excusing the error, not on the grounds of his own sloppiness, of course, but on the grounds that the fire in the car had taken hold much quicker than he had planned, indeed anyone, could have reasonably anticipated.

Since the previous evening he had had time to convince himself that the knife could not be connected to him – which was very likely to be the case. But now his brittle confidence had been dramatically shattered again. He was shocked when he read the newspaper headlines during breakfast. *'Carnage at the Circus'* read one dramatic headline. *'Body Discovered in Blazing Inferno'* was another. But what really caught his attention was another headline: *'Murder City'*. True, it was a smaller article and below the front fold but amongst the words of *'Murder City'* was the reference to the stabbing of Guy Hernandez at Grange Lodge, the home of Mr and Mrs Christopher Miller. He couldn't believe what he had read. He read the article again. Slowly. He felt physically sick. He was so shaken by this turn of events that he couldn't finish his toast.

'More coffee, sir?' asked the unsuspecting waiter.

'Does it look like I want more bloody coffee?' snapped Nicholas.

Other dinners glanced across at Nicholas disapprovingly. The waiter backed away.

Nicholas was incandescent with rage at what the newspaper article had revealed but he recognised that he had now drawn attention to himself. Preservation dictated that he needed to remain calm. Remaining calm was unbelievably difficult, but, he disciplined himself and resolved not to draw attention to himself again. He beckoned the waiter across and apologised. He ordered more coffee with a show of bonhomie. As he drank his coffee, he pretended to continue to read the morning papers. But he wasn't concentrating upon the contents of the papers now. He was concentrating upon revenge. He had been let down. The papers bore clear evidence of that. Worse, he had been betrayed, as every generation of his family had been betrayed over the years. His perfect plan, he reasoned, formulated with such care, had been ruined by the incompetence and the treachery of others.

Revenge is an extremely powerful motivator and Nicholas began to refine an instrument of that revenge.

His plan had been one of the many options he had had in his mind for some while, particularly since the glossy society pages had shown Christopher Miller hosting a charity reception at his home. To Nicholas, Miller appeared arrogant and complacent, comfortably surrounded by his wealth and well-heeled friends as they gathered for photographs in his lounge and the dining room. And the magnificent centre-piece of the dining table was plain for all to see – another family possession looted. But, he was determined as a smile creased his face, that the centre-piece would play a key role in Miller's undoing.

As he formulated his plan, he became calmer and he resolved to enjoy, if he could, the spa facilities offered by the hotel. He would walk casually through Clifton Village. He would relax and be seen to drink coffee in the various cafés and visit, with great curiosity, the antique shops. And take the return flight to Gibraltar the following day as planned.

***

The meeting or, more accurately, tense interview, had already lasted more than fifteen minutes. The Deputy Chief Constable was seated, in full uniform, behind an impressive, but cluttered, desk. Superintendent Kay Yin stood before the desk wearing designer jeans and a Balmain jacket. The Assistant Chief Constable (Crime), Robert Perrin, a slimmer version of the Italian politician and news mogul, Silvio Berlusconi, was also standing, but slightly to Kay's left clutching a bundle of blue and buff-coloured files to his chest.

'And it is said that you barked orders at the constables without any consultation at all,' said an unsmiling Miss Winters.

'This wasn't an incident that would have benefited from local knowledge or experience. It was a fire. No discussion was necessary. Prompt orders and action were,' replied Kay in a quiet and reasonable way.

'Yes,' replied Miss Winters as she thumbed Kay's personnel file in front of her. Miss Winters wasn't physically nor facially an unattractive woman, but her facial expression was worn before its years, hard and unyielding. 'Of course,' she continued in a disparaging tone, 'you were formally a, what was it, *Sub*-Inspector in the Royal Hong Kong Police, a *quasi-military* force.' She closed the file in front of her as she continued. 'But military, parade ground-style orders are not appropriate to the UK, Miss Yin.'

'I beg to differ, ma'am. They were and they were appropriate and timely.'

'And was standing on the bonnet of someone's private car appropriate?' she asked as if dealing with a child.

'Yes,' replied Kay simply as if no further explanation was required.

'And do you think that the car's owner would agree with you?' she challenged.

'As the vehicle was subsequently destroyed by fire, I don't expect the owner will be unduly concerned,' she replied evenly.

Frustration was beginning to be etched on the DCC's face. Miss Winters began to realise that challenging this bright superintendent in the presence of the ACC (Crime) was becoming an embarrassment to her. But ego and history clouded her judgement. She continued in the hope of badgering the young superintendent and gaining the upper hand, to salvage something from what she should never have started. 'Constable Giffen drew your attention to the person trapped within the blazing car, did she not?'

'I was already aware of the *body* in the car.'

'But you didn't think of utilising the circus' own fire engine?'

'Their fire engine was a 1960s vintage Austin Gypsy with a wooden ladder, two buckets of sand, two fire extinguishers, a war-time on-board Coventry Climax pump, and towing a water bowser. It was totally inadequate for such a task.'

'But it did have an adequate supply of water?'

'Which would have been totally unsuitable for a petrol fire.'

'But there were fire extinguishers?' she remarked as if making a telling point.

'There were two. One was foam, the other CO_2. Both could be used on flammable liquids, maybe on a fire confined to the engine compartment, but this fire had engulfed the car and was spreading to other vehicles. The two extinguishers would have been useless in such circumstances.'

'So you say,' she said dismissively. 'And so, you made no attempt to effect a rescue but ordered the constables to maintain a perimeter of what, thirty yards,' adding in a tone full of criticism: 'Far too extreme.'

'Not at all,' countered Kay. 'A total of twenty-four vehicles were damaged covering an area thirty yards by thirteen.'

The DCC's ill-conceived questions were constantly nullified by unexpected, detailed and concise answers. The longer the DCC allowed this exchange to continue, the more uncomfortable she became. Instead of seeking a way to conclude the interview on a dignified note, she foolishly changed tack. 'You chose to call PC Giffen away from her colleagues and forcefully reprimanded her, away from anyone who may have witnessed your ... ,' she checked the notes in the file before continuing ... "overbearing and aggressive manner".'

'I didn't know who PC Giffen was with. I simply thought it better that I should speak with her alone without a public presence.'

'But her view, supported robustly by the Police Federation, is that you were a bully.'

'Well, the Police Federation has a reputation for imprudently racing to the support of its members without doing their homework. No doubt the Federation will be better prepared when they represent PC Giffen at her forthcoming disciplinary hearing.'

The DCC sat back in her impressive chair. But she wasn't favourably impressed by this unforeseen turn of events. She was taken unawares. 'What disciplinary hearing?' she demanded, adding accusingly: 'It was *your* decision to give her advice, not to discipline her.'

'But there was a caveat to that decision,' she replied calmly.

'What do you mean a *caveat*?' she asked sneeringly as she attempted to fathom what Superintendent Yin's intentions could be.

'I made it clear to PC Giffen that I was prepared to give her advice on the assumption that she acknowledged the unacceptable nature of her conduct and, if that should be the case, then the matter would be closed. Clearly, she does not acknowledge the disrespectful and racist nature of her conduct.' She paused. 'She *will* be disciplined, ma'am.'

'I don't think that we need to go that far, Superintendent,' offered the DCC in an oily and conciliatory manner as she attempted to regain her composure.

'The report has already been submitted.'

A smile illuminated the DCC's hard face. 'That will be viewed as vindictive and simply a spiteful counter-allegation in response to this meeting here today.'

'I don't think so. I submitted the report to the Professional Standards Department this morning at a little after two, informing them that I would report further as to PC Giffen's reaction.'

'But you didn't know what Giffen's reaction would be.'

'I anticipated what her reaction would be and I now know it to be the case,' she replied quietly and calmly. 'What I also know is that PC Giffen has a track record of unsubstantiated complaints. She made a complaint against her PTI during her initial training. She complained about her patrol sergeant whilst stationed at Southmead. She seemed to have skipped the inspector rank. Then she complained about her chief inspector whilst serving at Hartcliffe. I had little doubt that she would not heed my advice and would make a complaint against me. That assessment was part of my report to Professional Standards and I will be informing them of this latest development accordingly.'

'This can potentially cause embarrassment to the force,' she said, a threatening chill in her voice.

'If I may say so, ma'am, the days of protecting the bad image of any force have long gone. We should demonstrate that we can keep our own house in order, particularly in respect of minority groups, and attract recruits accordingly.'

'Is this what this is about? A crusade?' she asked, her voice dangerously unsteady.

'I don't do crusades, ma'am. However, I'm surprised that I am not receiving your full support in this matter.'

The DCC recognised the danger. A potential Chief Constable who condoned racism would never become a Chief Constable. The DCC inflated herself as she sought to justify her position, her voice tinged with alarm. 'I have an absolute right to question you so as to gain a comprehensive picture of events.'

Prudence would have dictated that Kay should have merely agreed with the DCC's comment whilst, at the same time, controlling her anger, but she felt compelled to speak, yet conscious of ACC Perrin's presence and keen not to embarrass him. 'I understand that your mother's family is Irish?' The DCC didn't answer. She resented the mention of her beloved mother by this officer whom she considered an up-start. She knew what was coming, her stare both angry and ice-cold. 'Am I really to believe,' continued Superintendent Yin, 'that if PC Giffen had referred to you in a similar way that you would be so tolerant? I don't think so, ma'am.'

Perrin silently exhaled a breath, relieved that this young superintendent had not suggested that, in similar circumstances, PC Giffen could have referred to the DCC as a 'callous Irish bitch', but Kay's response had been measured and she now carefully glanced at her watch. 'If you would excuse me, ma'am, I have the first of two post mortems to attend.'

***

Grey rain clouds scudded across the sky, much darker over the distant hills, as ACC Robert Perrin sat with Chief

Superintendent Mark Faraday around the coffee table in Perrin's headquarters' suite discussing the latest case.

'I am hopeful that the PM on Guy Hernandez will be concluded by five, sir, although the tox screen will take a few more days.'

'And the fire victim? enquired Perrin.

'Tomorrow, sir. Mid-day.'

'And the fire brigade were helpful too, you say?'

'Yes. Fortunately they used some sort of chemical-mist spray on the car containing the body which starved the fire of oxygen, and, thank goodness, they didn't use high pressure water which could have destroyed so much evidence. If you wish, I could draft a letter to the Chief Fire Officer for your signature.'

'Yes, if you think it necessary,' he replied almost absent-mindedly, his thoughts elsewhere.

'It can't do any harm and they were helpful after the fire was extinguished.'

He looked up, curiously. 'In what way?'

'They neatly removed the roof of the car, then cut the driver's seat floor mountings and lifted the whole framework out with the charred body virtually intact, which we were able to carry to one of our SOCO vans - rather like a grotesque sedan chair, although shielded from and unseen by the public.'

Perrin reflected upon this ugly image for a short moment, then asked: 'No idea of cause of death?'

'Not yet, sir.'

Perrin leaned forward and poured more coffee into their cups. Faraday mouthed a 'thank you' and sipped the perfectly ground coffee. 'Whilst we are here, Mark, I need to talk with you about another matter.'

'Go on, sir.'

'It might get a little too personal.'

'You know that I'm pretty much an open book, sir.'

'Okay. Let me get straight to the point. Do you have any history with Miss Winters?'

Faraday's response was immediate. 'Yes.'

'I have sensed there was something and Miss Winters gave Kay a hard time earlier. What made it worse was she wasn't a match for your wife. Would you care to enlighten me?'

Mark Faraday thought for a long moment, wondering what would be appropriate and dignified, factual and objective to say. There was no mystery. He started at the beginning.

'When I was promoted sergeant I was posted to Broadbury Road. Miss Winters was there as a fellow sergeant, but with three or four year's seniority. Four, I think. We were both single and we went to the cinema and restaurants a few times. I was introduced to her family, invited to birthday parties, that sort of thing. She met my parents a couple of times and we celebrated a New Year together on one occasion.'

'But nothing came of it?'

'No. It was an on-and-off thing for eighteen months.' Mark paused for a moment in thought before continuing. 'I could never quite get to grips with where I stood or where the relationship was heading.'

'You broke it off?'

'I suppose I did. It wasn't acrimonious. Well, I didn't think so and I think she expected it.'

'But, maybe, she did not accept it.' He took another sip of his coffee before continuing. 'I sense that Miss Winters is a very proud woman. What may have appeared to you as a natural consequence of drifting apart, could have been seen by her as a slap in the face.'

Mark replaced his cup in the saucer and thought back over the years. 'I thought it had all been conducted quietly and in a dignified manner. She was, and I suspect still is, very ambitious and I don't think a long-term relationship was ever on the cards for her. Any relationship like that would have got in the way of her career ambitions.'

'You are probably right, but it remains the case that you *rebuffed* her.'

'And you think that still rankles?'

'As people get older they reflect on their lives, what they have done, what they have achieved, whether their lives have been a success or a failure. Other than her career, Miss Winters has no achievements to speak of. Like us all, she will one day be just another pensioner and member of NARPO,' said Perrin, referring to the National Association of Retired Police Officers. 'If I recall,' said Perrin, 'Miss Winters' promotions were rapid, originally transferring on promotion from Bristol to Cleveland as a superintendent, then to South Wales as a chief superintendent, then, within two years, to Greater Manchester as ACC, followed by her appointment as DCC with the Wiltshire force. That sort of domestic disruption demonstrates a very significant ambition.'

'Yes, I'm sure you are right.'

'And why are people ambitious, Mark?' he teased, but with a purpose.

Faraday reflected for a moment. He thought of his father. His father had been ambitious but only in so far as success provided security for his family and, also, a desire to help others less fortunate. 'Security,' I suppose, 'for the family.

And to contribute – like your staff officer who is a volunteer crew member with the RNLI. There's often a fear of failure I suppose,' he speculated, 'no one wants to look stupid. Often an ego thing. A desire to achieve. It could be any one of a host of motivators.'

'There lies the real question, Mark. Why do ambitious people need to achieve?'

Mark Faraday didn't answer immediately. He thought of Miss Winters and those individuals whom he would classify as really ambitious before he gave his answer. 'Not always, but often, the answer can be found in a lack of self-esteem. They are compensating for some perceived inadequacy or insecurity.'

'I think that you are absolutely right,' he agreed, reflecting again before he continued. 'If I may say, Mark, as a friend, you are not trusting when it comes to suspects, but you are otherwise too trusting – unlike Kay. I think that we will all need to be careful and cautious in our dealings with Miss Winters.' Perrin returned his cup and saucer to the coffee table before continuing. 'During the last twelve months, Miss Winters has applied for the top jobs in Norfolk and then Surrey, or was it Sussex, without success.'

'I'm sure it was Surrey, sir.'

'Yes, you are right, it was Surrey. Now she has moved side-ways in the same rank from Wiltshire to us, a much larger force of course, but a move which she hopes will allow her to fulfil her ambition, at the relatively young age of forty-two, and seize a Chief Constable's baton when our chief retires shortly.'

'I'm sure that would be her plan.'

'But her exchange with Kay today has reminded Miss Winters of her background – both personal and professional. Her father was a clerk in a pickle factory; Kay's father was an Assistant Commissioner. Whilst Anita is well suited to the politics of senior rank, she lacks operational credibility and appears vulnerable before a sharper mind. We need to tread carefully, Mark'

'Thank you, sir.'

Perrin rose from the coffee table, walked to the windows that gave him a splendid view of the Gordano Valley. The clouds had darkened even more. 'Thank you for your candour, Mark. That has been helpful,' then asked: 'Does Kay know about your association with Miss Winters?'

'Oh, yes,' he replied. He thought for a moment, adding: 'I guess Kay's presence in the DCC's office today, reignited some long forgotten resentment.'

'Resentment is rarely forgotten, Mark. Far from it. It's my experience that resentment, if anything, ferments over time.' Perrin returned to his desk. 'We are all supposed to be part of the "police family". When we loose an officer, we are at our very best and really pull together, but, at other times, we are not always like *Happy Families* are we?

Ego and ambition, jealousy and resentment always seem to get in the way.'

Chapter Four

Saturday, 12th April.

Murder Incident Room, Police Headquarters, Bristol, England.

THERE WAS A QUIET INTENSTITY pervading the Murder Incident Room. There was no frenetic rushing back and forth, no excited voices, just a subdued buzz of focused activity; with photocopiers whirling and telephones ringing; and whispered conversations and thoughtful concentration.

Detective Superintendent Kay Yin was at the mortuary observing the PM being performed on the charred corpse from the burnt-out car. In the Murder Incident Room, ACC Robert Perrin stood with Chief Superintendent Mark Faraday in front of the display boards, some electronic, containing photographs, diagrams, plans and documents; some connected by coloured lines and the key words: WHY? WHEN? WHERE? HOW? and WHO? Questions easy enough to pose but with, potentially, multiple and contradictory answers.

'You say that the murder of Guy Hernandez was an assassination, Mark?' queried Perrin.

'A killer could have stabbed him in the back, upper or lower. He could have stabbed him in the stomach or chest. But he didn't. To have done so would have been to risk the knife becoming entangled in the coat, the trouser belt, a mobile phone pouch or a wallet in a breast pocket. The assailant minimised the risks of bungling the killing stroke or getting involved in a mêlée with the victim. I believe the assailant knew exactly what he was doing. He stabbed Hernandez from the right, downwards, at an angle estimated to be between 42° and 46° directly into his carotid artery. It was the perfect killing stroke. He would have lost consciousness within five seconds and died within twelve.'

'Bloody hell!' exclaimed Perrin quietly, then asked: 'A trained killer then?'

'He could have been a trained killer. We don't know, but he appears to have had some knowledge or experience.'

Perrin studied the photographs of Hernandez and Miller, promotional, full- length photographs obtained from Young and Son and similar full-length family photographs from Mr Miller's private portfolio. The conclusion was clear. During an early evening it would have been very conceivable for a killer to confuse one man with the other. Perrin moved closer to examine the mortuary photographs of Hernandez's neck wound.

'A small wound. A small kitchen knife would you say?'

'I believe we have the knife, sir,' replied Faraday.

'We do?' said a surprised Robert Perrin.

'Let's move over here, if you would, sir.'

Perrin followed Faraday to a large table. Faraday picked up a brown coloured A4 exhibit envelope. He removed a photograph.

'The corpse in the burnt-out car was wearing a wide leather belt,' said Faraday. 'We believe it to be Spanish from the buckle design. More significantly, on this belt was a knife scabbard.' Faraday placed the photograph on the table. It showed the charred corpse with the scabbard, mostly destroyed by fire, but with the knife out of the vertical line but still held in place by the metal *chape*, the metal protective sheath at the pointed end of the leather scabbard. The next photograph that Faraday laid on the table was simply the fragments of the scabbard displayed as if they had formed part of a *Mary Rose* archaeological exhibition. Faraday removed the third photograph from the envelope and placed it deliberately and slowly on the table. 'This is the weapon found on the deceased, sir. A Fairbairne-Sykes Fighting Knife.' Perrin starred quizzically at Faraday. 'The knife was … '.

'Sorry, sir,' interrupted Detective Inspector Harding, I have Miss Yin on the phone and she would like to speak with you, Mr Faraday.'

'And we were getting to the interesting bit,' said Perrin. He turned to Mark. 'It's okay. See what Kay has to say.'

Within minutes Mark returned. 'Interesting development, but, if I may, it might be useful if I just continue where we left off.' He picked up the photograph in both hands, leaning it towards the ACC. 'This make of knife was used throughout the Second World War by the Royal Marines, the US Rangers and other allied special forces, but it was never initially intended for the military. It was designed by William Ewart Fairbairn and Eric Anthony Sykes, two British officers of the Shanghai Municipal Police for dirty, up-close-and-personal fighting in dark, back alleyways. It was unusual in that it had a substantial foil-grip hilt that provided for a good hold in a fight and a relatively short blade of just over five inches with a sharp stabbing point and sharp cutting edges. When the war came along, I think it was Fairbairn, became part of British special forces, the blade was extended to just over six inches then to seven and a half, the idea being that the blade should be capable of penetrating at least three inches of clothing before penetrating vital organs. As you can see, sir,' said Faraday pointing to the black and white scale laid alongside the weapon in the photograph, 'this weapon is just over five inches. We cannot be sure, but we could reasonably assume that the killer had no intention of stabbing Mr Hernandez through his clothing, but intended to stab him in the neck.'

'Are you saying that he is, after all, a professional assassin?'

'No. It could be a coincidence that he had access to such a weapon, literally thousands were manufactured in Sheffield and elsewhere, and he may not have known anything about its history. It could also mean that he knew precisely what he intended to do and chose the perfect weapon to do it. At this stage, sir, we just don't know.'

'Well, I now know all about this knife, but we still don't know the killer's identity or his motives. Any ideas?'

'If we could move to the main players and possible motives in a moment, sir, but for now I can tell you that the call from Kay confirms that the cause of death of the charred corpse in the car was as a result of a single shot, fired at a right-angle, to the left side of the victim's chest. Dr Stotesbury cannot be absolutely certain because of the condition of the body, but there appears to be no evidence of smoke inhalation prior to death. The bullet appears to have passed through the body, left to right, and hit the central, right-hand car door pillar. The round was certainly not a .22, something heavier, which is suggested by the indentation to the door pillar and the destruction of the deceased's ribs. Death would have been instantaneous.'

'The assailant certainly took a risk,' observed the ACC.

'Yes, he did, although he didn't shoot his victim in the head which was sensible as it would have caused a mess, possibly seen by passers-by, but he used a larger calibre weapon, the bullet of which could have easily passed through the metal skin of the driver's door. That was careless, reckless even. That means he is capable of making mistakes. That means that his conduct is very likely going to help us, sir.'

'But, we don't know for certain that the man in the car is Guy Hernandez's killer.'

'That is true, but it is one of the hypotheses that we are working on.'

'Okay,' agreed Perrin. 'What time will Kay be back?'

Faraday looked at his watch. 'About twenty minutes, sir. Can I suggest we wait for her? I don't want to step on her toes and we could, meanwhile, have some coffee.'

Chapter Five

Monday, 14ᵗʰ April.

British Overseas Territory, Gibraltar and Murder Incident Room, Police Headquarters, Bristol, England.

IT WAS NOT THE BEST OF NEWS for Hugh Thornton, Gibraltar's Commissioner of Police. Three weeks before he had had his routine annual physical check-up. And blood tests. Just four. The results had been excellent, although his B12 levels had been low. His doctor, Doctor Parikh, had suggested tablets. Hugh Thornton was content. Doctor Parikh was not.

'Low B12 levels aren't fatal but I would like to know why your B12 levels are low,' observed the doctor who ordered more blood tests. Just six.

'Any urgency, doctor?'

'Not really, Commissioner. As before, have them taken in the next two weeks.'

One week later – that was today – Doctor Parikh rang Hugh at his office. 'Commissioner, your results have come in. All extremely good. As before, your level of fitness and the results are what I would associate with a man twenty years younger.   One area of concern, however, is that your protein levels are high.'

'That's good isn't it? English fish and chips and a spoon-full of cod liver oil?'

'Not this high,' replied Doctor Parikh who got straight to the point. 'Have you ever heard of Myeloma?'

Thornton's reply was equally immediate. 'No, but it sounds horribly like a cancer to me.'

'It is, and you have it, well, I'm pretty sure you have it. There is no cure, Hugh, but it can be managed. I have arranged for you to see a specialist, a Doctor Rachel Hall at the Royal Bournemouth Hospital in Dorset. She's the Clinical Director no less. She's good. Has an excellent reputation, as does her team. Are you available to see her this Wednesday?'

'I can be,' he replied, his positive response that of an experienced police officer dealing with a crisis. 'I will speak to the Chief Minister.'

'Hugh, I want you to take down my mobile and home numbers. Between now and Wednesday you and Rebecca may have some questions. Just ring me any time you wish.' Doctor Parikh waited a long moment so that the Commissioner could record the numbers before speaking again. 'I have a couple of patients with Myeloma. There's no cure, I know that, but they are having a good, full life and Doctor Hall and I will do our very best for you. Meanwhile, I will draft the letters.'

Hugh Thornton thanked Doctor Parikh and replaced the handset. It was time to act. He pressed his intercom. His PA, Mrs Julie Levant, stepped into his office. Mrs Levant was stunning. She looked like Amy Winehouse but without the tattoos, the exaggerated hair style and eye make-up. She was tall, perfectly groomed, elegant and sharp. 'Julie, I'm in a bit of trouble and I have an urgent medical appointment in Bournemouth on Wednesday. See if there's a commercial flight tomorrow afternoon, returning Friday, would you, for my wife and me. If not, maybe we could hitch a ride with a routine RAF flight. Meanwhile, I will speak with the Chief Minister.'

Tears began to sting Mrs Levant's eyes. 'Is there anything I can do, sir?'

'Yes there is,' said Thornton with a bright smile. 'A nice cup of tea would be good and then no fuss please.' Julie stood at his desk. Thornton stood up and turned to his office window. For what seemed a very long time there was complete silence. The Police Commissioner looked out of his window. The sun was shining. He saw some of his officers below crossing the tranquil quadrangle of scented flowers and shrubs. All seemed so normal – as it had been seven minutes before. But Hugh Thornton knew that his world would never be normal again. Then he spoke without turning around. 'I need to work out how I am going to tell Bex,' he said, referring to his wife, 'and to make sure that if the news on Wednesday is really grim, then everything will be in place for her.' There was silence again as he turned to face his PA. 'I will need to tell Debbie and James,' he said, referring to their children, 'but, my immediate concern is Bex. Whatever I say will instantly change her life for ever … and if there is one person in this often grubby world who doesn't deserve that, it's Bex.'

***

Assistant Chief Constable Robert Perrin and Chief Superintendent Mark Faraday gathered in the office of the Senior Investigating Officer, adjacent to the Murder Incident Room.

'Take my chair, sir,' invited Detective Superintendent Kay Yin.

'No. That's fine, Kay. You are the SIO. We are comfortable here,' he said as he and Faraday occupied a pair of tubular-framed, but far less comfortable chairs in front of her desk. 'Thank you for the heads-up regarding what you have discovered regarding Mr Miller's political intentions, or intentions that others seem to have for him,' said Perrin with a rather cynical smile. 'As a result, the Chief Constable immediately phoned the Home Secretary. We now seem to be very popular with everyone in Whitehall and on everybody's Christmas card list. I've had a meeting this morning with the Chief as a result of a call she received from Sir George Sinclair, the Permanent Under-Secretary of State at the Foreign and Commonwealth Office. It seems that, what we believe to have been a murder attempt on Mr Miller is causing some diplomatic wobbles.'

'In what way, specifically?' enquired Faraday.

'Apparently, Mr Miller is highly respected in Gibraltar. His companies have played a major part in rejuvenating the older, run-down areas. He has been instrumental in the expansion of the dock facilities to the extent that they are used by US submarines and further development will facilitate their use by our new super-carriers, *The Queen Elizabeth* and *The Prince of Wales*. Miller has been called upon to use his diplomatic skills in dealing with some of the more contentious issues with the Spanish; he is involved in banking – a key area for Gibraltar; and he's a lawyer. Your information was quite correct, Kay. Miller has already been approached by Gibraltar's Chief Minister with a view to Miller's appointment as head of the newly created Economic Development Board. Spain, of course, is constantly finding fault with Gibraltar and its internal and external affairs, whether this is the airport's flight paths, fishing, artificial reefs, cigarette smuggling and so it goes on. It seems that Spain sees this new board as an influential instrument that will draw various Gibraltarian departments together to challenge Spain at every turn under Miller's strong, no-nonsense leadership. The FCO believe that Spain will latch on to anything that would cause Gibraltar embarrassment with such an appointment. The Home Secretary has made it clear that she does not wish to interfere with the independence of the police investigation and expects the police to follow the evidence wherever it takes them. That said, the Home Office and FCO want this whole issue of Miller, Hernandez, who ever, to be dealt with the utmost tact, discretion and sensitivity for which, I quote: "the British police service is rightly renowned".' Perrin shook his head in disbelief at the cynical remark and grinned. 'You both know how this will play out. If we get it wrong, we will be thrown to the dogs. If we get it right, there will be a nod in our direction, but little more. And so, this stays between us and I need to be updated on a daily basis at 6pm.' Perrin looked at Faraday. 'Are we all happy?'

'It's Kay's show,' responded Faraday, glancing towards his wife, not wishing to supplant her authority in any way. She nodded agreement. He answered for them both. 'I think we are all happy, sir.'

'Good,' said Perrin nodding, 'maybe, Kay, you could update me regarding the body in the car?'

'Of course, sir. Shall we step out?' The two men followed Kay into the Murder Incident Room and towards the display boards. 'The index number of the vehicle and the VIN identifies the registered keeper as Victor Jenkins, forty-two years of age,' she said as she pointed in turn to the photographs of the burnt-out car and the identification numbers, then the police mug shot on one of the electronic boards. 'Jenkins had an address in Easton, a small one-bedroomed flat with bathroom and kitchen-diner. He has four previous convictions: two for Drunk and Disorderly, one for Common Assault/Public Order and one for a Section 47 when he dislocated someone's jaw in a fight. His dental records confirm his ID. His pre-court antecedents record his service in the British Army, in fact, some of his dental work was carried out by the military.'

'What unit, Kay?'

'He was a Lance Corporal in the Royal Logistic Corp, but he had served a tour in Afghanistan. He was discharged for drunkenness and, since then, he had drifted, from one job to another. He had a spell as a forklift truck driver but that ended when he crashed his forklift, whilst drunk, and brought down sixty-four foot of warehouse shelving eighteen foot high. He later worked as a loader in a warehouse; then as a labourer with the local council, Highways Authority and local parks department ... .'

'A good choice for our killer do you think?' speculated Perrin.

'He's hardly a Royal Marine or member of the SAS,' she replied, 'but, nevertheless, he could be seen as a good choice.'

'Why?' he questioned.

'Mark,' encouraged Kay as she looked at her husband knowing that he was always attracted to the backgrounds of these sorts of individuals.

He needed little encouragement. 'He's a loner, sir. His life seemed to have revolved around itinerant contacts in a "greasy spoon" café near Old Market Street and a seedy pub in Bedminster.' Little stars appeared on a large computer screen in response to Mark's operation of a hand control. 'He seemed to have no friends as far as we can ascertain. And so, no one would miss him. He had no relatives, and so, no one would care. And he was a drunk, and so, no one would believe what he might say – even if he could recollect what he had said or done. If you wanted someone to do this type of job, someone with rudimentary skill plus an obscure background, then Victor Jenkins had a very attractive CV, although drink may have caused him to be unreliable.'

With a less able team, Perrin would have asked directly whether specific military units had been contacted, but simply enquired: 'And the army?'

'The SIB,' replied Kay referring to the army's Special Investigation Branch, 'are sending his file to us.'

'And anything useful from his flat?'

'Maybe, sir,' answered Kay. 'We found a RLC's cap badge and an Operational Service Medal with Afghanistan clasp in a bedside table. There were possibly two framed pictures hanging on the wall, but these are no longer there. There was a broken ring binder file with documents regarding his driver qualifications, a first aid certificate and other employment related papers. We are checking all of these. There was also a letter, dated seventeen years ago, which appears to have been written by his mother, describing his father in derogatory terms. There were copies of old job applications forms, letters from Social Security, a bundle of betting slips - we are checking the betting shops. But no bank or credit statements. There was no sign of a mobile but a mobile did go up in smoke in the car and there was a charger in the kitchen. There was a pen on the bedside table but no note pads or a diary, although there was one of those monthly tear-off calendars hanging from a nail on the back of the kitchen door. At the moment, the scribbled notations on the calendar are not very helpful but we might be able to cross-reference something over the next few days. The bathroom was filthy and the flat itself untidy. The kitchen area was grimy and the little fridge/freezer well stocked with micro-wave foods, but, the waste bin and waste baskets were completely empty. Our view is that Jenkins' flat had been searched and the contents of the bins and any other incriminating or useful items removed, but the calendar behind the kitchen door seems to have been overlooked.'

'Well, there's progress. It's frustrating, I know. Like walking through treacle. But there's progress and a lot of avenues to explore. If any team is going to crack this, it will be yours, Kay.' Perrin looked at his watch. 'Can you take me through the rest of these characters again,' he asked, pointing to the photographs displayed on the magnetic board.

'Of course, sir,' replied Kay. 'Here we have Mrs Christopher Miller, nee Maria Carluccio. She is thirty-four, but looks much younger and five years younger than her husband whom she married less than two years ago. A lawyer specialising in European law. She initially worked for a law firm in Madeira, a subsidiary of Stockley, Kray and Burgess, then moved to their Bristol office as an associate six years ago. Her grandparents were from Naples and moved to the UK shortly after the Second World War. Her parents followed in the family business as restaurateurs. Three restaurants in Bristol, one each in Cardiff, Bath and Taunton. They originally settled in Leeds but the local manifestation of the mafia drove them out nineteen years ago. One of their restaurants was petrol bombed. In a separate incident, her father was badly beaten-up and their other restaurant had its windows smashed. A lot of intimidation. They got out of Leeds and came to Bristol. There have been no similar problems here or since, although we are liaising with a DCI from the West Yorkshire force who was a DC on the case at the time.'

Perrin nodded in acknowledgement but was silent for a while as he paced up and down before he spoke again. 'I always wonder how that sort of experience impacts upon an individual, particularly a child or teenager … do they develop into timid individuals or imitate the successes of their assailants or become strong and very self-reliant …'

'Is that a profitable line of enquiry, bearing in mind that she was nearly the victim here?' interrupted the Deputy Chief Constable who had entered the Murder Incident Room quietly and unnoticed.

Kay didn't answer. Robert Perrin did - in as pleasant a tone as he could muster. 'And what do we owe the pleasure?'

'I like to keep abreast of developments, Robert, particularly if the Chief should be absent and I have to take *command* of the Force.' She turned to Kay. 'Is Mrs Miller a suspect?' she asked in an imperialistic tone.

'She's a *person of interest*, ma'am.'

'A *person of interest*.   And how will that aid the investigation?'

Her reply was instant and not intended to offend, although the DCC took the reply as an oblique reference to her own humble background. 'It's often instructive to look at an individual's past which can provide a clue to their later intentions and behaviour.'

'And does that also apply to Mrs Mia Vickers?' she asked sneeringly.

'Mrs Vickers was born in Holland,' replied Kay patiently, 'and married an English merchant navy officer. The ship upon which he served as First Officer sank in the North Sea. The ship was loaded incorrectly. She was top-heavy and turned over in a storm. The subsequent litigation against the ship's owners and port authorities who were responsible for loading the vessel, was handled by Mr Miller. Since then she has been employed as Mr Miller's housekeeper. She has an impeccable background, hard-working, undertakes a great deal of charity work and attends the United Reform Church in Henleaze.'

'But still up there on the board?' she challenged.

'Of course,' she replied calmly. 'We are now running two murder investigations in tandem and it's a reminder to the team that there is always a chance for a useful cross-reference, but also to negate the possibility of a conflicting cross-over.'

'Like Colonel Fraser here, I suppose?' she said pointing to a photograph on the board, 'Hardly a suspect or *person of interest*.'

'The colonel heads-up Fraser Security, ma'am. He's of interest to me because I can't understand how a company that is contracted to Highgrove House and Gatcombe Park,' she continued, referring to the Gloucestershire homes of Prince Charles and Princess Anne respectively, 'can have installed such a sloppy security system.'

Every one of the DCC's questions to Kay where parried which only increased the DCC's annoyance and frustration. 'And three teams I see deployed to the circus. Why?'

'Just six detectives, ma'am. I was keen to have circus people interviewed quickly before they left town. Victor Jenkins could have had a connection with the circus. He could have sought temporary employment with them or maybe he might have sought to leave town with them.'

'What, in disguise as a circus clown or trapeze artist? Hardly likely, Miss Yin,' she said scornfully, then turned her attention to the ACC. 'There needs to be a tighter grip here, Robert,' she said as she walked towards the door. 'This investigation is drifting. Drifting. More grip is required. More grip.'

The DCC's public behaviour towards ACC Perrin was utterly disrespectful and so, Kay attempted to lighten the atmosphere and continued as if the DCC's remarks were unimportant. 'Let me brief you on some of the other characters, sir,' suggested Kay Yin airily, pointing at the board as the DCC power walked out of the Murder Incident Room. 'Alex Hernandez, is the brother of the deceased. He runs a garage in Port Talbot. He has previous convictions for car ringing and receiving stolen motor parts. Otherwise, no direct connection, but enquiries continuing.'

Kay pointed to the next photograph to the right, alongside that of Mr Miller. 'This is Miss Sarah Withers. Twenty-seven. Very attractive and with a marvellous pair of legs, so I'm reliably informed,' she said, smiling and raising an eyebrow. 'Unmarried but with a flotilla of admirers. Usually toy-boys. Usually six or seven years her junior. But there is no indication that she was romantically or sexually involved with Mr Miller who is twelve years her senior.'

'And ground staff?' asked Perrin pointing to the logo *'Heaven on Earth'*.

'The Millers uses this company. High-end. Uniquely, *'Heaven on Earth'* clients approve the staff used, and so, the same two groundsmen for the last four years.'

'Access to the house then?' queried Perrin.

'Not normally,' she said pointing to the ground floor plan of Grange Lodge pinned to another board. 'The house has a workshop and store with integral outside-access-only rest room, kitchenette and toilet. There is an *action* pending to interview both men, as there is with a plumbing company who recently attended because of a boiler system failure. Still lots to do.'

Perrin checked his watch for the third time. 'Okay, thank you. We have forty minutes. We had better finalise our preparations for the press conference.'

Chapter Six

Tuesday, 15th April.

Bristol, England.

THE PRESS CONFERENCE HELD ON THE PREVIOUS DAY had gone well. There had been a good response which generated many very positive lines of enquiry to follow.

The media liked Robert Perrin. He looked good. He looked Italian. He looked sharp. Sharp. Not cheap. He had a certain charisma. He had an engaging smile. But there was something in his eyes. A knowingness. He was articulate and the media had come to trust him.

The media liked Mark Faraday. He looked good too. Very English. Calm. But alert. He exuded reliability and confidence. Not arrogance. When fielding questions, even the inane, he was respectful. Not condescending. The public and the press warmed to that.

The media, however, had focused upon Detective Superintendent Kay Yin. She was different. Not from the usual mould. She was Chinese. She was petite. She was beautiful. She was bright. She spoke quietly. There was an unknown aura about her. But she impressed. The media recognised her grasp of events, her no-nonsense and resolute but realistic approach.

For the moment, the media were prepared to accept that the city was in safe hands – but, as always, only for the moment.

***

Numerous calls had been received by the Murder Incident Room in response to the press conference request for information regarding any unusual behaviour by co-workers, friends or neighbours. One neighbour reported suspicious activity in a neighbour's garden shed; another reported unusual items of washing hanging on a clothes line. A co-worker reported an unusual change of clothing by a colleague – all worthy of investigation – and there were calls from numerous launderettes and dry cleaning companies. One call had been received from the Avon Gorge Hotel and the *action* was able to be taken by Kay, who linked up with Mark prior to their meeting with Mr Christopher Miller, at his request, at his offices.

Both officers were invited into the office of the hotel's general manager, Mr Turnbull, and sat to the right of a large antique desk. The office walls were decorated with numerous awards from travel companies and hotel and restaurant associations, as well as a collection of miniature national flags and photographs of Mr Turnbull with the Lord Mayor, the Prime Minister and, what appeared to be a group of smiling Chinese guests.

'It might be nothing, of course,' said a rather rotund and balding Mr Turnbull, 'but one of our guests, a Mr Nicholas Milano, deposited a jacket, a wind-sheeter type of jacket, and a pair of trousers at reception during the late evening of the 10th and asked for them to be dry cleaned overnight. Usually, our guests would simply leave any clothing they required cleaning in the laundry bag in their room with their requirements listed on an attached form. Their laundry would be removed by Housekeeping in the morning and returned to their room that evening.'

'And this aroused your attention?' probed Kay.

'The guest said that he had spilt wine on the jacket and trousers. He may have, of course, in a bar or restaurant, but he did not check-out until the morning of the 12th. Since the police press conference, I began to wonder why he would not follow the usual routine. He is an annual guest and I would have assumed he would be familiar with the arrangements, standard in most hotels. As I say, it may be nothing, but I pass it on to you for what it's worth.'

'We are glad you have, Mr Turnbull,' said Kay, 'this is just the sort of information we rely upon. It may be nothing, but we are grateful for your call,' then asked: 'You say he is an annual guest?'

'Yes, usually once or twice a year for three or four days at a time. He has been a guest with us for the last six or seven years for the Bristol Wine Fair,' adding unnecessarily, 'He's in the wine trade.'

'And when was his previous stay with you, Mr Turnbull?' she asked.

'It would have been March.'

'When did he arrive?'

Turnbull glanced at his desk-top computer screen. 'On the 19th,' he replied.

'I see', continued Kay. 'On his most recent visit, was there anything else that may have drawn attention to Mr Milano, for example, his dining companions, his behaviour?'

'In the past, he has had an attractive female companion join him. If I recall, that was so in March, but on his last visit he dined alone. He is normally most charming but the waiting staff,' replied Mr Turnbull, 'have described him as being agitated on Thursday evening and at breakfast the following morning. In fact, he snapped at one of the waiters on the Friday who had simply asked him if he wanted more coffee.'

'And you say that would have been out of character?' enquired Kay.

'Oh, yes. As I say, he has always been most charming, particularly towards female staff.'

'Could we see his account please?' asked Faraday. 'Is that possible?'

'Of course, I can bring it up on the screen here.' Turnbull's podgy fingers moved the cursor across the screen and tapped a sequence of keys. 'Here we are,' he said as he angled the screen towards the two officers.

The officers leaned in. Kay noted Milano's restaurant times, then asked: 'This item, *Glover of Clifton*, that's a florists, isn't it?'

'Yes. Close by and very convenient for us. We advertise their services and they provide our floral displays at a special discounted rate,' he said, clearly pleased to allude to the attractive commercial arrangement he had secured.

'Seventy pounds seems a reasonable amount to pay for a bouquet of flowers,' suggested Faraday. 'Do you know if they were delivered to someone or did Mr Milano collect the flowers from reception?'

Turnbull ran his finger along the screen. 'Here it is. These would have been delivered to reception and then collected, I assume, by Mr Milano on the 11th.'

'Can you tell us who the receptionist was who took the order?' asked Kay.

'According to this, it was Daphne. In fact, she is on duty now. I saw her as I arrived earlier.'

'Could we speak with her do you think?' she asked.

'Of course,' replied Turnbull, please to help but slightly bemused as to what useful information the receptionist might be able to provide. Mr Turnbull picked up his phone and called reception. Shortly there was a knock on the general manager's door. Daphne entered. 'Daphne,

nothing to worry about but these are police officers.'
Daphne looked uncertain.

'Hullo, Daphne,' said Faraday, getting up from his seat and
shaking Daphne's hand but then resumed his seat. Daphne
was short.   Faraday was tall.   Faraday didn't want to
unwittingly intimidate Daphne.

'We need to ask your advice regarding one of the hotel's
recent guests,' asked Kay. Daphne relaxed a little. There
didn't seem to be a complaint from a guest, she reasoned
and was simply being asked for advice. But she still looked
a little anxious. 'A Mr Nicholas Milano ordered a rather
expensive bouquet of flowers during the evening of the
10th, last Thursday evening. Can you recall?'

'Yes, I can,' she replied, looking from Kay to Turnbull, then
back to Kay.

'One would have assumed that such an expensive bouquet
would have been for a special occasion, an anniversary, a
birthday, something like that. Did Mr Milano ask your
advice about the choice of flowers or did he mention the
occasion, by any chance?'

'No, he didn't ask me about the flowers. He selected them
from the *Glover of Clifton* brochure and said that he wanted
to pick them up from reception the morning of the 11th but
he actually collected them on the morning of the 12th.'

'I see,' replied Kay, nodding encouragingly. 'And do you
have any idea what occasion the flowers were for?'

'I think it was a funeral, ma'am.' Kay and Mark did not exchange glances.

'A funeral,' remarked Kay easily. 'Well they would certainly be a splendid tribute, but why do you think they would have been for a funeral, Daphne?'

'The gentleman said so,' she said as if the answer was self-evident.

'Can you recall actually what he said?' asked Faraday patiently.

'Yes, sir ... I think so.' She thought for a moment. No one hurried her. 'Yes, he said something like: "Very sad, a bereavement you know. I think the family will like these". He seemed pleased with what he was doing, you know, doing the right thing,' she added with a shrug.

'That has been very helpful, Daphne,' said Kay before turning to the general manager. 'If it isn't too much trouble, Mr Turnbull, I would like to take a very short statement from Daphne. A matter of a few sentences. Just how long she has worked here and in what capacity, when she came on duty on the 10th and her recollection of her brief conversation with Mr Milano. If I can do this now it will save a detective calling later on and disturbing Daphne again.'

'Of course,' agreed Turnbull helpfully.

Kay stood and went to the door. 'I will leave you with Mr Turnbull, sir,' she said to Faraday. 'We should only be about fifteen minutes.'

Kay and Daphne left the office as Turnbull and Faraday continued at the screen. 'Meanwhile, Mr Turnbull, I see that Mr Milano ran up a higher than average drinks tab on the evening of the 10th.'

'Yes, he certainly did.'

'And I see that he made a particular request for his shoes to be cleaned?'

Turnbull stared at the screen and agreed. 'Yes. Yes, he did.'

'And his room was single occupancy?'

'Yes, that's correct.'

'Has that always been the case?' continued Faraday.

'No, on previous occasions, I believe he may have shared with a lady.' He raised his eyebrows as if he and Faraday would understand these things, adding: ' … not always the same lady.'

Faraday made a mental note as he continued to search the screen. 'He didn't appear to use the internet or make calls from his suite, but were any messages left for him at all during his stay with you?'

'Give me a second,' he said and searched the screen. 'No messages.'

'Okay,' continued Faraday, 'can you tell me how Mr Milano left the hotel on checking-out. Did reception arrange a taxi for him, for example?'

Turnbull searched the scene again. 'Yes, here we are. Our preferred taxi company. I have the details here.' Faraday made a note.

'And, lastly, would it be possible to speak to Housekeeping and whoever was responsible for dry cleaning?'

***

Kay drove as Mark called Detective Inspector Harding during the journey, arriving at Queen Square some twenty minutes before their scheduled appointment with Christopher Miller. At Miller's request, their visit would be announced as a courtesy call. It would prove to be much more than that.

Kay parked facing directly into the square and towards the equestrian statue of William III where Mark took the return call from DI Harding. Faraday listened as Harding spoke.

'Okay, John, thank you,' said Faraday as he closed the call. Then turned to Kay. 'John has checked. No funerals listed for anyone by the name of Milano or Miller in the greater Bristol area between the 8th and 30th, yet Nicholas Milano ordered flowers for a bereavement. Whose bereavement?'

'What do we know?' asked Kay rhetorically. 'The taxi company have told us that they took Milano straight to Bristol International Airport but, en route, he asked the driver if there was a children's hospital in the city, and he then left the flowers with the Children's Hospital adjacent to the BRI,' she said referring to the Bristol Royal Infirmary. 'The hospital says that they couldn't recall Milano - they have so many gifts of flowers - and certainly not the details on any gift label and so they didn't have any idea of the original intended recipient.'

'And we have nothing at all to connect Milano with Victor Jenkins,' said Faraday checking his wrist watch. 'We better go in.'

Entering Queen's Chambers was rather like entering 10 Downing Street with its black, wrought-iron arch and ornate lamp at the front step. The Georgian building was beautiful, with dark high doors, a sweeping staircase, a glittering chandelier and graceful yet complex, pale blue and white, ceiling mouldings. On the ground floor was a little corridor off to the right of the main black and white tiled marble hall, down which could be found the most modern, and smoothest, of lifts. On the top floor, the officers were greeted by the vivacious Miss Sarah Withers who showed them firstly into Mr Miller's office. Whether Miller had adopted a gambler's poker face, it was not clear, however, there was not the slightest hint of intimacy between Miller and his PA when they spoke or when she removed papers from his desk, or later when she brought in a tray of tea to the conference room.   It appeared to be all-business. Friendly and relaxed, but, all-business.

The officers sat at a beautifully polished walnut conference table that would not have looked out of place on the BBC's *Antiques Roadshow* or in an episode of *Downton Abbey*. For a brief moment Faraday wondered how the table could have been brought up to this top floor but assumed that it would have been dismantled, then reassembled. The room was oblong with a high ceiling and tall windows giving an impressive view of the tree-lined square and which allowed silver bars of the afternoon sun light to stream in. They spoke in relaxed and reassuring generalities, of Mrs Hernandez; of the forthcoming inquest; of the successful redecoration of the hallway at Grange Lodge and the replacement of the carpet; the press conference and alluded to some of the lines of enquiry that were now being followed before they moved to the main purpose of the meeting.

Mr Miller removed a sheet of paper from a brown leather folder. 'I have here the details of four individuals and their companies with whom I have had professional dealings, who may, I emphasise *may*, harbour some ill-feelings towards me.' For a short moment he held the single sheet of paper in his hand. 'I'm not sure to whom I should hand this?'

Faraday was going to say that Kay was the SIO, but sought to reassure Miller of the information's security from the outset.   'That's for Kay's *safe-keeping*,' said Faraday, gesturing towards his wife.

Miller laid the piece of paper on the polished table and almost reluctantly pushed the paper towards Kay. Kay picked it up and glanced at the list of forty-two names as Mr Miller continued. 'We spoke about trust, Miss Yin, when we first met. I am trusting you to ensure that the details of these four individuals aren't just chatted about casually or the individuals subjected to embarrassing interviews.'

'Mr Miller,' said Kay as she scrutinised a list, 'the four names in a slightly different font will be simply listed on our data base, along with the other thirty-eight, as individuals with whom your companies have had recent dealings, names which are already in the public domain. Should these four individual's names crop up, the system will be programmed to automatically notify me and no one else. Are you happy with these arrangements, sir?'

'Not happy as such,' he said cautiously, 'but I am relying upon your discretion.'

'Of course you can,' she replied emphatically, hoping to reassure Miller before asking: 'Can you tell me something about them?'

They discussed the four individuals and their professional connection to Mr Miller, one of whom opposed Miller's view that Gibraltar should adopt a more Bermudan model of transparency and link banking more closely with insurance services. Another was not at all happy that Miller was proposing that Gibraltar should seek to triple tourism within ten years, as Singapore was planning to do, the view being that this would fundamentally alter the character of Gibraltar. The third had been, as Miller put it, 'out-manoeuvred' by him in securing a very lucrative port-related contract, and, the fourth had been refused a loan of nearly thirteen million sterling by the bank of which Miller was a director.

Satisfied, the officers moved seamlessly to discuss his extended family. There was little to discuss although informative and provided context. Miller's parents had both died at an early age, his mother at forty-seven years and his father a year later at the age of fifty-two. He had no brothers or sisters. There had been an uncle and aunt on his mother's side, both of whom had died in a canoeing accident whilst salmon fishing near Ketchikan in Alaska. There was a 'distant cousin' who was apparently not a cousin at all, but a childhood neighbour in Madeira, although Miller said that he had lost contact with him many years before. Mark and Kay nodded as if spectators listening to an interesting and colourful family history, but part of their mind was calculating whether any of this, apparently inconsequential, background information could impact upon their murder enquiries. And, usually, background information did.

More tea was offered, but the police officers declined. Miller smiled as he looked, firstly at Mark, then at Kay. He had recognised their synchrony.

'Something amuses you, Mr Miller?' she asked with an encouraging smile.

'I'm intrigued,' he said, relaxing a little, pleased that the matter of the four potential *persons of interest* had been dealt with. 'You are husband and wife, yet work together. There must be professional disagreements from time to time?'

Miller was a lawyer by training and the officers instinctively wondered whether he was simply showing an interest or was there a more spurious intent. Again, they did not exchange glances but both recognised the inherent danger with familiarisation and the need to say just enough, but not too much, to say as little as possible whilst learning as much as possible, and to always remember that the Millers would remain – at least - *persons of interest.*

'We have worked together for a number of years,' replied Kay, 'before we were married and since, but there has never been an issue.'

'I'm just thinking of colleagues who have set-up companies or law partnerships with their spouses and, in every case I can think of, there were difficulties.'

'No, not with us,' replied Faraday casually.

'But surely ... ,' continued Mr Miller hesitantly, ' ... I am assuming you have always held the higher rank, Mr Faraday. You must have had occasion to over-rule your wife?'

'Never. Not at work,' he said, adding light heartedly, '*nor* at home.'

Miller smiled before asking: 'But what would happen if this murder enquiry was floundering?'

Both wondered whether this question had been prompted by Anita Winters, but Faraday responded as if the question was quite a reasonable one to pose. 'Chief constables and senior officers are often under tremendous pressure from the media, the public and politicians to get an early result and this will bring pressure to bear upon the Senior Investigating Officer,' he said, 'but it would be rare to over-rule the SIO. If the enquiry was stalling then the usual procedure would be to bring in a review team. In any case, Kay and I meet regularly with the ACC (Crime) and discuss a multitude of matters. Kay might ask for advice or seek resources. We might make suggestions or test a hypotheses, but trying to second-guess the SIO is usually counter-productive.'

'I don't follow,' he queried with a frown. 'Counter-productive?'

'Yes. Very often initiative and imagination can be stifled by interference, even well-meaning interference. Usually, all that is required is a gentle hand on the tiller. What is always required, however, is support, not only in terms of resources, but also when the going gets rough and the SIO is under pressure.'

Miller fiddled with his cup and saucer, thinking. 'If I may say, you seem to work instinctively together. There's no ... what is it ... no edge.'

Kay didn't answer immediately. She reflected for a moment before answering. 'It's about shared values, I suppose, and we don't have big egos that get in the way, Mr Miller. I am immensely proud of my husband. I am comfortable that he is a chief superintendent and has an MBE. It might be an issue for others but it has never been an issue for us.'

'And I am immensely proud of Kay. It hasn't been an easy run for her. In some respects she was an out-sider. She had held inspector rank in Hong Kong and reverted to being a constable when she joined us, a service that was still male dominated and female detectives tended to be in the minority. More recently, the police service has become increasingly career-competitive whilst, at the same time, the number of officers in each rank has been drastically reduced. And so, everywhere you turn it is heavy lifting.'

'And would you think of setting up a law partnership with Mrs Miller?' asked Kay, guiding the conversation back towards the Millers.

'Never really given it a great deal of thought with Maria working in Brussels. I'm not sure,' reflected Mr Miller. 'Certainly that would not be on the cards whilst there may be the prospect of a Gibraltar appointment.' Miller smiled as he thought of his wife. 'Maria has an excellent brain and she is a very good organiser and planner. We would probably complement each other. I tend to see the opportunities, bring the parties together, undertake the negotiations, then leave the organising and planning to others, but Maria is very hands-on. As a domestic example, our housekeeper had occupied a rather nice, large room on the first floor with the almost exclusive use of a bathroom, which I thought was more than adequate. Once we were married Maria thought Mrs Vickers deserved more and planned a two-roomed en-suite flat for her. The same with the complete redesign of the kitchen and the imaginative workshop facilities for the groundsmen. There is never a need for a project manager when Maria is around. She has a very persuasive personality. Maria is very focused and determined and gets things done.'

Miller returned his cup and saucer to the tray which Mark and Kay interpreted as a signal that their meeting was drawing to a close. Kay slipped the sheet of paper in her briefcase as Faraday stood up from the table, as he did so he looked across the room behind Mr Miller and admired a painting entitled 'Waiting for the Verdict' by Abraham Solomon, depicting a scene in 1857 where an impoverished defendant, surrounded by his distressed family, awaits the verdict of the jury as his barrister appears ominously at a doorway.

'You like the painting?' asked Miller.

'It's very … very emotive, I suppose,' suggested Faraday.

'Yes, I suppose it is,' he said, then paused in personal thought for a few moments. 'There is another by Solomon entitled "Not Guilty", but I think "Waiting for the Verdict" reminds me of a lawyer's responsibilities. It was given to me by my father when I became a lawyer … shortly before he died.'

Faraday nodded, pausing for a respectful moment or two, but, he was a policeman and never missed an opportunity to gather information and so asked: 'And this one here?' as he moved towards the end of the conference room and a gilt-framed manuscript hanging on the far wall. 'The fine detail is remarkable,' Faraday observed as he studied the beautifully engraved and illustrated British coat of arms and those of Gibraltar, with scenes of the enemy's *Grand Assault* and the defender's famous *Sortie*, the capture of the *San Miguel* and the *Relief of Gibraltar* during The Great Siege of Gibraltar that lasted from 1779 until 1783.

'It lists a number of military officers,' explained Miller, 'who were singled out for recognition by the Governor, General Sir George Augustus Eliott, and one of whom could have been my great, great, great-grandfather and was later appointed Deputy Military Governor.'

Mark and Kay scanned the manuscript and both saw the name, third from the top of a list of twenty-two, but they made no recognition of it or exchanged knowing glances. 'I'm sorry, I can't readily make out your name,' commented Mark with apparent confusion.

'Here it is: Milano, Colonel Henry Bartolomeu Milano. The name was Anglicised in 1940 to Miller.'

'Oh, I see. And it occupies pride of place here.'

'Well, I think it's rather magnificent but it's all in black ink and Maria didn't want it in our home. She thought it a little gloomy for our lounge so it's here.'

Kay casually engaged in a distraction, not wishing to appear overly interested in Colonel Milano. 'Well, Mark has a *Certificate of Lunacy* on our lounge wall. Now that *is* gloomy.'

'You're not being serious?' he challenged incredulously.

'Oh yes, dated 1880,' responded Mark, 'and addressed to the Commisioners in Lunacy, authorising a Mary Brett … I think that was her name … to be detained because she was grumpy and grumbled a lot, refused to take a bath and wandered around the streets not properly dressed.'

'This is a joke, surely?' he challenged lightly again.

'Oh, no,' replied Mark. 'It seems ridiculous now but that was all the evidence that was required then. And what is even more worrying is that it was signed off by her brother, a retired naval officer, Captain Spencer Brett. As a result, poor old Mary was sent to Bailbrook House, a local lunatic asylum,' then added with a huge smile, 'All I can say is that it's a good job I wasn't around then or I would probably have been locked up in Bailbrook House with her.'

'Wouldn't we all,' scoffed Christopher Miller, pulling a make-believe anxious face.

But Faraday hadn't forgotten his main task. 'You said that Colonel Milano "could have been" your great, great, great-grandfather?' probed Faraday, apparently absent-mindedly, whilst looking intently at the manuscript.

'The truth is I don't know if I am directly related. I suspect that there would be some loose connection somewhere.'

'And the name was later Anglicised you say?'

'Yes, in 1940.'

'Was that year significant?' enquired Mark.

'Yes, I suppose it was. The family were all living in Gibraltar which was being bombed by the Germans. There was also the worry that General Franco's Spain would take the opportunity to attempt a seizure of The Rock and so all women and children, and some men, were evacuated during the July and August of 1940 either to England, Jamaica or Madeira. My family went to Madeira. There had always been a large English ex-pat population there because of the wine trade. There had been a good deal of inter-marriages and many non-English locals changed their names. It was good for business, apparently. They even have a name: Anglo-Madeirans.'

'And is this where your distant cousin lives?'

'Probably. Although I wouldn't really know. He wasn't really a cousin at all. The family referred to him as a "cousin", rather like the old lady in the local confectionary shop was always referred to by everyone in the town as "Aunty Agnes". I haven't seen my distant cousin for probably thirty years and I wouldn't recognise him if I did. In fact, I can remember Aunty Agnes's name because she always gave me sweets, but I can't even recall his name. Michael? Vincent? I can't recall,' he said rubbing his eye with his index finger.

Mark didn't pursue the matter but was well aware that there is always a difficulty in telling a lie in that the sub-conscious mind acts automatically and independently of the lie, and so, body language can give the liar away. The eye rubbing gesture is the brain's attempt to block out the deceit or for the liar to avoid looking at the person to whom he is telling the lie.

Whatever, Mark had heard enough and didn't want to emphasise his interest in the 'cousin'. He smoothly changed tack. 'And the ship there,' he asked, pointing to a beautiful scale model in a glass display case, 'is there a family connection too?'

'Yes, there certainly is,' he replied enthusiastically, pleased for the conversation to have moved away from the 'cousin'. 'This is a 1/200th scale model of the *Ulster Monarch*, "taken up from the trade" and pressed into service by the Admiralty for the evacuation. Tragic really. Built by Harland and Wolff, Belfast, in 1929, I believe, and the only one of her class to survive the war. But, she did her job and evacuated hundreds to safety including my mother and father and his mother and father.'

'That's really rather nice,' remarked Faraday, 'nice to have your special treasures here.'

'It is. I find it inspirational at times,' he said modestly, but then added with some pride, 'but, the really special treasure is *"Dirty Nell"*.'

'*"Dirty Nell"*?' Now Mark and Kay did exchange glances of questioning amusement.

'Yes, I don't know the origins of the name, but it is totally inappropriate for the most elegant and graceful table centre-piece I think I have ever seen. It is in our dining room. A porcelain figure of a beautiful, naked woman serenely reclining on a rock above a wild sea with her hands clasped behind her head. It's just under three foot high and nearly four foot long.'

'And it's a treasure you say?'

'Oh, yes. Thousands of them were produced in the States in the 1880s and mainly used as decorations in taverns, bordellos, speak-easies and casinos. When they were first produced they were marketed under the title of *"Perfection on the Rocks"*, a twist on "scotch on the rocks" I believe, which was appropriate bearing in mind the premises where they would often be found. I think they were seen at the time as erotic, virtually pornographic, titillating pieces for the punters, but I've never seen it as that. It is utterly beautiful.' Miller was on a roll. He was somehow proud of *'Dirty Nell'*. 'Being porcelain, and remembering where they would be found, most where damaged or broken beyond repair over the years. As a result there are believed to be only four left in the world, one of which is in the Metropolitan Museum of Art in New York and even that one has a slightly chipped right big toe. You see, they look as if they were made of metal but they were porcelain coated in a satin bronze by a process known as *liquid metal coating*, as a result they were often mishandled and accidentally damaged.'

'And valuable?'

'Ours is in mint condition,' he said proudly. 'I have been offered two million, but it's not for sale. Sentimental and inspirational, I suppose. You see, my great-grandfather secured a very profitable partnership with two Bristol horse dealers and haulage contractors to part-own one of the Bristol coal mines, known as Speedwell Deep Pit, which went on producing coal until 1936, and the deal-maker was the gift of *"Dirty Nell"* by the other partners, the two brothers that is, to my great-grandfather.

'What a fascinating story,' said Faraday genuinely. 'It was kind of you to share this with us,' he remarked as they shook hands.

'And you can rely upon my discretion, Mr Miller,' said Kay as they walked towards the door.

'Please give me a call any weekend,' offered Christopher Miller. 'We are often at home for a coffee and I would be delighted to introduce you to *"Dirty Nell"*.'

On that positive note, Mark and Kay left Miller to his thoughts. They returned to their vehicle and Mark drove towards the M5 motorway and the Murder Incident Room. He knew where Kay would need to be and what she would need to prepare. But it wasn't just Christopher Miller who reflected upon their meeting. Mark and Kay had their own thoughts too.

'I'm wondering,' said Kay, 'whether Miller really had no recent knowledge of his "cousin".'

'I'm sure that he knew his "cousin's" name but whether he had recent knowledge of him, then I'm not so sure,' replied Mark. 'He appeared happy enough to discuss the details of the Gibraltar Siege, although he didn't immediately point out the name of his ancestor. But, it begs the questions: Is his "cousin" actually Nicholas Milano? And did, or does, his "cousin" know him?'

'Those are the critical questions as is the reason for the denial, the lie,' Kay said as Mark turned off the motorway at Junction 19 and drove along The Portbury Hundred. Then she continued. 'And why was Miller so interested in our relationship? Was he just curious? Was he comparing our relationship with that of his with his wife? Was he harbouring doubts about their relationship? Maybe we should take him up on his offer of coffee, what do you think?' she said with a conspiratorial grin.

'I think it would be extremely discourteous not to do so after such a generous offer,' he said with a smile, 'although I just have a slight feeling that he wants to be a little too close to us, maybe so that he hopes to be just a step ahead all the time.'

'Well, he gave us a great deal of his time,' reflected Kay. 'His desk gave the appearance of a busy man, and I assume he rarely wastes his time. His PA removed plenty of files but plenty remained on his desk. Whatever, more intrigue and facts to consider and more *actions* as a result.'

And Faraday held one particular intriguing query in his mind.

***

It was ten minutes past seven in the evening when ACC Perrin had been called to the Chief Constable's office. The DCC, Anita Winters, was already there.

'Thank you for coming in, Robert,' said Chief Constable Emily Woodland. 'Anita has some concerns regarding this Hernandez murder enquiry. Anita thinks the enquiry is, as she puts it, drifting.'

'Maybe Anita would like to explain how she has arrived at that curious assessment?'

The DCC didn't give the Chief Constable an opportunity to answer. She stood confidently having prepared what she considered to be a water-tight case. 'It has clearly been drifting,' she said, 'because the main suspect, Nicholas Milano, is now in Gibraltar and effectively out of our reach. The SIO has clearly not been focusing. From what I have been able to observe, the whole investigation is conducted on a scatter gun approach, where she launches all sorts of enquiries in the hope of hitting the target. Miss Yin seems to be treating Mrs Miller and a security specialist, to name but two, as suspects and orders the interviews of over sixty circus workers,' adding, as if persuasively: 'I'm afraid that Robert's personal involvement with Faraday and his wife has affected the objective oversight that this delicate investigation demands.'

'Nicholas Milano is a *person of interest* and is not out of reach,' retorted Perrin, 'but, before we approach the Foreign and Commonwealth Office, before we get the all-clear from the Chief Minister and interview an army officer, we need to be in possession of some compelling evidence.'

'Your team is unlikely to secure *compelling* evidence by concentrating upon Mrs Miller,' she said with an air of triumph.

Perrin didn't comment but asked, 'What do you mean "my personal involvement"?' he demanded, his face flushed.

'We all know that you gave Yin away, some may feel inappropriately, at the Faraday wedding. You and Barbara have had supper at the Faraday's apartment and they have dined at your home.'

'This is "politically correct" nonsense,' replied Perrin. 'They are an interesting and amusing couple. We have a lot in common. Both have travelled a good deal as have Barbara and me. Our daughter and son-in-law are the same age as

Kay; Kay's father was an Assistant Commissioner (Crime) in Hong Kong and Barbara's father happened to have served with Mark's father in the fire brigade, coincidentally, at the same station at Ashton Gate for a number of years. The sadness is that we would dine together more often but you have previously made comments suggesting favouritism. Now we are in the ridiculous position of being wary of having a normal social life outside the police service in case that quite normal behaviour is perceived by *you* as favouritism.'

'You agree then that you have shown favouritism?' questioned the DCC.

'How?' challenged Perrin.

'You have never invited *me* to your home, Robert,' she said haughtily.

'And I can assure you that I won't ever do so,' he replied with a no-room-for-manoeuvre glare. 'Do you know why? Well let me tell you, madam,' he said, an angry frustration infecting his tone. 'When I first introduced you to my wife, you were rude and disrespectful towards her.'

'I was *no* such thing.'

Robert Perrin was rarely angry but there were exceptions: dishonesty and lying, bullying and disloyalty, and, disrespect directed at his family. He remained calm but anger laced his icy reply. 'You were dismissive. You asked Barbara how we met. She replied that it was when I was serving as an

Inspector and Barbara was a Special Constable. And you replied: "Oh, only a Special Constable. No real understanding of policing then." You were unwelcoming and rude.' Robert Perrin turned and offered the Chief Constable three plastic files containing a two-page briefing report. Perrin directed his next comment to the DCC. 'You say that Miss Yin is not focused. Well, the briefing files I have just given to the Chief are focused, encapsulating the current enquiries succinctly, with copies should the Chief require them when she attends the FCO tomorrow. Miss Yin has now brought to my attention a startling revelation as a result of a meeting that she and Faraday had with Miller this afternoon, details of which are contained in these files. She was not asked to produce these files but used her initiative, anticipating the Chief Constable's requirements. You can show an interest in this murder enquiry, Anita, but you are being disruptive and interfering. You need to back off.'

Perrin walked to the doors. He stopped and turned, addressing the Chief Constable. 'I hope Miss Yin's performance at the press conference and the contents of her briefing files will satisfy you as to her competence, ma'am. Both Mark Faraday and Kay Yin are fine and capable officers. Together, they are exceptional.' Perrin turned to the DCC. 'It's a great pity, Anita, that you don't confine your energies to doing your own bloody job and allow me to get on with mine.'

Chapter Seven

Saturday, 19th April.

Bristol, England.

THE MILLERS WORE AWKWARD SMILES. Mark and Kay did not. Maybe the Millers had anticipated an early visit. But not this early.   Nevertheless, Mark and Kay would assume that they would have prepared.

'Please come in. Welcome to our home,' said Christopher Miller flamboyantly – maybe too flamboyantly - as he stood back and allowed them to step into the hall, the smell of fresh paint still evident in the air. 'Shall we go straight through to the dining room and *"Dirty Nell"*?'

'That would be good, although there are a few police matters we should deal with first,' suggested Mark in a very business-like tone.

'Oh, right,' replied Christopher Miller warily. 'Let's all go through to the lounge,' although he had hoped that he would have been able to have created a more relaxed and advantageous atmosphere from the beginning.

The lounge gave superb views over the beautiful rear garden. One wall of the lounge was dominated by Neville Johnson book shelving, whilst another, a beautiful Portland fluted-stone fireplace. There was a pine coffee table on which was a superb arrangement of fresh-cut white lilies, peach and mauve alstroemeria, carnations and red roses. A light-grey nine-seat sofa was arranged in an L-shape of five and four, decked with a collection of either dark grey or purple-coloured cushions. On one wall was an original Ken Keeley of Time Square.

'I have some more information which we would like to share with you,' said Faraday disarmingly as they took their seats. 'Between the 7th and 12th of April, a man by the name of Nicholas Milano was a guest at the Avon Gorge Hotel,' he said reading the notes in his leather file, before looking directly at Christopher Miller. 'Have you been in touch with him, Mr Miller?'

Mr and Mrs Miller had not expected such a prompt and direct question. They exchanged resigned glances before Mr Miller, his chin thrust forward, replied with undue forcefulness, thought Faraday. 'No, *certainly* not.'

'He hasn't contacted you or attempted to contact you, sir?'

'As I said, *no*.' But he revealed a 'tell'. Faraday's question had been too quick for Miller's brain to prevent his reflective and instinctive glance to his wife, albeit so slight, but which was virtually impossible to hide.

'But *you*, Mrs Miller, *you* have met with him,' said Faraday with an absolute certainty that was not justified by any evidence at all, 'and he *has* been in contact with you, hasn't he?'

Faraday's assumption had been correct. 'Yes, he has,' she responded smoothly and without hesitation, like a practiced lawyer taken unawares.

'Thank you for openness, Mrs Miller. I want to continue in that vein.' As Faraday removed a pen from his leather file he added virtually philosophically, but with an ominous purpose: 'The reality is always that everything we do is known to someone, a neighbour, a PA, a friend, a driver. There are *never* any forever hidden secrets, there are just secrets waiting to be discovered. And when they do surface, as they will, a *person of interest* can easily be promoted to *suspect*, and we would wish to avoid that if we can.'

'Now, just a minute,' interrupted Christopher Miller tersely, 'are you threatening to arrest my wife?'

'Mr Miller,' replied Faraday coldly, 'the other day you told me that you were unaware of your "cousin's" first name. That was untrue. *You* knew his name,' said Faraday, again with a certainty unsupported by the slightest evidence. 'Lying to the police during a murder investigation is extremely imprudent and could very easily bounce *you* up from *person of interest* to *suspect*.' Mr Miller was about to protest but Faraday raised his hand and continued without a pause. 'We said to you both at the beginning of this enquiry that we would be as open with you as such an enquiry would allow. I am being open with you now. If you consider my comments to be a threat, then I am also seeking to remove the threat of embarrassing you both personally and professionally.' Faraday allowed this prospect to hang in the air as he turned to Mrs Miller. 'I need to know what type of relationship you have, or have had, with Nicholas Milano. Would you care to tell me now?'

A stillness filled the room. Maria Miller stiffened in her seat. She blushed and for a moment she felt embarrassment as she considered her response, wondering what she should or should not say. Anyone, she thought, would envy her life-style since meeting Christopher. And why, she wondered, had she ever been reckless enough to become entangled with Nicholas Milano and place her trust in such a man. Excitement, maybe even danger, she knew was the reason. Faraday allowed her time to wonder, to gather her thoughts together, before she spoke, whilst Kay studied her. She was endowed with a natural beauty, enhanced by careful make-up. Her finger nails were immaculately manicured, her hair perfectly styled and her jewellery was tasteful and reassuringly expensive.

'It all started,' she said, 'whilst I was working at Stockley, Kray and Burgess in Madeira. Nicholas came to the firm as a client,' she continued reasonably, her composure restored. 'He sought advice regarding issues of trade regulations, particularly the restrictions which he felt were inhibiting his wine business. The EU legislation is immensely complex,' she explained, 'but we were able to help his company. He was handsome and charming, immaculately groomed and witty, with an easy and ready smile. We were both single,' adding vaguely, 'we met socially,' before continuing. 'My family had experienced some significant difficulties when they were establishing their restaurant businesses in the UK. As a teenager, it was an unsettling and confusing time for me. I could see the worry and distress that was being caused to my parents. In fact, at one period the family were actually frightened, and my parents could not disguise that or shield us from it. Nicholas had a very different story to tell, but the impact upon him was similar, I think. His family history, the background against which he was raised, was one of family quarrels and recriminations that were unsettling and confusing for him. The family specialised in the wine trade, a trade that had been badly affected from time to time by a fungus called *oidium* and a root-boring insect called *phyloxer*, and even floods. These real or potentially damaging occurrences hung over the family business, and its success or failure. It was a constant worry for the Milanos. There was a meeting of minds, I suppose. Initially, we had much in common, but Nicholas,' she paused before she continued as if reluctant to malign him, ' … was shallow and self-absorbed. He was a gambler, mainly poker and roulette and, as we know, the "house" always wins. His gambling became a source of friction between us, although somehow, he always managed to keep his financial head above water.'

Maria Miller adjusted her posture on the settee, but her movement did not cause her husband to relax his reassuring grasp of her hand, as she continued: 'He was very close to his mother whose extravagancies he often funded and he was extremely proud of his family name being associated with The Great Siege and, as a citizen of Gibraltar, he was able to secure a commission in the Royal Gibraltar Regiment.'

Her thoughts for a moment seemed to drift but then Mrs Miller continued reasonably. 'He served two tours in Afghanistan. During his second tour, I was offered advancement to our main Bristol office and I thought that this would be a good opportunity for us to go our separate ways and start over. Nicholas was so wrapped up in the regiment that he didn't seem to be too concerned that I was relocating. Once I had settled in Bristol, Nicholas would visit two or three times a year on wine business and we would meet up, but once the UK's military commitment to Afghanistan lessened, Nicholas wanted to resume the relationship on a much closer and longer-term basis. I did not. Last year he came to Bristol twice and I rather cowardly ignored his calls. He texted again in February and these calls I ignored too. On the 11th April he texted me. Excuse me a moment.'

Maria Miller rose elegantly from the settee glancing back towards he husband as if to say: 'trust me, I know what I am doing', and walked to the kitchen, retrieving her mobile from her handbag. Christopher Miller remained seated but looked uncertain and bemused. Maria returned to the lounge, scrolling through her messages. 'There are no secrets here, Mr Faraday. Here we are,' she said as she handed her mobile to the policeman, her perfume enveloping the officers, 'at 09:37 on the 11th : "You bitch. You married that bastard".'

Both officers read the screen. 'He did not know of your marriage?' asked Kay sceptically.

'I assume not,' she replied understandably. 'But I'm not surprised. It was low key. A small family gathering in San Ferdinando,' then responding to Kay's questioning look, added, 'in Italy, on the outskirts of Naples.'

'And he didn't contact you on the 7th, 8th, 9th or 10th?' persisted Kay precisely.

'No,' she replied firmly. Kay thought that odd but saw no immediate purpose in pursuing the point, mindful that the text message could have been triggered by reference on the 11th to *Mr and Mrs Christopher Miller* in one of the local newspapers. She changed tack.

'Nicholas has homes in Madeira and Gibraltar I believe?' enquired Kay.

'Yes, in Funchal, a very nice property he owns jointly with his mother, and an apartment on Europa Road in Gibraltar.'

'I suppose it would depend on an individual's income but, would these properties be considered expensive?'

'They would, I suppose. The Madeira property is substantial and luxurious and any apartments on the southern part of Europa Road are always sought after as they offer splendid views over the Straits towards Morocco.'

Kay wondered how familiar Mrs Miller had been with these two properties, but continued. 'You said that the family were always quarrelling. What was that all about?' she asked.

Mrs Miller thought for a moment before clarifying. 'Quarrelling would be the wrong word, more a constant negativity which became the norm because of its frequency.'

'And the root of this negativity would have been what?' probed Kay.

'It was a lot of nonsense as far as I could gather,' she said, pleased that the conversation had moved away from Nicholas Milano and onto safer ground. 'Obviously I wasn't aware of all the details but it seemed that, way back, there was one particular ancestor who had been responsible for one, or even two, illegitimate children and this may have complicated the issue of inheritance and the direction of the business. It was a constant source of conversation and recrimination.'

'Did these illegitimate children have any real bearing on the family fortunes?' she queried.

'I don't think there was any actual evidence of illegitimate children, but they were a family who had developed a habit of always blaming others or events for any problems that they may have encountered. There was bitterness, particularly in respect of divorces. This bitterness seemed to have been encouraged by Nicholas' mother and grandmother. And then there was Nicholas' divorce. But, on the surface, the family maintained a dignified and charming image. They were well off, and, of course, had the attractive connection with the heroic Great Siege.'

'And so, are you saying that despite all their bitterness and negativity, Nicholas and the family were successful business people?'

'They were very knowledgeable and, what is the word … yes, they were canny, but Nicholas, he was not a business man. He tended to look upon the family name and business as a convenient backdrop to his pleasant, casual life-style. I think you would describe him as a charming, but rather indolent, pleasure-seeker who revelled in his connection with Colonel Milano.'

'There was a direct connection then, with Colonel Milano?' continued Kay.

'I'm not sure there was, and Nicholas deliberately didn't make any effort to confirm the connection in case he found none.' All four smiled at the wisdom of that course.

'And you, Christopher, said that you may be directly connected with Colonel Milano?' questioned Faraday recalling their previous conversation.

'I'm not sure that I am either. I have never seen any actual evidence, a family tree, letters or photographs. I suppose I should enquire for curiosity sake. Maybe if we had children or I was in the army it might have more relevance, but I have just assumed that there would have been a connection. You see, Gibraltar is a very small place. Even now, I think the population is less than a tenth of that of the city of Bristol, so, there is always likely to be a connection, but it isn't really that important to me.'

'But important to Nicholas?' challenged Faraday lightly.

'It helped to open doors for him,' replied Mrs Miller, 'and … and ensured that he was … he was accepted.'

Kay wondered how insecure Nicholas Milano must be before asking: 'His text to you indicates an angry individual?'

Mrs Miller didn't answer immediately. She was thoughtful before replying. 'I had never seen him angry as such. Agitated, preoccupied, maybe. As I said, he seems to have been able to keep his head above water most of the time but EU regulations and tariffs were … a worry to him. He would become agitated, partly because he didn't really understand any of it – or simply didn't want to. And then there were some gambling debts and he was financially supporting his mother, all of which would be costing him about €2-3,000 per month.'

Mrs Miller didn't really answer the question but Kay pursued the more critical avenue. 'And so how did he manage to keep his head above water?'

'I think he had, how would you say … he had his fingers in other pies.'

'Such as?' queried Kay.

'I really don't know, but the numbers never seemed to add up. When I asked him about his debts or expenses he would say confidently: "Don't worry about it. It's all covered". He seemed rather smug about it as if he had a very clever scheme in place that was making him money.'

'"It's all covered" in what way do you think?' persisted Kay.

Mrs Miller thought for a long moment before answering. 'I really don't know. It was as if the whole finance thing was catered for by … by some sort of monthly arrangement, maybe a dividend, some sort of regular credit, a debt repayment, a legacy. But I don't know.' Kay tucked this issue away in her mind as she changed focus again.

'What else did he have cause to be bitter about?' asked Kay.

'Very little, and that is what made our relationship strained. He was sometimes quite irrational. He was handsome and charming. He had a good family name. He wasn't rich but he was certainly financially very comfortable indeed, but he was sometimes … unrealistic.'

'Unrealistic? In what way?' Faraday queried.

Mrs Miller thought for a moment. 'An example would be the army. He … he quietly resented the regular regimental officers I think. He was in command of 'B' Company, I'm sure that it was 'B', whatever, it was the reserve company, and so as a reservist there was no opportunity for him to hold a higher rank than that of captain which he thought … yes … he thought he was owed.'

'And what do you think people think of him and his family?' asked Faraday.

'He's a charmer,' she replied, a little too warmly and readily, then tried to distance herself from any suggestion that her ready response indicated a residual affection. 'I think people generally would consider him to be a vain man, but good company. The family? Affluent and influential. A little eccentric possibly, but respected.'

Mark looked at Kay. She nodded. 'Thank you both for your candour,' he said as he closed his leather file then added, his eyes smiling with amused curiosity. 'Maybe you would like to introduce us to "*Dirty Nell*".'

The dining room was large, with gold striped wallpaper and *Summer Evening* cream gloss paint, uncluttered and strangely calm. Sun light flooding in through the tall, triple patio windows, their delicate, pale-grey, floor-to-ceiling drapes stirred in the gentle breeze. The eighteen foot long dining table was perfectly set for twelve guests. Although large, the table didn't dominate the room. In the centre of the dining table was '*Dirty Nell*'. Three foot high by four foot long. It was '*Dirty Nell*' that dominated the table and the room. This centre-piece was graceful and elegant, serene and innocent, captivating and compelling. Not at all pornographic. Just utterly beautiful.

Chapter Eight

Monday, 21st April.

Bristol and London, England.

ROBERT PERRIN DIDN'T LIKE DRIVING. Mark Faraday and Kay Yin did. An Assistant Chief Constable would rate a staff car and driver which would allow him to work on papers as he travelled and avoid the delays and interruptions of rail travel. But Mark volunteered to drive up to London with Kay driving on the return journey, thus saving the use of a police driver.

Kay had amended her briefing paper which had been e-mailed to the Foreign and Commonwealth Office, although her brief case contained hard copies. The staff car was an unmarked grey BMW 5 Series and the officers were in plain clothes. Perrin sat in the rear left-hand seat, his grey double-breasted suit jacket in a carrier in the boot. Mark chose an Epson, single-breasted grey sharkskin suit with navy and red striped shirt and red patterned tie, with Kay wearing a blue Smyth blazer and trousers and black loafers.

They spoke continuously, discussing the Chief Constable's visit to the FCO on the 16th and the latest developments. Kay referred to a much more detailed briefing file she had prepared for Robert Perrin as she spoke. All *persons of interest* had been interviewed and could, with the exception of Mr and Mrs Miller, be safely eliminated from their enquiries, she explained. Forensics had confirmed that the mud at the entrance porch of Grange Lodge was identical to that found at the boundary wall. The local authority's CCTV near Grange Lodge had provided no useful information, although Victor Jenkins' vehicle had been sighted on eleven occasions parked at various locations near Queen's Chambers in the five weeks prior to the murder of Guy Hernandez. Nicholas Milano had also been identified as walking along Whiteladies Road at 11.05am and again further along the road at 11.53am on the 8th, near The Jersey Lily, the public house named after Lily Langtree, the mistress of Edward VII when he was the Prince of Wales, and in Clifton Village at a variety of location between 10.34am and 5.17pm on the 11th. Enquiries with the circus had only identified one individual of interest to the police who had been wanted on warrant, but nothing to connect the circus with the death of Guy Hernandez or Victor Jenkins, although two stall holders, the coconut shy and the hi-striker, remember a boisterous Jenkins being at the circus on the day of his death, but no recollection of Milano. The hotel room used by Nicholas Milano was subjected to forensic examination but nothing was discovered that would help the officers' enquiry. The calendar hanging on a nail behind the kitchen door in Victor Jenkins' flat was endorsed with scribbled notes, mainly regarding betting fixtures and shopping lists, but nothing apparently to connect Jenkins with the murder, with the exception of a time: '6' endorsed in the 9th of the month square and '730' in the 10th square, together with the impression of the figures '6844', scrawled at an angle, corresponding with 8th, 14th and 20th of the previous month. The brain-numbing task of searching CCTV footage was continuing.

Significantly, enquiries in the Old Market café frequented by Jenkins revealed that he had had a dispute with Theodore 'Boats' Leahouse – 'Boats' attracted this name because of his huge feet! Worryingly, Leahouse was a known associate of John 'Dusty' Miller who had convictions for possessing and supplying firearms. During interview, Leahouse would agree to having had an argument with Jenkins over an unpaid loan but denied any involvement with the supply of firearms to Jenkins and refused to comment on any involvement with 'Dusty' Miller, but believed that Jenkins had managed to buy a Croatian weapon from a rival source during the previous month. This was never substantiated but could have been a comment by Leahouse to divert attention away from his own criminal activities. Whatever the source, the officers were obliged to conclude that Jenkins may have obtained a firearm, although no firearm had been found in Jenkins' flat or in and around his burnt-out vehicle.

Enquiries with the security chief of Greaves, Scutt and Pinnock, wine merchants of Denmark Street, Bristol, confirmed Nicholas Milano's business appointments which, together with his hotel reservations seemed to provide Nicholas Milano with a water-tight alibi for the time of the murder of Guy Hernandez, although not that of Victor Jenkins.

As they sped along the M4, Faraday mentioned his interview with Housekeeping staff on the 15th, particularly a young Greek chambermaid, Nefeli Alexandratou, who remembered the fragments of a torn-up photograph that she had found in the waste basket of the room occupied by Nicholas Milano. This information resulted in Faraday's subsequent search of rubbish bags stored in the hotel's basement which led to the finding of Milano's hotel-issued tooth brush and a torn-up photograph of Nicholas Milano and Maria Miller captured in a friendly, holiday-style pose with the Clifton Suspension Bridge in the background.

Kay spoke of her phone call with DCI Seward of the South Yorkshire Police. Seward recalled Mrs Miller's family and the petrol bomb attack upon one of their restaurants. Tellingly, Seward mentioned an incident that occurred at about the same time when Mrs Miller was fifteen years of age. It was reported by her school that Maria had been subjected to bullying by some boys. Apparently, Maria had been referred to as a 'gawky Italian slut'. On one particular occasion, Maria was followed home after school by four boys who, in an alleyway, pulled her hair painfully and pushed her violently against a wall. Maria responded by picking up a length of wood from a rubbish skip and forcefully struck one of the boys on the upper arm. Significantly, Maria did not run away but stood her ground against the four older boys who promptly ran off. There was no police action but the incident became common knowledge around the school. Robert Perrin, Mark and Kay discussed this incident and wondered whether young Maria's conduct demonstrated courage, quick-wittedness, determination or even ruthlessness – or, maybe, a combination of all four.

Mark and Kay spoke of their interview with Mr and Mrs Miller and the text message from Nicholas Milano. Mrs

Miller had said that 'there are no secrets here' yet, it seemed that Mr Miller had been unaware of the text. The three officers speculated as to why Christopher Miller had never researched any possible family connection with one of the heroes of The Great Siege, Colonel Milano, which they thought could easily enhance his political ambitions in Gibraltar. They also wondered why Nicholas Milano had not called Mrs Miller on the 7th, 8th, 9th or 10th, concluding that it would be wise for them to assume that it was to avoid any traceable link between the two. Consequently, Mrs Miller was promoted from *person of interest* to *suspect*, particularly as it appeared that she was the only person likely to gain from Mr Miller's death and inherit £8.7 million.

***

The Foreign and Commonwealth Office, situated on King Charles Street, impressed. Designed by George Scott in the Italianate style, this Grade One building was intended to impress and intimidate. The magnificently imposing paintings that adorned the walls, the dark oak panelling, the sweeping grandeur of the marble Grand Staircase with its purple carpet – all impressed. Impressed and cautious, the officers were not, however, intimidated as they waited to be summoned into the presence of Sir George Sinclair, the Permanent Under-Secretary of State, although they were to find that he looked uncannily like Sir Winston Churchill and possessed an equally gravelly voice.

Even so, the officers privately acknowledged that Sir George's office was rather splendid with dark oak panelling, an imposing conference table and a magnificent desk. Sir George was standing at the windows as they entered and warmly shook their hands. He then occupied his chair behind his magnificent desk inviting the three officers to sit immediately in front of him in the most comfortable of leather button-backed chairs, with the finest of coffee poured from a Queen Anne pot by his secretary.

Pleasantries concluded, Perrin invited Mark to summarise. He did so. He spoke firstly of the media strategy and 'holding' statements given by the police, matters that he thought would be upper most in Sir George's mind - they were. 'Fortunately, the death of a junior employee from a car dealership does not seem to have attracted the media's attention,' said Faraday, 'but what has is the assumed attempted theft of a £100,000 Maserati. Subsequent press articles have concentrated upon the number of high-end car thefts in Bristol and the UK, and the illegal export market to right-hand drive Commonwealth countries, particularly Nigeria. This has resulted in robust denials from Nigeria which have simply served to fuel a continuing debate in the press. Consequently, there has been little attention directed towards Mr Miller, with much more interest towards Nigerian gangs,' adding, 'and we have done nothing to dispel that interest.'

Sir George nodded approvingly as he asked: 'And no reference has been made to the fact that Mr Victor Jenkins was shot?'

'No, Sir George' replied Faraday. 'The coroner is aware. The usual procedure was followed with an inquest being opened then adjourned. Meanwhile, the press release had concentrated upon the macabre nature of the fire.'

'But the view is that the killing of Mr Guy Hernandez was premeditated?'

'Yes. That is so. There is evidence to suggest that Jenkins carried out rudimentary observations upon office premises owned and frequented by Mr Miller. The nature of the attack upon Hernandez shows premeditation, although no sign of it having been frenzied or personal.'

'A murderous task that remains to be completed then?' observed Sir George.

'We think so.'

'And another assailant could be waiting in the wings?' speculated Sir George.

'Yes,' replied Faraday, 'although if Nicholas Milano is behind this attack and he is no longer in the UK, such a re-run would take some time to organise. Meanwhile, Mr and Mrs Miller have secured the personal protection services of Fraser Security.'

Sir George nodded approvingly. 'And you say that there is not sufficient evidence to arrest Nicholas Milano?'

'If Milano should come to the UK, there are "reasonable grounds" to arrest him.' Sir George looked up as if to ask an unspoken question. Faraday took the opportunity to explain. 'Firstly, his association with Mrs Miller and a possible family link to Mr Miller. Secondly, Milano is known to have a possible link to the scene of Victor Jenkins' death – it's a loose link, I agree. Thirdly, there is our need to protect the public. However, I doubt very much that the Gibraltarian authorities would place such a liberal interpretation on our view.' Sir George nodded in agreement as Faraday continued. 'If Milano returns to the UK we would interview him, sir. Alternatively, we could interview him in Gibraltar, although I am assuming that you would not wish us to draw attention to members of the Miller/Milano family.'

Sir George smiled, a smile of agreement. 'Quite so, although an opportunity seems to have presented itself that would place you, Chief Superintendent, in Gibraltar.'

'An opportunity, Sir George. I don't quite follow?' queried Faraday.

'I think you know the Commissioner of Police,' said Sir George, scanning his open file, 'Hugh Thornton?'

'Yes, I do, sir. We attended the same Senior Command Course eighteen months ago. He and his wife have stayed with us on a number of weekends and Kay and I have visited him in Gibraltar twice.'

'Do you know that the Commissioner is unwell?'

'Yes, sir. Myeloma.'

Sir George removed another sheaf of papers from his file, reminding himself of the contents. 'He will shortly be undergoing chemotherapy at the Royal Bournemouth Hospital necessitating weekly hospital visits, followed by a stem cell transplant – or maybe it is the other way around. Whatever, the Dorset Police have been very good and have allocated him one of their VIP houses in Queens Park Avenue. The Deputy Commissioner is currently attending his SCC at Bramshill,' he said, referring to the Tudor mansion in Hampshire that is the Police Staff College, 'and will not return to Gibraltar for another four months. As a result, the Chief Minister, the Foreign Secretary and your Chief Constable have determined that you, Mr Faraday, will be appointed the temporary Commissioner of Police.' He leaned forward across his desk and asked in a gravelly voice. 'Are you prepared to undertake such an important role for us?'

For a moment Faraday was speechless. This was completely unexpected. He glanced towards Kay who nodded gently. 'Of course, sir,' he replied.

'The population of Gibraltar is about thirty thousand and the police force numbers only one-hundred and thirty, compared with your current responsibilities for the city of Bristol where you command seven-hundred and forty-nine staff. But,' he paused as he peered over his glasses, 'it is only right that I should tell you that your forthcoming responsibilities are not minor.' Sir George relaxed back into his chair as he continued: 'Gibraltar is small, village-like, in some respects insular. Everyone there seems to know everyone else, the road sweeper will be on first name terms with the Chief Minister, the councillor will know the shop keeper and the taxi driver — well, he will probably know everyone or be related to them. You will need to tread very carefully to be accepted. And then there's the military. The military have always been sensitive about their security role and there is always room for disagreement between the Military Governor and the Chief Minister, disagreements in which you may find yourself in the middle. There will be a royal visit during your tenure and Spain, of course, continues to be petulant and those difficulties will increase.' Sir George studied another piece of paper from his file. 'A bright young constable at the border crossing saw, what appeared to be, ordinary workmen making routine repairs to the frontier gates. What he also heard was one worker address another as "Brigada", that is Senior Sergeant — a Spanish army rank. MI6 confirm that the Spanish intend to seal off the border within the next three weeks.' Sir George reached across his desk and held up a maroon leather file. 'I have here a briefing file for you, Commissioner Faraday.'

Faraday stood, accepted the file and resumed his seat 'What it does not contain,' continued Sir George, 'are my very clear instructions to you that you must not take your appointment as Commissioner as an opportunity to investigate Mr Miller,' then added after a short pause, 'should, of course, information come to you attention regarding Mr Nicholas Milano or Mr Christopher Miller that you would consider pertinent to Miss Yin's enquiries or are likely to cause Her Majesty's government embarrassment, you will naturally bring these facts to the attention of the Chief Minister, and, the *immediate* attention of Mr Perrin and myself.   Do we understand the operational parameters?'

'Yes, sir.'

'And you, Miss Yin,' said Sir George fingering a copy of Kay's briefing file, 'believe that Nicholas Milano is behind all of this?'

'My instincts lead me to believe that to be the case, sir.'

'Well, I am minded to believe that your instincts are correct, Kay,' he said charmingly with a smile that, unfortunately, developed into a lascivious leer.   'You will, therefore, continue your Bristol investigation accordingly … ah, subject, *of course*, to Mr Perrin.'   Sir George remained silent for a short moment.   'There is the question of Madeira. There is always the possibility that Milano may wish to retreat to Madeira.   Would you also be able to make discreet enquiries on that delightful island if that should prove useful?'

There was no hesitation in her response.   'A man does come to mind, sir, a retired police officer of discretion and ability.'

'Discretion and ability you say?' he said, warming to her response.

'Proven discretion and uncanny ability, sir,' she replied.   'He had a nick name, "Have 'em in, Craven".   His record of arrests was staggering.   You see, he had the ability to think like a crook. If he had been a crook and not a policeman, I doubt very much whether we would have ever caught him.'

Sir George smiled. He liked what he had heard. 'He seems the ideal candidate for the tasks you may have in mind, Miss Yin. I leave that to you, but emphasise that your operational parameters remain as those pertaining to Gibraltar.'

'I fully understand, Sir George.'

'Meanwhile, it may be nothing of course, just the thoughts of someone whose family have spent their professional lives in the military and Diplomatic Service, but something you may wish to bear in mind.' He shuffled some papers together and placed them in a file on his desk before continuing in a relaxed and virtually amused tone. 'My grandfather served with the South Waziristan Scouts before transferring to the 1st Punjab Cavalry. My father also saw service in Afghanistan. I too was based in Pershawar whilst serving in what was, and still is I suppose, the North West Frontier, where the hill tribes are sturdy fellows who have fought and mistrusted each other for centuries, engaging in internecine blood feuds with considerable enthusiasm.' He closed a file and replaced the cap on his fountain pen. 'Throughout the sub-continent there are more than two-hundred languages spoken with a thousand dialects. Urdu is widely understood, of course, but interestingly in the context of our discussion, Miss Yin, in the Pushtu language of the most incendiary of the hill tribes, the word *dushman* means both "cousin" and "enemy". Why you may wonder, Miss Yin?' he asked rhetorically with a wry and experienced smile. 'It is because of their strongly held belief, confirmed over the generations, that it was inconceivable that a cousin could be anything other than an enemy.'

***

Maurice Underhill, Sir George's private secretary, had heard all of the conversation through the adjoining door which had been left slightly ajar. He entered the office and occupied one of the comfortable chairs vacated by the police officers.

'Did you manage to hear everything?' Sir George asked of Underhill who gave the appearance of an undertaker.

'Yes, I did, Sir George. They seem a sound trio, don't you think?'

'Yes, I believe so,' replied Sir George confidently. 'Perrin provides a protective umbrella. He is shrewd and competent and delightfully paternalistic to the others.'

'And the others?'

'Their personal files make for very compelling reading, including the "closed" sections. They are an impressive pair. It is clear that Faraday and the beguiling Miss Yin are dogged and determined, resourceful and imaginative, but also reliable and loyal with a sense of duty – duty,' he reflected, 'a much ridiculed notion nowadays but important nevertheless. When they detect the scent they will dig and dig. Their record indicates that they will both sail close to the wind if required and, I anticipate, they would breach the parameters I have set if the circumstances demanded, but they would not be fool-hardy and, the last thing they would want to do is to let Perrin down.'

'And you are not involving MI5 and MI6?'

'We could, but I think it best to leave them out of this one. The Gibraltarians wouldn't take kindly to our spies spying on them.'

'Only if it were to be found out, sir.'

'It would one day, Maurice, be assured of that.'

'And you think that Faraday and Yin will discover the whereabouts of the letter?'

'I believe they will,' he said with some certainty, adding jocularly, 'If the contents of the letter are revealed I would have to resign, like Lord Carrington, and find myself another job.'

'That significant?' asked Underhill seriously.

'Oh yes,' he replied equally seriously. 'The contents of the letter would destroy the historic and romantic edifice upon which Gibraltar's self-belief has been built.'

Chapter Nine

Wednesday, 23rd April.

The island of Madeira and Bristol, England.

'HOW CAN I HELP?' It was the way he always answered his phone. No name. Non-committal. But Brian Craven would always be willing and able to help Detective Superintendent Kay Yin. He was the man that immediately came to her mind when at the Foreign and Commonwealth Office speaking with Sir George Sinclair two days before. Brian was a former uniformed constable. He had never aspired to be a detective or senior officer. He remained a constable for all of his thirty years of service. Throughout, he tended to be contemptuous of senior ranks who he once described as 'purveyors of irrelevances', people who revelled in the trivia of bureaucracy but had little real understanding of the business of policing. This was certainly unfair, but Brian stubbornly held to that belief. As a result he had been, to some extent, an outsider and a loner but his innate stubbornness and focus on the bad guys resulted in him being a remarkable thief-taker. There were a few senior officers whom Brian did respect, Chief Superintendent Faraday and Detective Superintendent Yin were amongst them, both of whom would be seen on the streets in full uniform late at night, both of whom would race to the assistance of an 'officer down', both would be prepared to appear in court to support officers presenting their evidence or stand by officers who were the subject of criticism but had acted honestly and in good faith.

Kay had phoned Brian Craven saying that she needed 'a good man', a phrase she would always use when they served together and she needed a reliable and discrete officer for a particularly sensitive task. Brian had obligingly listened as Kay had told him that she needed his help in deciding upon the purchase of a holiday property on the island of Madeira and she would send him some details for his opinion. He knew this to be utter nonsense, but readily agreed. That was all she needed to know. During the next two weeks, Kay would send him the property details concealing the assignment. Later, Brian would receive instructions that all correspondence would be routed to Faraday through the home address of Mrs Julie Levant, using her maiden name of Ricardo.

***

Kay drove Mark towards their home in Stoke Bishop in her Golf GTi. They had left Faraday's divisional headquarters at The Grove a little after four and had driven through the afternoon sunshine to the City Centre, onwards towards the imposing Council House and up the steep hill that is Park Street, dominated at its summit by the Wills Memorial Building tower which housed the university's School of Law and the School of Earth Sciences. They intended to have a quick salad snack in their apartment before heading out to Force HQ and a meeting with the ACC (Crime). But their early journey home would not be wasted. They had been trying to solve a quandary for a number of days now.

Their route took them around The Triangle, turning left towards the mock-Grecian Victoria Rooms and past the Royal West of England College of Art, then towards the Artillery Ground and on to Whiteladies Road. For most of the journey Mark had sat in silent thought.

'Take the next left, my love?' he suggested.

Kay indicated and turned into Apsley Road. She read Mark's mind and turned next left into St John's Road, which ran roughly parallel to Whiteladies Road, then into Pembroke Road, until they reached Whiteladies Road again.

'See if we can pull in just past the rail station?' he asked.

'I'm there', she said anticipating the stop. She parked neatly outside the small library but didn't switch off the engine. Mark turned around in his seat, lowering his head to look out through the car's windows. Why, he thought, should Nicholas Milano want to wander up this road on the 8th? It was the question that had occupied their mind since Nicola, one of her ablest of detectives, had identified Milano after ploughing through hundreds and hundreds of hours of recordings from the numerous CCTV cameras situated throughout the city.

'We know that Milano's behaviour didn't alert the CCTV operators to target him specifically, they were sweeping the area and he just happened to crop up twice,' mused Faraday. 'There is no indication from Milano's conduct that he was waiting for anyone or had met someone; was interested in any particular premises or visited any specific address.'

'And so why was he wandering up this road between eleven and noon? puzzled Kay. 'We know from the hotel's records that he had lunch at a little after one o'clock. And so, why Whiteladies Road?'

Silent thoughts filled the car. Then Faraday spoke again. 'And none of the coffee shops and restaurants recognised Milano's photograph,' he said as Kay moved out into the traffic, anticipating again his requirements, Faraday peering left and right as she did so. 'The other premises are chemist shops, hairdressing salons, clothes and furniture shops ... ,' he said as he peered about, '... estate agents, auctioneers and building societies. There's even a hardware store ... an art gallery ... a few charity shops, plus a couple of churches.'

'And banks,' suggested Kay as she pulled in to the near-side kerb by the auctioneers and across the road from the Methodist church.

'Yes. There are three and they will have security cameras. We had better have them checked out.'

'Can do and I'll check again with the Avon Gorge Hotel,' agreed Kay, 'and see whether Milano paid by cash or by card which would indicate his bank. If it was a bank he visited, then he could have been making a deposit or withdrawal.'

Faraday remained silent for a long moment. He pondered the possibility of a deposit or withdrawal and his thoughts wandered. 'What's bugging me is Victor Jenkins' flat. We know he paid cash for his car and his flat would have been cheap to rent, but Jenkins had been unemployed for months. It begs the question: How did Jenkins have the money to pay for his car, pay the rent for his flat and live? It would be useful if we knew how much his rent was and how he paid, but we haven't been able to contact the absentee landlord.'

'No. He's not co-operating and lives in Lanzarote. Been there for months.'

They paused their conversation, both deep in thought. 'Whatever,' continued Faraday, his thoughts refocusing on Jenkins, 'if the rent is really cheap then Jenkins would probably be doing enough little jobs on the side, sufficient to pay the rent. If not, he's getting his money from someone and, my guess is, Captain Milano.'

'I will have Nicola chase up any CCTV recordings in and around Jenkins' flat for the 7th to the 12th, particularly the 9th and 10th. The '6' and '730', endorsed on the calendar in his kitchen, could be times of meetings ... meetings with Milano,' suggested Kay.

'Yes, and 7.30pm on the 10th would be about the time Victor Jenkins was killed.'

'If that is so, was there a meeting on the 9th at six o'clock, and for what purpose?'

Chapter Ten

Wednesday, 30th April.

British Overseas Territory, Gibraltar and Bristol, England.

THE BRITISH AIRWAYS AIRBUS 320, one of the two-hour thirty-seven minute flights from Bristol, made a gradual decent over the sparkling blue waters of the Bay of Algeciras on its final approach to North Front Airport, Gibraltar, considered to be the fifth 'most extreme' airports in the world - and one thousand feet shorter than Bristol airport's main runway.

As the A320 approached, Gibraltar seemed to act as a reassuring beacon, a 1,398 foot high mass of Jurassic limestone standing defiantly stark against the perfect pale blue sky, atop the two and a half square miles of the British Overseas Territory, ceded to England in perpetuity by the Treaty of Utrech in 1713.

The flaps on the trailing edge of the A320's wings extended fully, creating maximum drag and reducing lift, before the aircraft made its perfect landing, crossing the Winston Churchill Avenue, the main north-south street, that dissected this single short runway. Then the Rolls-Royce engines seemed to roar as the redirected air from the turbines created the reverse thrust that brought the aircraft to a gentle halt.

Passengers disembarked, the aircraft was quickly unloaded and Mark Faraday retrieved his three suitcases in the cool Arrivals area. Passengers, trollies and suitcases moved slowly across the marble floor towards the exit, and, at HM Customs the procedure was unhurried and relaxed. When it was his turn, Faraday stepped forward, placed his passport in front of the official who asked him the purpose of his visit. 'I am to take over temporarily as the Police Commissioner and will be here for about four months.'

The official glanced at his screen, nodded, then handed Faraday his passport with a knowing smile. 'Welcome to Gibraltar, Commissioner.'

In the Arrivals hall, Superintendent Antonio Quattromini stood immaculate in uniform jacket, not shirt-sleeve order that would have been quite appropriate, and saluted smartly clearly determined to demonstrate a respectful welcome. A good, reassuring start, thought Faraday. They warmly shook hands and walked towards the exit to emerge into the bright, warm sunlight again.

Quattromini's car was parked a little to the left. They loaded the car, then drove along the narrow, bustling roads to the apartment allocated to the new Commissioner at Europa Point where there was ample residents' parking. They parked and Faraday stepped out of the car and, for a brief moment, admired the sea-scape view, savouring the air which was fresh and salty. Both officers removed the suitcases from the boot and walked the short distance to the main entrance, then mounted the few steps to enter the entrance hall - wide, deep and cool - with its marble stairs and Spanish-style iron chandeliers. The apartment, on the third floor, was comfortably furnished, light and airy, with a single balcony leading off the lounge and master bedroom, affording a splendid and restful view towards Morocco, just eight miles distant.

Superintendent Quattromini had thoughtfully had the fridge/freezer and larder filled with all the immediate necessities, and had prepared a briefing file with details of the apartment's cleaning company's schedules, near-by shops and stores, café and restaurants, laundrettes and clothes retailers, plus a bottle of Santo Nykteri, together with a Royal Gibraltar Police cap badge.

'I will leave you to get settled in and collect you at two, if that is convenient for you, sir?'

'That will be just right, Antonio, and thank you for preparing everything for me. A great welcome and all very thoughtful.'

Once the superintendent had left, Faraday pulled his suitcases into the master bedroom and placed them on the bed in a neat row. He unlocked and unzipped the cases and threw back the lids, removing all the items and carefully placing each item into an appropriate drawer or on an appropriate hanger. Faraday had brought with him his own uniform, although his new insignia of rank, identical to those of a UK Commissioner, had been put on his epaulettes by the Severnside tailors store, together with the lapel gorget patches, and a brand new chief officer's cap with two rows of silver oak leaves to which he was able to affix the badge of his new force.

He checked the bathroom and deposited his toiletries. He surveyed the master bedroom and placed one of his favourite photographs of Kay on the bedside table. Satisfied – for the moment – he made tea and sat on the balcony reading the briefing file that Superintendent Quattromini had prepared. Faraday highlighted various words and sentences, making notations in the margins or at the foot of each page, adding little boxes that would require questions, actions and little ticks to be inserted upon completion.

At 2pm Faraday stood outside the apartment carrying a black briefcase containing Quattromini's file, together with that provided by the Foreign and Commonwealth Office. The sun shone brightly, but it wasn't oppressively hot, just pleasantly warm with an easy breeze. Faraday was dressed in blazer and wore a tie. It was probably inappropriate, but Quattromini had worn a tie and so would Faraday – today at least. He did not wear his uniform, which would certainly be inappropriate, as he was not to be sworn-in until the following day.

They drove along Rosia Road to the police headquarters and Faraday wondered whether Colonel Henry Bartolomeu Milano had once walked along this very road near the Clock Tower or had stood atop its fortifications. Located at New Mole House, the police headquarters was a modern complex, although the arched entrance way with its two traditional blue, wall-mounted, police lamps, formed part of the original fortifications. The building exuded strength, a sense of purpose and reliability – like the fine force that was the Royal Gibraltar Police.

At the main entrance, Faraday made a point of introducing himself to the receptionists and front office staff and anyone he met en route to his office on the first floor. There he met Mrs Julie Levant, the commissioner's PA, who exuded a smiling competence. She was utterly professional and welcoming, although, understandably, a little unsettled. Faraday was ushered into his new office. It was a good size, cooled by a quiet and efficient air conditioning system, well furnished with a six-seat pine conference table in front of his matching desk. Mrs Levant and Faraday sat at this table and talked, mostly about Hugh Thornton's usual work routine and scheduled appointments, with Faraday allowing that conversation to roll as they drank tea. Then he explained the way he normally worked, his dyslexia and the reliance he would place upon her. He had been assured by Hugh Thornton of Mrs Levant's discretion and that she had signed The Official Secrets Act, and so he then spoke of the need to make arrangements to receive correspondence from Madeira, and that it would be expedient to use her home address and maiden name, if she was in agreement. 'This matter essentially concerns an incident in Bristol, a matter with which I am still involved,' he explained. 'There is no need for you to know the details, other than for me to assure you that this matter does not reflect badly in any way upon our force or Commissioner Thornton.'

Mrs Levant readily agreed to the clandestine postal arrangements, pleased that Faraday had taken her so readily into his confidence. They talked of the schedule of visits and meetings that Antonio and Julie had arranged – and there were many: the Chief Minister, Faraday's formal swearing-in as Commissioner the following day; meetings with the Military Governor, councillors and local government departmental officials, the officer commanding the Royal Gibraltar Regiment, and the various police units.

'When you speak with the regimental adjutant, would you say that I would very much like to visit their museum – I assume they have one?'

'They do,' replied Julie Levant. 'Is there anything in particular that would interest you, sir?'

'Oh yes, but there is no need to tell them,' he said with a grin and a mischievous wink. Julie smiled. She was sure that she would enjoy working with Mr Faraday.

As their meeting drew to a close, Mrs Levant remarked: 'Mr Thornton has cleared the top of his desk for you … it looks so bare,' she observed as her voice became a little strained. 'The right pedestal drawers,' she continued, 'have also been cleared for your use. The left pedestal drawers are locked but the keys are on this ring together with the keys to my office and yours, of course.'

Faraday took the keys from her but asked: 'Where are Mr Thornton's family photographs?'

'I put them in a box, sir, in the foot of the clothes locker.'

'No, that won't do at all,' Faraday said not unkindly as he glanced around the office. 'Hugh always spoke about his photographs. Get them out and put them on the bookcase, please. This will always be Mr Thornton's office. I'm just the caretaker. It's where they belong in readiness for his return,' said Faraday, partly because he knew that his friend would not want his precious photographs shoved away in a dark locker, but also because he wanted to make a confident statement to Julie Levant that Hugh Thornton would be returning to resume his rightful command.

Faraday rose from the conference table as Julie retrieved Thornton's photographs from the locker and arranged them on the bookcase shelving, whilst Faraday placed his briefcase on the leather-topped desk, opened it and removed two framed photographs of his own. One was of his parents. The other was of Kay. He sat in the commissioner's chair, then repositioned the computer terminal and telephone console, finally placing the two photographs in front of him, but slightly off-centre to the right, so that every time he reached for the phone he would see her photograph.

'May I, sir?' asked Julie Levant, gesturing towards the photographs.

'Of course,' replied Faraday, picking up one of the frames. 'These are my parents.'

'I can see the resemblance. They look a fine couple.'

'They were. We were very lucky children.' He took back the photograph and placed it thoughtfully and carefully on the desk before handing his PA the second. 'And this is Kay, my wife.'

'My goodness, she is *so* beautiful … if I may say so.'

'Yes, in more ways than one, Julie. She brightens my life.' He paused for some while, his thoughts drifting. 'Anyway, enough of this.' He checked his 'to do' list and discussed its contents.

Lastly, he explained that Inspector Purchell from the Severnside Police would be arriving in two days' time as his staff officer and would share his office. He also explained the role of the staff officer.

'Additionally, Inspector Purchell will have some duties in connection with the Bristol affair. We can talk a little more about his role when he arrives. Meanwhile, I have a meeting scheduled with the Superintendent and we will be drafting a letter to all staff outlining some of my thoughts for my tenure here and also explaining the presence of Inspector Purchell and his duties. When it's done I would like you to look at it and tell me what you think.'

'Thank you for taking me into your confidence, Commissioner,' she said, 'and I will do my very best to serve you as I have Mr Thornton. If you wish, I will arrange for another desk and an additional secure filing cabinet,' she offered perceptively.

'Thank you, Julie, and before I forget, the telephone people will be here tomorrow to install an additional phone. Again, all to do with the Bristol affair.' But Faraday thought it unnecessary to explain that the new line would be a secure one to the GCHQ relay and collection station on *The Rock*.

***

Holly Lamb had a nice desk in a pleasant, open-plan office occupied by eighteen of her co-workers, most of whom were female, all of whom were friendly and supportive. Her desk was near the main entrance doors to the office. This allowed Holly the freedom to come and go as she pleased and, situated against the windows, it afforded her a pleasant view of Isambard Kingdom Brunel's masterpiece, the Clifton Suspension Bridge, which the Victorian engineer had described as *'my first love, my darling'*.

This was Holly's third day back at work with the insurance company. They had not been full days. Just mornings. 9am to noon. Her work load had been light and measured. Co-workers had made a point of joining her at the coffee station, but only one at a time. They had been advised not to crowd her. They had contrived a friendly distance. They had not overwhelmed her – or so they hoped.

The office was spacious. It could not be described as crowded in any way. It was light and airy and benefitted from a southerly aspect. But for Holly, she had begun to feel trapped again as she had before her break-down. Her hands would sometimes tremble and she would chew her lower lip. She tried to focus on her work or look at the photographs on her desk, photographs of her parents, or her cat, Bounty, or favourite Cornish holiday destinations. She would push her over-sized glasses up her little nose and glance at the clock. Co-workers would smile reassuringly towards her from time to time. And Holly would smile a practiced reassuring smile in return.

At noon Holly carefully tided her desk, placed her unfinished files in her 'IN' tray and took her neatly completed work to Miss Hastings, her supervisor. For a few moments they discussed the well-prepared files before Holly waved to her co-workers who waved enthusiastically in return.

'See you tomorrow, Holly,' they said cheerfully.

'Yes,' she replied with her pretty smile, 'see you tomorrow.'

It was such a beautiful day near the graceful suspension bridge of twin stone towers and vast wrought-iron chains. The sun was shining. Lovers were walking hand in hand; parents were pushing buggies and old folk were sat on the park benches watching the world go by. Constable Colin Bradshaw was enjoying the sun too as he walked from the direction of Leigh Woods towards Clifton and the city, across the 702 foot expanse of the road and pedestrian suspension bridge that spanned the Avon Gorge and the river more than 240 feet below. The water of the river was muddy-grey but this did not distract from the magnificence of the rugged limestone rock face and the river's winding beauty, often so brilliantly captured by artists such as Frank Shipsides and Glyn Martin, nor the elegance of the houses on Sion Hill beyond. But Constable Bradshaw was not distracted from his primary duty. Old folk or young children tended to be distracted by the bridge itself or the views from it and, the elderly and children and vehicles were never a good mix. And the occasional drunk or rowdy youth would sometimes need his timely attention. In short, the officer was constantly aware of his surroundings. He was also aware that the public mainly acted in a range of predictable ways. Their laughter. Their mannerisms. Their gait. Of course, a child would look and walk quiet differently to that of a teenager or the elderly, but, their individual behaviour would all be within a predictable range.

Holly Lamb's look and gait were of a combination that alerted Constable Bradshaw as he walked by the northern tower. They were frighteningly predictable. Her gaze was focused but seemingly upon nothing at all. Her posture was erect. Her gait purposeful and resolved. Her direction was towards where the great bridge's chains were anchored to the solid grey rock. Constable Bradshaw knew that if he climbed over the black, kerb-side railings and ran across the carriageway to his left and towards her now, his overt action would very likely spur her to run the remaining yards to the cliff edge. Anxiously, he walked slowly on for a few more paces towards Clifton and, as he past her on his left, he turned sharply, discarded his helmet, bounded over the railings on his side and sprinted the short distance across the carriageway behind her but, as he reached the pavement and vaulted over the second set of black railings, Holly, trance-like, had already mounted the low wall at a sign that proclaimed: *'Plant Lovers' Paradise'*, and within two or three short seconds, had thrown herself from the bridge. Witnesses said that she seemed to have an angelic smile as she cast herself into the air. But any angelic smile was brief as she hit the rocks some twenty feet below, bouncing before hitting more rocks forty feet further down, only for her body to be ensnared in the metal netting designed to capture any loose rocks, and amongst the fragrances of the Common Rock Roses, the Oxeye Daisies and the Bristol Rock Cress.

For the spectators, the scene was either horrific or a cheap sensation, something to be captured on a mobile phone and shared with others for their morbid entertainment. Later, for her co-workers, the knowledge of Holly's death was greeted by a mixture of shock, disbelief and sadness. For Holly's parents, it was a gnawing guilt for encouraging her return to work, of an unbelievable grief at the loss of their only child, together with uncontrollable tears. For Constable Colin Bradshaw the death of Holly Lamb was sickening. But for now he had duties to perform. He would remain at the scene. His tears would come later, together with an unjustified but ever-present guilt that he could have done more.

An ambulance attended as did the local fire and rescue service who maintained a Rocks Rescue Recovery Unit equipped with their harnesses, abseiling and safety ropes; belays, descenders and cammings; a 'R-N-R' orange-coloured plastic stretcher and a black body bag. Within forty-three minutes they had recovered the battered body of twenty-two year old Miss Holly Jane Lamb in as dignified a way as they could professionally achieve. They also recovered, entangled in the wire mesh, an American revolver, a Forehand and Wadsworth .38 *Hammerless*.

Chapter Eleven

Tuesday, 6th May.

Police Headquarters, Bristol, England.

IT WAS NOT A PLEASANT MEETING between Assistant Chief Constable Robert Perrin and the Acting Chief Constable, Anita Winters. In the absence of the chief constable, Miss Winters was enjoying her brief moment of supreme power. Perrin had asked for a continuance of the phone tap on the Millers' home phone. With the justification already fully documented, the decision needed to be considered, of course, but should have been very straight-forward. Instead, Miss Winters required the ACC (Crime) to justify his request in the minutest of detail, ponderously giving every comment he made exaggerated thought. After nearly forty minutes, Miss Winters gave her consent before bombarding the ACC with a barrage of questions regarding the Hernandez/Miller case, lamenting the apparent lack of progress.

***

Doctor Ruth Jennings from HQ Forensics had had coffee with the Senior Investigating Officer. Ruth had brought good news, well, useful news. Now Detective Superintendent Yin was briefing ACC Perrin in his office.

'The weapon recovered from the Avon Gorge was a Forehand and Wadsworth .38 *Hammerless*, an American five chamber revolver,' she said, standing alongside the seated ACC at his desk.

'You say "hammerless", then how is it fired?' asked Perrin with a frown.

Kay produced a photograph from her folder. 'The weapon does have a trigger and hammer, sir, but the hammer is concealed under the casing of the weapon itself,' she explained, pointing at the mechanism. 'It is ideally suited as a pocket weapon. Light weight. Eighteen ounces. With a three inch barrel and a concealed hammer which wouldn't catch in the lining of a pocket or snag as it was being pulled out.'

'I've never heard of Forehand and Wadsworth,' adding light-heartedly, 'they sound like a pair of music hall performers.'

Kay smiled at the man who had walked her up the aisle when she married Mark Faraday. 'A music hall,' she said in mock bewilderment. 'Whatever is a music hall?'

'I deserved that.'

'And I probably deserve a clip around the ear, sir,' she replied with that captivating smile. 'Anyway, the manufacturers were based in Worcester, Massachusetts, and this weapon would have been produced any time between 1890 and 1902.'

'And so the dates of manufacture means that the weapon would be classified as an antique and, therefore, doesn't require a Part One Firearms Certificate,' he replied knowingly.

'Normally, yes, sir, but Mark and I have been talking about this. The real question is, we think: who would want to carry such an un-cool weapon? I doubt whether it would be a bank robber, a burglar or a gang member. Bank robbers and gang members can pick up a modern automatic hand gun for as little as fifty pounds. And so, why throw away a weapon that could be on sale in an antique shop for three-hundred pounds or more?'

'And your conclusion?'

'Our conclusion is that either the weapon was stolen originally by a crook or gang member and then used or discarded as not being cool enough. However, we tend to favour another explanation.' Perrin glanced at Kay full of expectation. 'An apparently respectable person,' she said, 'could carry such a weapon in the knowledge that he or she had a ready-made excuse for possessing such a weapon, namely, that it was an antique.'

'Hum,' he mumbled thoughtfully before gently probing: 'And a .38 you say?'

'Yes, sir.'

'But if it's a .38 calibre and is capable of firing modern ammunition, then it cannot be classified as an antique, can it?'

'You are absolutely correct, sir, although Ruth has detected lead at the end of the barrel - only at the end of the barrel - as if there was, at some stage, a plug of lead inserted. If the owner of the gun was stopped by the police, he or she would probably be able to baffle an enquiring constable into accepting that this weapon was an antique, had been deactivated by means of metal poured into the barrel and incapable of firing. The fact that the weapon is the *Hammerless* model would add to the illusion. I doubt very much whether patrolling officers would be aware that deactivated weapons are proof-marked by a Proof House and a Certificate of Deactivation issued.'

'A precautionary tactic do you think?'

'A sensible precaution. Certainly a possibility, yes.'

'And likely to be the sort of heavier calibre weapon used to kill Victor Jenkins.'

'Again, a possibility.'

'How likely?'

'It's a very viable possibility. Ruth Jennings tells me that, bearing in mind the recent weather, temperatures, humidity and the relatively exposed position in which the weapon was found, the condition of the gun indicates that it was unlikely to have been in situ for more than three weeks. We have contacted the Parks Department and the steel netting at the Avon Gorge is regularly inspected. They have checked their records and tell us that some of the retaining bolts were replaced at this particular location a little over six weeks ago. I think we can reasonably assume that this weapon was discarded within the past six weeks.'

'And antique shops?'

'We are contacting all Bristol antique shops. We are also trawling web pages and have e-mailed antique shop networks in France, Spain, Italy, Gibraltar and Madeira and are liaising with Interpol regarding any thefts of such a weapon or if such a weapon had already been used in the commission of a crime. It's a long-shot but something might crop up.' Kay removed another photograph from her folder and placed it in front of the ACC. 'What is interesting is that whilst the weapon was clearly wiped down and no finger prints have been found, there are minute smears of a powdery substance found in the grooves on two of the screw heads,' she said, pointing to the two white arrows on the photograph, 'as you can see, one near the chamber itself and one on the butt. Ruth is working on this as we speak.'

'Any idea what it might be?' asked Perrin intriguingly.

'Ruth says that its consistency is that of dust or powder with some sort of greasy substance binding it together.'

'Oil used to clean a gun, maybe?'

'Ruth has discounted that possibility, but we will have to wait a while before we know for sure, although this case is amongst those at the top of Ruth's long list.'

Chapter Twelve

Monday, 12th May.

The island of Madeira and the British Overseas Territory, Gibraltar.

BRIAN CRAVEN WAS NOT CONSPICUOUS. Brian was inconspicuous. He was, therefore, ideal for the task that had been set for him by Superintendent Yin. He was neither short nor tall. His build was slight. Not intimidating. His hair and complexion were neither too dark nor too fair. He appeared benign. Not inquisitive or enquiring. He was one of those people whom others tended to ignore. He was everyone, yet no one. He merged. Merged into the background wherever that might happen to be. A city centre. A municipal park. A harbour-side restaurant. A café in a shaded square of banana and fig trees. Today, it was a café in a shaded square of banana and fig trees. Saint Benedict's Square.

Brian sat at a table under a tree festooned in electric lights with coloured bulbs. At the adjacent table was seated a group of ladies whom he had grown to know, not as friends, of course, but as part of the local social élite, as he typed into his laptop or scribbled notes whilst studying tourist information brochures, as if innocently compiling text for English Sunday newspaper travel supplements. It was not difficult to gather information about the Milano family. There were gaps in his knowledge, of course, because the Milano family was not the sole topic of the conversation of these ladies, although Grace Milano ensured that mention of her family, and particularly her son, Nicholas, always figured prominently at their gatherings. There were also gaps in Brian's knowledge because he made a point of not visiting the café every day but, clearly, Grace Milano was a, if not *the*, person to be seen with and, during the past three weeks, Brian had been able to manoeuvre himself to such an extent that he had been within ear-shot of Mrs Milano on eight occasions, sometimes seated at an adjacent table with his back to her, or sometimes near to the side of her table, or sometimes facing in her general direction. But what she said wasn't always important. What was in many ways more important was what the other ladies had said about Grace Milano and her son - in her absence.

***

At fifteen minutes to eleven the previous evening, the Guardia Civil closed the border between mainland Spain and Gibraltar. It wasn't a quiet affair. The Spanish press were there in significant numbers. They took many photographs of posing Spanish officials - the local Municipal Police, Guardia Civil and the army - all with beaming smiles, wearing their very best uniforms and jostling for centre stage. This morning, the Gibraltarian and UK papers ensured that the pictures that had the most prominent position on their front pages where those that depicted the Spanish authorities as if they were participating in some sort of comic opera whilst, in the background, stood two young Gibraltarian constables, immaculately smart in their traditional British 'Bobby's' uniform and full of quiet dignity – as directed by Commissioner Mark Faraday.

In liaison with the Military Governor and Chief Minister, Faraday implemented a pre-prepared operational order, including the posting of public notices and a press release. The operational order dealt with, amongst other things, any possible demonstrations either side of the border, the security and distribution of fuel and food, the repatriation of Gibraltarians from Spain and Spanish nationals from Gibraltar, violations of Gibraltar's borders and territorial waters by the Spanish or any blockading by Spain and the mutual aid that could be provided by the Royal Gibraltar Regiment. These well-rehearsed plans now fell neatly and calmly into place.

Gibraltar's First Minister wrote to the Spanish government. The Spanish government did not respond. The British government did respond. They sent three additional *Typhoon* multi-role jet fighters armed with *Harpoon* anti-shipping missiles and *Mauser* cannon to The Rock in order to ensure the safe passage of civilian and military aircraft and re-routed to Gibraltar a Duke-class Type 23 frigate, *HMS St Albans*, armed with *Sea Wolf* low altitude, anti-aircraft missiles. It was, possibly, slightly an over-the-top response but the British Prime Minister was determined to make the point that Gibraltar and the UK would not be bullied.

What was of more immediate significance to Faraday, however, was Julie's announcement that Detective Inspector Frobisher of Special Branch required an urgent meeting. Frobisher was ushered into the Commissioner's office.

'There's been a development, sir. Could I have a word do you think?' asked Frobisher, standing with his back to the closed door, briefcase in hand, with all the appearances of a lawyer about to enter a court.

'Of course. Sit down, James.'

'It's highly classified, sir,' he said glancing carefully towards Inspector Purchell who, apparently unconcerned, continued to draft a report at his desk.

'It's okay, James. Peter has all the appropriate clearances.'

Frobisher hesitated for a moment before continuing. 'Right, sir,' he said, although clearly uncomfortable with what he viewed as unnecessary openness.

Faraday moved from behind his desk, picked up a pad and pen, and sat at the small conference table. The inspector waited until Faraday was seated before taking his seat.

Once seated, Inspector Frobisher placed his briefcase on the table and spoke. 'You will be aware that we are constantly monitoring voice traffic in liaison with GCHQ, sir. One operation is in respect of an individual who uses the code name "Hobbit". For the last two years there has been regular traffic between Hobbit here in Gibraltar and what we believe is a Guardia Civil unit in Algerciras. Most of this traffic consists solely of eight digits followed by three digits. Our assumption has been that the eight digits represent the time, day and month and the three digits a location or person. Many of the calls are via mobile phones to and from an individual calling himself "José" at roughly monthly intervals, although sometimes more often, for example prior to a visit by a Royal Navy vessel or a UK government minister. Today we intercepted a message to José.' Frobisher unlocked his briefcase, felt inside and removed a small digital recorder. 'It was *in clear*, sir,' he said as he pressed a button with his thumb and held up the recorder for all to hear. Faraday leaned in as Purchell looked up from his desk.

'This is Hobbit. You've closed the bloody border. You know you should have given me a warning. How am I going to manage before the 28th? You arrange something and arrange it now.'

Frobisher switched off the recorder and continued. 'Most of Hobbitt's previous messages have been on the 24th, 25th or 26th of the month and the previous digital codes have, we think, been in respect, primarily, of meetings and, maybe, also payments.'

'But now you think it more likely to be payments?'

'It could be, bearing in mind his comment: "how am I going to manage?".'

'And Hobbit is getting desperate, you think?'

'I think so, yes, sir. In his desperation he became careless and used a phone kiosk.'

'And you have the handset?' enquired Faraday with a raised eyebrow.

Frobisher smiled, pleased that his action would be approved. 'Yes, we do, sir. We didn't want to waste time so we removed it this morning with … with a pair of pliers, sir. I have reported it to the telephone company as vandalism.'

'I'm pleased you have reported it, James. Vandalism is becoming a great worry to me,' said Faraday as he smiled approvingly before asking: 'Fingerprints?'

'PNC has no record but the SIB do. SIB took some while to respond and the good news is that we have a match.' He hesitated for a moment, realising the sensitivity of what he was about to reveal. 'The prints belong to a … a Captain Nicholas Milano of the local regiment.'

Faraday was mindful of what Sir George Sinclair had said that *'everyone there seems to know everyone else'*. At this stage he would be guarded in trusting his staff, none of whom he really knew, and continued as if understandably curious. 'And what do you know about this Captain Milano?' he asked reasonably as his pen hovered over his pad as if eager to make notes.

'He is a Gibraltarian, a successful wine merchant who lives in Gibraltar and Madeira with a commission in the Reserves.'

Faraday made a note. 'Any previous indication that Milano might be a traitor?'

'No, sir. Milano,' he added somewhat defensively, 'comes from a successful and very famous family whose heroism was pivotal during The Great Siege.'

'That's okay,' said Faraday without censure. 'I assume that you will be reviewing all the past traffic?'

'I have an officer working on that as we speak.'

Faraday nodded before asking instinctively: 'And the bad news?'

For a few seconds, DI Frobisher was surprised at his perception. 'Milano has just landed in Madeira.'

Faraday thought for a moment. 'Are you saying that he moved quickly and the SIB didn't?'

'In fairness to the SIB, I didn't make my request a priority, sir, as I didn't want to draw particular attention to our enquiries. I merely said that our request was in respect of vandalism. I hadn't … '.

'James,' interrupted Faraday, 'I don't engage in unhelpful post-mortems. It is probably better that the military are unaware of our suspicions, at least at this stage. Other military personnel may be involved. I will have to inform the Chief Minister, of course, but not until I have something more substantial to report.' Faraday remained silent as he stood up from the table and walked behind his desk to stare out of the window and across the quadrangle. Frobisher was about to speak but Purchell raised his hand to silence him, knowing that Faraday would be mentally juggling with options, preferably in silence. Frobisher remained silent although he was still having difficulty in understanding how Faraday worked.

'Do you use a pocket book or desk diary, James?' asked Faraday eventually.

'Both, sir,' replied a bemused Frobisher.

'Do you have your pocket book with you now?' he asked as he continued to look out of the window.

'Yes, sir,' he replied, although not comprehending the reason for the question.

'Good,' replied Faraday as he turned back towards the inspector. 'Do you know where Milano lives?'

'Yes, I do, sir,' responded Frobisher, although Faraday knew from his conversation with Mr and Mrs Miller that Milano lived in an apartment very near his own on Europa Road.

'Well, I think you and I should visit his home address. I shall endorse your pocket book to the effect that I believe that a serious offence, namely treason, may have been committed and we will search his address accordingly. It will be low key. I will need a few minutes to change into civvies, meanwhile, how are your cat burglar skills, James?'

'Pretty good, sir,' he confirmed with a wry smile, 'although they won't be necessary today.'

'And why should that be?'

'I know the janitor of the apartments.'

Excellent, thought Faraday with a grin – *everyone seems to know everyone else*. 'We'll use your car, James, if you would. I'll see you out front in ten.'

Once DI Frobisher had left the Commissioner's office and out of ear-shot, Faraday spoke to Inspector Purchell. 'Discreetly update Kay on the secure line, please. Now if you would.'

***

Faraday was standing near the DI's car when he answered Frobisher's call. He then walked casually towards the apartment block and entered through the open front doors. He was aware that his photograph had appeared in the local *Chronicle* and so he crossed the vestibule and walked up the stairs to the fourth floor – he didn't want to take the lift that could result in him travelling with a nosy neighbour eager to engage the new Commissioner of Police in conversation. On the fourth floor, Faraday walked along the carpeted corridor towards apartment number 409. The door was ajar. He pushed it open and closed it quietly behind him. Frobisher was in the hallway. They gloved up.

The apartment had two bedrooms, one of which was the master. The king-sized beds in each room were neatly made-up. The smaller bedroom of the two had a feminine feel about it. In the master, a black and white photograph of Maria Miller in a silver frame was on the bedside table alongside the phone. The spacious bathroom was tidy with hand towels and bath sheets neatly folded. Blue toilet cleaner had been poured around the rim. The kitchen was beautifully and expensively fitted, the sink and surfaces of which were spotless. Cupboards were well stocked with food in tins and air-tight containers, but the fridge had been emptied. The lounge/dining room was very large and uncluttered, the French doors of which gave a spectacular view across the rocky foreshore towards the Atlantic Ocean. The brown leather, antique-looking, furnishings were clearly extremely expensive and a number of oil paintings adorned the walls, most of which appeared to be by local artists of local street scenes. One in particular was of a *baroque quintas.*

Frobisher tried the handle of a door in the lounge without success as Faraday opened the French doors and stepped out onto the balcony, then re-entered the lounge. 'Is that door locked, James?'

'Yes it is.'

'Well, it isn't a cupboard, James. There's another window along the balcony and the shutters are closed. See if you can find a key.' Faraday returned to the kitchen and searched the cupboards and drawers as Frobisher searched the lounge.

Frobisher found the key first. 'Sir, I have it,' said DI Frobisher a few minutes later, holding up a key and a carved sandalwood box of a Moroccan style in which the key had been concealed.

'Okay. Let's see what might be in Aladdin's cave,' said Faraday as Frobisher inserted and turned the key. There was a click. Frobisher turned the handle and pushed open the door. The room was still and silent. Dark and cool. Faraday moved to the window and adjusted the wooded shutters to allow the bright sunlight to stream in to reveal a pleasant room, furnished as a study with a comfortable, easy chair at the window to their left and a large desk, facing into the wall, immediately in front of the two officers. On the wall at the front of the desk was a framed manuscript regarding The Great Siege, identical to that hanging on the wall in Christopher Miller's Bristol office. Also on the wall, immediately below the manuscript, were two glazed, identical wooden picture frames. One contained a pair of shoulder epaulettes with three golden stars, the other a military decoration.

Faraday pulled out the leather, high-back swivel chair in front of the desk and sat down. 'These aren't the Bath stars of a British army captain?' said Faraday slowly, although he had already grasped their significance.

'No,' replied Frobisher hesitantly as if reluctant to acknowledge what they represented.

'Spanish?'

'Yes, sir,' he replied, clearing his throat. 'They are the eight-pointed stars of a Spanish colonel.'

'And the decoration?' asked Faraday drily, examining the *Cruce del Mérito Militar* consisting of a silver cross, surmounted by the Spanish royal crown, the round central disc depicting the coat of arms of Castile, Leon, Aragon, Navarre and Granada together with the escutcheon of the House of Bourbon-Anjou, suspended from a grey-coloured ribbon with a red central stripe and yellow stripes on both outer edges. Immediately below the royal crown could be seen a small tablet upon which was engraved a date.

'I can go to Wikipedia, sir, to clarify, if you wish?' suggested Frobisher, although he had a general idea of what it was, but not its significance.

'Yes, do that,' Faraday replied tetchily.

'Give me a moment,' replied Frobisher as he removed his iPad from his shoulder case and occupied the chair near the window. Faraday remained at the desk but turned to face into the room, his anger smouldering. As he waited he recalled the comment made by Maria Miller that she considered Nicholas Milano to be vain – and he knew that the vain will always seek recognition. 'I have it, sir. It's the Cross of Military Merit.' There was a careful pause before he added: 'The one with the yellow stripes is awarded to officers for … for *"service that involve high personal risk".'*

'I'm sure there was a *high personal risk*, James,' Faraday said contemptuously, adding, 'and I assume the date is the date that this honour was awarded?'

Frobisher checked his iPad again. 'That's correct, sir … I think that we can assume that Milano has been at it for at least two years.'

Faraday swivelled round towards the desk. To the right of the blotter was an ornate brass desk lamp with green shade, to the left a brass pillar, about the same height as the lamp, on top of which was a Norman-like knight wearing chain mail and standing in a heroic pose. But what absorbed Faraday's attention was an elongated brass plate, with two screw holes, that had been propped up on the desk, against the wall, just behind the leather-bound blotter. He turned completely around so as to face Frobisher head-on, holding the brass plate between his right fingers and thumb. 'This is the sort of thing that you would have screwed to your office door, isn't it?'

'I'm sorry, sir,' asked Frobisher as he craned forward in an attempt to read the inscription. 'What does it say?'

'"Colonel Nicholas Milano, Deputy Military Governor, Gibraltar".'

Frobisher was stunned. He too remained silent, his anger mounting as Faraday's lessened. For Frobisher, whose home was Gibraltar, this was unbelievable treachery by a man holding the Queen's commission. For Faraday, he was able to be more dispassionate and objective.

'I hadn't anticipated this, sir.'

'Nor had I, James,' replied Faraday, partly to reassure Frobisher that he wasn't incompetent, partly because it was true. 'A secret cupboard or drawer, maybe. Something hidden behind a wardrobe or picture. But not this. I think we should now search every inch of this apartment much more thoroughly,' said Faraday, 'but do not leave any trace of our visit.' Faraday stood but didn't move. He was deep in thought.

'Sir?' said Inspector Frobisher after nearly two minutes of silence.

'It's okay, James. My mind was wandering. Many of the answers will be here, I think,' he said apologetically as thoughts spun in his head. Then he smiled, certain as to what his next instruction to Frobisher would be.

'Shall I take the smaller bedroom and lounge, sir?'

'No. No, James. You take the master bedroom, kitchen and lounge, if you would, and I will take the smaller bedroom, bathroom and study.'

Faraday and Frobisher began to systematically search their respective rooms. They made written notes and took photographs on their mobile phones. They noted the contents of kitchen cupboards and bathroom cabinets; of brands and sizes of the clothing in drawers and wardrobes. They examined behind the air conditioning vents and extractor fans in the kitchen and bathroom. They removed nothing with the exception of a laptop. There was no need. Photographs were taken of the desk calendar, the contents of drop files, of a neat group of letters in date-order, apparently written by his mother to Nicholas, and a little note book containing a matrix of figures that had been secured by Velcro pads underneath the top drawer of the right-hand desk pedestal.

Finally, Faraday checked the answerphone. There were seventeen messages. He noted the messages verbatim on his pad, in particular one of Tuesday, 22nd April:

'Nicholas, I need to see you when you come to Bristol. I have the present.'

Faraday recognised the voice immediately. It was Mrs Maria Miller. Faraday made no reference to this message to DI Frobisher nor that he recognised the voice, but continued to make his final inspection of the study, particularly the contents of drop files.

'I have domestic details here, James, from the drop files,' remarked Faraday. 'I will need you to check all landline calls made in the last two years. And his mobile phone provider, in particular any mobile designations of foreign providers. You know what to do.' Faraday thought for a few minutes as he examined the details contained on the photographs he had taken on his phone. Faraday concluded that Frobisher would be reticent to involve too many officers with his enquiries. He would want to do much himself, but there was an urgency. 'There's a great deal to do, James, and so put someone else on this, too, if you think it necessary. I will leave it to you.'

'Okay, sir.'

'Check for commonalities and possible webs of relationships,' continued Faraday, 'although I doubt whether his phone records will tell us much. I think he would have been cautious but may have become complacent and sloppy if this has been going on for a number of years. More revealing will be the bank accounts, and so kindly track expenditure and patterns, as well as his passport and airline manifests.' In all, their search of the apartment took them nearly two hours.

'I'm worried, sir, about what this could mean?'

'And so we should be, James. Has there been any chatter?' he asked of intelligence intercepts.

'Nothing out of the ordinary. There is some low grade traffic from various people who are sympathetic to Spain, all of whom are migrant workers. But we are as confident as we can be that we know who they are and what they are doing.'

'Any Spanish military activity, exercises, that sort of thing?'

'There has been a greater presence of the Guardia Civil at the border. But the increase in numbers is small and seems to be there to kerb any possible demonstrations by Spanish workers who would normally be employed in our docks or restaurants or on construction work.'

'And no military exercises taking place further inland?'

'Not that we are aware of, and our own military do keep us well informed of that sort of thing.'

'The Spanish prime minister was talking only last week about joint sovereignty again,' said Faraday. 'It could be a smoke screen, of course. My main concern is an increase of Spanish incursions into our territorial waters which might result in some trigger-happy behaviour by the Spanish. For the moment, I don't think that the Spanish would be as fool-hardy as to attempt any sort of land grab. In any event, Colonel Contaldo,' he said referring to the commander of the Gibraltar garrison, 'is very confident that we could give the Spanish a good dusting and repel any attack mounted by them,' added Faraday as he remained seated considering his next step. 'Okay,' he said finally. 'This essentially remains between Inspector Purchell, you and me. We will not be keeping the military in the loop at this stage. I will, however, ask for a meeting with the Chief Minister when we get back. Meanwhile, get the technical guys to put in surveillance cameras, if you would please. If we have searched his apartment, others may be like-minded, and so our cameras are not to be installed in the vents but in the smoke detectors or in the air conditioning control panel, something like that.'

For a moment Frobisher assumed that Faraday's instruction indicated his lack of reliance on the competence of the usual Special Branch officers at the airport. 'But we will know if he returns, sir.'

'We probably will, but there's always a chance that he will attempt to sneak in to Gibraltar under the cloak of the military somehow and we could miss him. In any case, I want to know if this apartment attracts any other visitors.'

***

Back in the Commissioner's office, the three officers sat around the small conference table. Faraday up-dated Purchell, showing him the photographs they had taken on their phones, photographs now transferred to the desk computer, whilst Frobisher rang the detective who was checking Hobbit's messages. Frobisher instructed the officer to check back all traffic for the past five years, as well as Milano's travel patterns – but discreetly. Meanwhile, Julie brought in more tea and chilled fruit juice and glasses. She had sensed the change in atmosphere and looked anxious - maybe anxious that Faraday had discovered a fault with Commissioner Hugh Thornton's conduct, she thought. As Julie placed fresh cups and saucers on the table, Faraday scribbled a note: *'Everything is good. Nothing to worry about.'* and slipped it on to her tray as she left.

'What is intriguing me, James, is the name "Hobbit",' remarked Faraday as Julie closed the door. 'You told me when we were in his apartment that you had met Captain

Milano when you were invited to the Regiment's Officers' Mess. You thought him a little arrogant and rather superior, didn't you?'

Frobisher thought for a few seconds. 'Silly point-scoring really, sir,' clarified James Frobisher as Peter Purchell discreetly tapped into his lap-top computer. 'He tried to make a point that he was a captain and an inspector's rank was somehow equivalent to that of a first lieutenant. He seemed to think it was amusing to introduce me, twice, as: "and this is Lieutenant Frobisher, I mean, Inspector Frobisher".'

Faraday thought of what they had discovered in Milano's apartment before continuing. 'He sees himself as a colonel, but also emulating his ancestor do you think?'

'Colonel Henry Bartolomeu Milano was, at some stage, the Deputy Military Governor under General Eliott,' offered Frobisher. 'It's certainly a possibility.'

'I think that Captain Milano's aspirations are more than just a coincidence,' suggested Faraday, 'but, if he is as arrogant and superior as you believe him to be, is he really likely to use the code name of "Hobbit", the title of a childish fantasy novel, written by who was it, Tolkein? Surely he would use a name like "Grey Fox", "Lone Ranger" or "Sun Downer". It just doesn't fit with his personality and background for him to use the name "Hobbit".'

'When Hobbit was first used, I did look up the details of the author. I had assumed that Hobbit was appropriate as

Tolkein's book reflected some of the author's World War One experiences of his personal journey and heroism.'

'But is it "Hobbit", sir?' asked Purchell looking over his computer screen. 'As I understand it, we have only ever heard the name, not seen it written?'

'That's correct, isn't it, James?'

'Yes, that's true, sir,' he replied cautiously.

'So, what are you thinking, Peter?' asked Faraday.

'What if it is O-B-I-T?' he said, checking his screen. 'You see an "Obit" is an obscure medieval term for a form of death duty or inheritance tax.'

Faraday thought for a moment before commenting. 'If it's obscure, it is unlikely to be random, and it will have been thought through and be significant,' suggested Faraday. 'If you think of his study, it was like a fantasy set: the Norman knight in heroic pose; the manuscript on the wall; the Spanish epaulettes of a full colonel; the military decoration, a decoration awarded specifically for conduct involving high risk; and the brass door plate. All of this must, surely, have a symbolic significance.' Faraday remained silent for a short moment, right elbow on the table, head in his right hand – thinking. Frobisher and Purchell looked at each other and smiled in silence, waiting, waiting for Faraday to continue. 'I am sure that "Obit" is symbolic,' said Faraday thinking of the words of Maria Miller when she spoke of Nicholas Milano's bitterness, and that he considered himself deserving of a higher rank than that of captain - which 'was his due'. Then Faraday spoke again. 'Maybe Captain Milano considers himself entitled to some sort of inheritance that is his due.'

Chapter Thirteen

Tuesday, 13th May.

Bristol, England; British Overseas Territory, Gibraltar and the island of Madeira.

IT WAS LATE EVENING when Kay spoke with Mark. On the secure line. From Bristol. 1,068 miles away. Two hours thirty-seven minutes flight-time apart. Whilst the line should have been secure they had agreed, nevertheless, to speak in a rudimentary code, often referring to the ACC as 'father', Sir George as 'uncle', Christopher Miller as 'son' and Captain Milano as the 'prodigal son'. They had pseudonyms for the other players too. Against that background, Kay spoke of her meeting with Assistant Chief Constable Robert Perrin and his subsequent call to Sir George Sinclair at the Foreign and Commonwealth Office. Mark spoke of his meeting with the Chief Minister and his instructions to make discreet enquiries into the activities of Captain Nicholas Milano, but not to alert the local military garrison. And Kay had more startling information.

'The SIB file on Lance Corporal Victor Jenkins arrived yesterday and it's very revealing'.

She had his full attention now. 'In what way, darling?'

'Jenkins was a truck driver with the Royal Logistic Corp. In the section in the file dealing with his deployments, Jenkins is listed as having served in Morocco on Exercise *Jebel*

Sahara and also in Afghanistan. In June, elements of the Royal Gibraltar Regiment, under the command of Captain Nicholas Milano, were deployed to Afghanistan and, part of their role was to provide security for convoys. On the 23rd July, a RLC convoy, in which Jenkins was serving, was attacked. A roadside IED exploded damaging the second and third trucks in the convoy killing four RLC soldiers. The convoy then came under heavy fire, particularly the lead truck that had been left isolated. In the fire-fight, seven of the enemy force were killed and another five ran and scrabbled for shelter in a ramshackle goat-herd's, stone-built dwelling. The fire-fight continued for another twenty minutes or so. Then silence. When Jenkins and others soldiers stormed the tumbled-down building, only two of the enemy remained alive. During the later interrogation of one of the enemy, an allegation was made that Jenkins had shot dead the other prisoner. There was an enquiry and Jenkins was exonerated on the evidence of – you've guessed – Captain Nicholas Milano. Milano's evidence was that the dead man had raised his weapon as both he and Jenkin's entered the building and Jenkin's had very properly shot the man dead.'

'Is there anything to contradict Milano's version of events?' he asked.

'No, nothing at all.'

'Whatever the truth of the matter, whether Jenkins had acted entirely properly or had murdered the prisoner, Jenkins would have been indebted to Milano,' Faraday suggested.

'Absolutely,' she replied, adding, 'and we have had more good news. We had a hit on the Forehand and Wadworth .38 *Hammerless* revolver.'

'Brilliant, how so?'

'We had a positive response from an antique shop in Hay-on-Wye, a small town in the Brecons. They are sending us details.'

***

Grace Milano lived in a delightful *baroque quintas*, a traditional Madeiran small mansion with green-painted wrought-iron balconies and louver shuttered window, near the Rue do Sardo in Funchal. Brian Craven knew this. Brian was across the road. In the little boutique café. Sat in a window seat. Drinking coffee. And he saw Grace's visitor too. Her son, Nicholas.

Chapter Fourteen

Thursday, 15ᵗʰ May.

British Overseas Territory, Gibraltar and Bristol, England.

MAJOR HERBERT ROWSE ARMSTRONG was five foot six inches tall. He was neat and dapper. He was a solicitor. The only solicitor in British legal history to be hanged. Hanged, in 1922, for the murder of his spiteful, over-bearing and nagging wife.   He was a small man, made even smaller by a wife who spent most of their married life humiliating him.   The Armstrongs lived in the Welsh Border town of Hay-on-Wye.   The mention of Hay-on-Wye reminded Faraday of the case, a case in which Mrs Katharine Armstrong was poisoned with arsenic administered by her mild-mannered, bespectacled husband.   Faraday was not overly preoccupied with thoughts of Major and Mrs Armstrong, but if a major was capable of murder, would not a captain be equally capable, he thought.   It was just one of thousands of thoughts that whirled around in his fertile, dyslexic mind as he entered the Officers' Mess at Devil's Tower Camp, the home of the Royal Gibraltar Regiment, at 12.30pm.

Faraday wore civilian clothes for lunch, not his police uniform with the insignia of rank identical to that of an army general, which he thought might seem rather pretentious, particularly as this visit was a social one. And the visit proved to be a very congenial social occasion as he enjoyed an extremely leisurely buffet lunch with Colonel David Contaldo in the pleasantly cool Mess. Contaldo was a tall, dark-haired man, with a handsome face and rather prominent nose, of Mediterranean appearance that hinted at his Italian roots. They talked of family and holidays, of Europe and the United States, of England and Spain, and of the forthcoming Royal visit. They shared family photographs on mobile phones and diary entries were made of future social meetings.

After a comfortable lunch, Faraday and Contaldo walked to the regimental museum. It was fascinating. It would also be revealing. They examined together old but bright, colourful uniforms, ancient but burnished weapons; they lingered at oil paintings and artefacts; admired the old regimental standards and poured over musty records.

'This might interest you,' said Contaldo, pointing to a display featuring a Fairbairne-Sykes fighting knife. 'This weapon was designed by two of your forbears serving with the Shanghai Municipal Police, William Fairbairne and Eric Sykes. Both later became members of British Special Forces in the Second World War, one retiring as a colonel, the other a major. So significant was this weapon that one made of solid gold forms part of the memorial to Special Forces in Westminster Abbey.' As they moved towards other displays, Faraday reflected that Captain Milano was very likely to have more than a passing knowledge of the Fairbairne-Sykes knife. Meanwhile, Faraday had seen the manuscript and manoeuvred his way towards it.

'What an intricate piece of work,' commented Faraday pointing to the framed manuscript hanging on the wall between a breech-loading Ferguson rifle and a muzzle-loading Baker rifle, a manuscript identical to those to be found in Christopher Miller's conference room and Captain Nicholas Milano's study.

Contaldo was delighted to explain the significance of each part of manuscript depicting the Great Siege: the *Grand Assault*, the heroic *Sortie*, the capture of the enemy's ship, the *San Miguel* and, finally, *The Relief of Gibraltar*.

'And the names here?' asked Faraday pointing at the central list of names as if their significance was unknown to him.

'Ah, yes. These are officers who particularly distinguished themselves during the siege.'

'Oh, I see,' replied Faraday innocently. 'And, I suppose, there could be descendants of these distinguished officers still living in Gibraltar?'

'Certainly. There are to my knowledge at least three families, including one of our own officers, Captain Nicholas Milano.'

'What a remarkable piece of history,' remarked Faraday casually. 'The captain must be a natural centre of attention for new comers to the regiment, I assume?'

'Well, he certainly is,' acknowledged Contaldo. 'He doesn't brag, of course, that would not be acceptable at all. But people do seem to gravitate towards him. He's a charmer and when asked, he speaks of it emphasising, probably a little too much, the romance of it all. He's a little vain, perhaps,' he added with a tolerant smile, 'quietly basking in the reflected glory of his ancestor, so to speak.'

'The romance of it all, you say?' probed Faraday ever so gently.

'Well,' replied the colonel understandably, 'I suppose there is a certain romance. It is clear that Nicholas is very proud of his ancestor who was deputy to the Military Governor, General Sir George Augustus Eliott, who had married a rather beautiful lady by the name of Anne Drake, a descendent of Sir Francis Drake.'

'Oh, I see,' replied Faraday with a smile, absorbing the important information but, at the same time, revelling in the history. 'It's these sorts of colourful connections that illuminate history, I think,' remarked Faraday admiringly, 'and provide an intimate, human aspect. It's a great story, Colonel.'

It was a great story, but Faraday had heard enough about history. He was now keen to understand more about the regiment's more recent activities. They moved from display cases to cabinets, maps to charts, manuscripts to scrolls, finally to the present day.

'As you see,' said Colonel Contaldo, pointing to a collection of photographs, 'the regiment has served with NATO and the UN, and in Afghanistan. We have been honoured to have mounted the guard at both Buckingham Palace and Kensington Palace and train regularly, in fact, for the past thirteen years, with Moroccan forces, and attend the Infantry Battle School at Brecon,' adding with a touch of pride, 'an unforgiving, usually wet and very tough environment for us from the much warmer Mediterranean, as you can imagine.'

Faraday scanned an array of photographs displayed on a wall, alongside a trophy cabinet. 'I see that the Milano name is prominent again, Colonel?' he said, pointing to one particular photograph.

'Oh yes. Captain Milano is no slouch. He has always been keen to play an active part in the regiment.'

They discussed the significance of the photographs and the regiment's achievements further before Faraday glanced at his watch. 'Colonel, I have overstayed my welcome.'

'You certainly have not and it has been a pleasure, Commissioner.'

Both men exchanged further pleasantries before Faraday left, a military car taking him back to his police headquarters. Once inside New Mole House, Faraday sprinted up the stairs to his office.

'Is everything alright, Commissioner?' asked a startled Julie Levant.

'It couldn't be better, Julie.'

'Would you prefer tea or a cold drink?' she asked, standing at the open door.

'Tea would be perfect, thank you,' said Faraday as he occupied the chair behind his desk. He opened the bottom desk drawer to the right and reached in and grasped the red handset. He pressed four buttons and waited just a few moments. Kay answered.

'Hi, sweet heart. How's you?'

The call was unexpected but Kay recognised that there was no tension in his voice and relaxed. 'I'm fine. And you?'

'Everything is good here and we've had a significant development.'

Julie Levant entered his office with tea. She noted the red telephone handset. 'I think I will close the door and leave you alone for a while.'

Faraday nodded and smiled before continuing his conversation with Kay. 'Nicholas Milano was on a military training course in the Brecons. The course finished on the 14th March, but he then had the option of one week's leave in the UK or returning to Gib. Most of his colleagues spent their week exploring the hot-spots of Cardiff or London,

Bristol or Birmingham. What Milano did, I haven't a clue, but I think we should get someone up to Hay-on-Wye with a photograph of Milano.'

Chapter Fifteen

Friday, 16th May.

Bath, England and the island of Madeira.

MARIA MILLER LIKED TO SHOP IN BATH, the Georgian city just thirteen miles east of Bristol. Deputy Chief Constable Anita Winters liked Bath too. She lived there. And so they met for lunch in the Dower House Restaurant of the Royal Crescent Hotel, the premier hotel in the city which once played host to President Ronald Reagan. In such idyllic surroundings conversation was easy and flowed effortlessly, but Miss Winters really knew very little of Mrs Miller, although she would never admit that she was a poor judge of others. The truth was that Miss Winters was out of her depth and conceited enough not to recognise that fact. She certainly did not have the astute, calculating and objective mind of a lawyer and, what was in her mind was distorted by a combination of ego and envy. Obliviously, Miss Winters ate her delicious lunch of Smoked Scottish Salmon whilst Mrs Miller enjoyed her Chicken Caesar Salad, followed by Strawberries with Vanilla *Ivy House* Clotted Cream, in these perfect surroundings overlooking the hotel's secluded Walled Garden.

Throughout their meal, the DCC was on her own ego trip. It was understandable that Miss Winters would take the opportunity to recount to, an apparently receptive, Mrs Miller her career struggles as she ascended to her present rank. She quietly but, nevertheless, with a certain restrained drama, alluded to the heavy burden of her responsibilities that she strove to bear lightly. She expressed, feigning discretion, her disappointment with some of her subordinates. And, mindful of Mr Miller's prominent position with the local Law Society and Mrs Miller's role within the Bristol Lord Mayor's charity supporting disadvantaged youths, she spoke of her hopes of advancement to do further good and suggested opportunities for mutual support.

Maria Miller listened attentively but, in reality, she didn't care for Anita Winters. They had little in common. The DCC was hard working but with little substance; her ambitions not compatible with her abilities. In contrast, Mrs Miller had depth in both personality and innate abilities. Nevertheless, the DCC had presented an opportunity not to be missed and Maria skilfully manoeuvred the conversation towards the enquiries conducted by Mark Faraday and Kay Yin.

'And are you disappointed with Chief Superintendent Faraday and Superintendent Yin,' adding innocently, 'they seem sound enough?'

'Everything is not always as it seems, Maria,' she replied as if confiding in one of her closest of friends.

'In what way?' asked Maria Miller full of spurious curiosity.

'Let me assure you, Maria,' replied Winters in a quiet but pompous tone, 'I have had to speak with the Chief Constable about them both and I have now been able to put this enquiry back on track, although I had felt for some while that there had been a lack of direction, with an often inappropriate focus.'

'"Inappropriate focus"?' Maria Miller gently solicited.

DCC Anita Winters paused before replying as if reluctant to continue, although she was eager to do so. She looked around the restaurant warily like a conspirator involved in the Gun Powder Plot, then spoke in hushed tones. 'Yin tends to consider everyone associated with this case as a suspect in the hope of stumbling into the perpetrator by chance.'

'Oh, goodness,' she said in amused alarm. 'Does this mean that she suspects *me* too?'

'Maria, Miss Yin suspects *everyone*,' she mocked as if her contact with Kay was akin to a teacher dealing with an underperforming and disappointing child. 'Unfortunately, the main suspect, a man by the name of Nicholas Milano,' she said, waving her hand dismissively in the air, 'apparently some sort of obscure, distant relative of your husband, has fled to Gibraltar, temporarily out of reach,' she said, unaware that Milano was now in Madeira, 'but, you can place your confidence in me, Maria, I have made sure that there is now a proper focus.'

***

Brian Craven had sent his daily reports to Julie's home by special delivery. These were read by Faraday and formed the basis of his secure-line calls with Kay Yin.

Craven confirmed that Milano was spending most of his time in his mother's *baroque quintas*, which was so convenient for his regular visits to the Casino da Madeira, an ultra-modern building which looked more like a futuristic cathedral than a casino, where Craven was on more than speaking terms with the voluptuous Vânia, a croupier. Vânia had gradually, and whilst engaged in ill-concealed seduction to their mutual satisfaction, informed Craven of Milano's regular routine of drinking *Jack Daniels* on the high stools of the rather gaudy Palm Bar before going to the fourth floor, and the Bahia Restaurant, with its spectacular views over Funchal. Vânia had confided that Milano was one of the more successful gamblers but, more importantly, through Vânia, Craven had identified a man whom Milano would often meet in the Palm Bar – José, who was an estate agent with an office in Gibraltar.

Chapter Sixteen

Saturday, 17th May.

Bristol, England.

NICHOLAS MILANO HAD A RECKLESS STREAK. He called Maria Miller from his mobile. He needed to know more about her husband and Grange Lodge. He had rung her home on Thursday and the call had been answered by the housekeeper, Mia Vickers, and so he pretended he was from a double-glazing firm. Mia quickly brought the conversation to a close as Nicholas knew the suggestion that he was selling double-glazing would. He rang again on Friday but the call was diverted to the answer-phone. He did not leave a message. Today, he rang at a little after mid-day when he judged that Maria would probably be in the kitchen alone, and would answer the phone promptly. She was alone. She answered the phone promptly.

Nicholas Milano spoke smoothly. He possessed a voice that instantly charmed. His silken words disarmed and seduced. Memories floated readily into Maria's mind, a mind disturbingly receptive to his words.

'Nicholas, you shouldn't be calling me,' she said eventually, a trace of anxiety, or was it regret, in her voice.

'But I *had* to,' he said slowly and seductively.

'No. No, Nicholas. I'm married. You must know that.'

Hatred began to absorb Nicholas' mind on hearing those words of confirmation. Words that confirmed her betrayal of him by marrying Christopher Miller. But he had anticipated mention of her husband and had steeled himself so as to control his emotions. There was a pause. 'I *only* want to see *you*,' he said softly and reasonably, adding, temptingly, 'just for a few … just a few *special* moments.' Maria's mind was in turmoil. She thought of his winning smile. A smile difficult to resist. Erotic memories flooded back again disrupting her reasoning. She remained silent in a haze, a haze of emotion-filled thoughts. For a fleeting moment she remembered their passionate liaisons, thoughts he interrupted. 'I shall be visiting Bristol *very, very* soon.' He allowed the prospect to linger for more tantalising moments before suggesting reasonably: 'How can just a *few* moments between friends in the Avon Gorge Hotel be the cause of any harm?' he suggested, deliberately mentioning the hotel that was the scene of so many of their fervent interludes. There was more silence as he allowed her to think of that hotel. 'Maria, I *need* to see you.'

The thought of being needed by another human being, particularly a charming and handsome human being, began to overwhelm Maria. Her heart began to race. She began to breathe heavily. But, that was his mistake. He had miscalculated. Her racing heart had served to alert her like a smoke alarm. Such a liaison, even a fleeting one, would endanger her and, somewhat reluctantly, reason resumed its seat. She resisted the temptation. 'I can't meet with you, Nicholas,' she said firmly. 'You must have heard of the murder that was committed at the front door of my home. We are both suspects, you and I.'

The confirmation that he was a suspect shocked Nicholas but he remained unruffled. 'How can *you* be a suspect, *my dearest*?' he said soothingly.

'Why?' she asked with quiet exasperation, as if she was likely to be overheard. 'Because … because the police believe that my husband was the intended victim and I am the only one who can gain from his death, can inherit.'

'That is *so, so* ridiculous, my dear,' he replied sharply but reassuringly, then continued on his quest. 'What harm can come of two old friends meeting in such an open way in a hotel? To *comfort*, to *reassure* each other.' There was silence for more moments as he allowed her to think of the human pleasures of being comforted and reassured. 'I cannot forget you, Maria. We *must* meet when I come to Bristol.'

'Nicholas, Nicholas. Please,' she said, desperation in her tone. 'You are not listening. Don't you understand?'

'What is there to understand?' he asked cunningly.

'I was speaking, Nicholas … I was speaking with the Deputy Chief Constable yesterday. You … you are a suspect too. The police, they think that you have fled to Gibraltar.'

'Gibraltar,' he replied, careful not to divulge where he was, 'but I will come to Bristol. I will come to *you*, Maria,' he said, his words laced with temptation. 'Surely you remember our plans?' his smooth words taking her thoughts back to an earlier and easier time. 'We had plans, Maria. We were embarking upon something that was beautiful and dangerous. And you *wanted* to meet.'

'But that was only to return a ... .'

Nicholas Milano interrupted her. 'We have unfinished business to conclude, Maria.' Then the line went dead.

***

The phone rang in the Senior Investigating Officer's office. Detective Superintendent Kay Yin picked up the receiver. It was Doctor Jennings from Forensics.

'Hi, Kay. It's Ruth. Have you a minute?'

'Of course. Is it good news?'

'Oh, yes. I have some preliminary results on the revolver. The powder-like substance that we found around one of the screw heads on the butt, and a smaller amount near the chamber, is some sort of make-up foundation. We are narrowing the range, probably expensive, but I should be able to have a match within the next few days.'

Chapter Seventeen

Monday, 19th May.

Police Headquarters, Bristol, England and the island of Madeira.

IT WAS TWENTY TO EIGHT IN THE MORNING. 'I assume it must be very important, Robert?' asked Chief Constable Emily Woodland, as Assistant Chief Constable Perrin closed her office door behind him.

'Yes, ma'am, it is rather.' Robert Perrin stepped forward and placed three sheets of A4 paper on the chief constable's desk. 'As you know we have tapped Mr and Mrs Miller's home phone for a little while now. This is a transcript of a telephone conversation on Saturday between Mrs Miller and a man called "Nicholas" whom we believe to be Captain Nicholas Milano.'

Emily Woodland raised an eyebrow, then lowered her head and read the double-spaced document with rapt attention. There was no smile on her face as she looked up a few minutes later. There was no need to question the significance of the text. The content was clear. 'What do you recommend, Robert?' she asked slowly.

'Nothing at this stage, ma'am, other than to continue to monitor the calls.'

'And Anita?'

'Again, nothing at this stage. I think we should pretend that nothing is amiss.'

The chief constable picked up the papers again thoughtfully. 'Agreed. Thank you, Robert. And Chief Superintendent Faraday and Superintendent Yin will have to be told, won't they?'

'They need to be in the loop and they are discreet.'

'I hate this, Robert,' she said as she rose from her seat and threw the papers across her office in frustrated disgust. She placed both of her fists on her green, leather-topped desk starring at the other papers on her blotter, considering what she had read and its implications. Eventually she looked up and at the ACC. 'There is one consolation,' she said eventually, 'at least I can rely upon you, Robert.'

'And Faraday and Miss Yin.'

'Yes. I've grown to realise that.'

Robert Perrin stooped and collected the discarded papers from the floor and placed them neatly on her desk. 'Thank you, ma'am. I will keep you up-to-date.' He turned and was about to leave, but paused, adding: 'I don't like Anita, as I think you must know, but I *am* sorry. You don't need this.'

'The Police Service doesn't need this, Robert, but we are at where we are at. And, be assured, I will deal with it.'

***

Nicholas Milano had first met Harry Holt, five years previously when he had sailed over to Morocco and had driven to Guelmin and onwards to Ouzzazate, south of the Atlas Mountains and the gateway to the Sahara Desert, a country that enchanted him and appealed to his romantic inclinations, a location used for scenes in many films including *Lawrence of Arabia*, *Gladiator* and James Bond's *The Living Daylight*. As far as Nicholas was concerned, Harry may have been English. But probably not, he thought. His name was unlikely to have been Harry Holt. But it didn't matter. To Nicholas he was his friend, José.

But his name was Harry Holt, an Englishman with a natural charm and fake tan enriched by the Mediterranean sun. Three years before Nicholas had met Harry, Harry had been engaged in his latest drug smuggling run from a little Moroccan cove twenty-two miles east of Melilla. These runs had been hugely profitable in the past. His last one had not. Near the island of Mallorca his hard-worked launch developed engine trouble. Harry's drifting launch had attracted the attention of the Spanish Servicio de Vigilancia Aduanera which dispatched one of their *Gerifalte*-class customs cutters to render assistance. It was the type of assistance that Harry had hoped to avoid. Harry found himself rescued, then arrested and charged with drug smuggling and detained in the Centre Penitenciari de Mallorca, Palma, to await trial. After five months, and now fluent in Spanish, the authorities allowed Harry to savour a modicum of freedom by allowing him to work in the prison's kitchens.   Some fellow inmates resented this favouritism but Harry had a ruthless streak and scolded a disgruntled assailant with paella – one of his specialities - the paella that is, not the scolding.   Or maybe it was. Whatever, two months later the authorities dropped all charges against Harry and arranged for him to work in Valencia for an estate agent - and the Spanish intelligence services – as José Torno. The estate agency was ideal for his new clandestine role. Harry would meet clients who would divulge details of their background, aspirations and financial status, usually without a second thought. This proved to be a very useful source of information for someone involved with the intelligence community. And, he was able to help his clients achieve their aspirations – at a price, of course. Harry could also meet subversive and perfidious contacts at a wide range of locations and properties without attracting suspicion. Harry soon became valued as a natural salesman as well as becoming a more than useful 'asset' to the intelligence services. After one year, Harry was transferred to an estate agency in Gibraltar where he identified Nicholas Milano as a potential intelligence source and had decided to follow the captain when he travelled to Ouzzazate. Their mutual attraction to Morocco served to cement their relationship.

Ouzzazate had been a good place for their first encounter. Isolated. Discreet. Safe. Today, their meeting place was less exotic but, nevertheless, equally discreet and much more sophisticated.

Belmond Reid's Palace, or simply Reid's, appealed to Nicholas as a romantic and superior place, a place where he believed he naturally belonged. It was also, in fact, strangely discreet. Guests of Reid's, this world famous hotel, would not expect a fellow guest to be a traitor to his country. True, guests would range from wealthy retirees to families of means from the world of commerce, including those whose commercial enterprises involved ruthlessness, double-dealing and corruption, but, heaven forbid, not traitors to the State. And so, Captain Nicholas Milano sat confidently on the black and white marbled Tea Terrace and looked over the scented, sloping gardens and across the glittering waters towards the harbour of Porto Santo. He was satisfied that, here on the beautiful island of Madeira, he was beyond the reach of the British authorities. He was confident too that there was little evidence to implicate him in the murders of Guy Hernandez or Victor Jenkins. He also consoled himself with the thought that any liaison between the British police and the Portuguese authorities would be protracted, and, if it proved necessary, his friends within the Centro de Inteligencia de las Fuerzas Armandas would encounter few difficulties in spiriting him away to Morocco. Reid's was certainly the place for Nicholas Milano to wait, the hotel that had once been frequented by Sir Winston Churchill and the heroic Antarctic explorer, Captain Robert Falcon Scott, but, more appropriately for Nicholas' image of himself, movie stars such as Gregory Peck and Sir Roger Moore.

And Brian Craven was waiting too. Nearby. Not on the hotel's Tea Terrace. Not in the hotel's lush gardens. No, he was resting his elbows on a wall, binoculars in hand, a paper cup of coffee at his side, his Fiat 500 at the kerb, near the Avenida do Infante.

It was late afternoon when Nicholas checked his watch. At the appointed hour, he took the lift down from the hotel's Upper Gardens to its private jetty. José was there on board the sleek power boat with that giant, Gunter, at the controls. The boat was a *SeaRay 220*. Not too big. Not too small. A craft that most of the guests would overlook as they admired the much larger *Dynacraft 46* and the *Birchwood 33* cabin cruisers anchored nearby. José and Nicholas embraced. Good friends eager to drink the champagne waiting in the ice buckets; to gossip and conspire; to exchange the brown envelope bulging with €10,000 in used bank notes. Once Nicholas and José were seated, Gunter skilfully manoeuvred the boat away from the jetty, slowly but not too slowly, without attracting unnecessary attention.

Their passage was stately as José apologised to Nicholas for his inexcusable lapse in failing to warn him of the closure of the Spanish-Gibraltarian border. They discussed the failure to kill Christopher Miller. For these failures there were no recriminations from either party, just an understanding between professionals that plans rarely run smoothly. Nevertheless, Nicholas was keen to demonstrate his worth to his pay masters and handed José details of the military preparation and schedules for the forthcoming visit to Gibraltar by the Duke and Duchess of Cambridge. They discussed some proposed regimental reorganisations, the deployment of a small SAS team for an up-coming exercise and the plans to modify the South Mole to accommodate the new British super-carriers as they drank more champagne and rounded the headland of Ponta da Cruz. As they continued towards Câmara de Lobos, José asked Nicholas to explain his 'cunning plan'.

'I have a simple, workable plan, with no risk at all,' replied Nicholas eagerly, 'that will be guaranteed to discredit Christopher Miller.' José smiled encouragingly as he poured Nicholas another glass of champagne. 'At the moment, Hugh Thornton, the Commissioner of Police, is under-going treatment in a UK hospital, the Royal Bournemouth Hospital. Bournemouth fits so neatly into my plan,' he continued enthusiastically. 'We know that Miller and the Chief Minister and Thornton are on very close terms. My plan will very simply ensure that Miller will be exposed as a cheap crook who sought to enhance his personal wealth in a deceitful and devious way. Let me explain in more detail,' he said, extending his arm so that José could re-fill his glass.

Nicholas explained his plan. José listened intently. José acknowledged that the plan was brilliant in its conception and simplicity. It would be a headline-stealer, they knew, in the UK, Spain and Gibraltar. All that Nicholas required José to do was to ensure that the Spanish press were appropriately briefed beforehand. To that end, Nicholas helpfully provided a series of photographs and a draft press release.

José shook his head from side to side and smiled in admiration. 'That is a really excellent plan, Nicholas. Our superiors will be pleased with you,' adding warmly, 'Congratulations. Congratulations. Your continuing work for us is well worth the increase of payments from €5,000 to €10,000.'

Nicholas was relieved that his demand for an increase, based primarily on his possession of the letter, had been agreed. 'We should celebrate,' suggested Nicholas, 'and Gunter should too,' he added, conscious that Gunter had not shared the champagne.

'Later,' replied José, 'Gunter is concentrating on the tide and currents which are tricky here near Cabo Girāo.'

'You are *so* mean, José. Be generous,' said Nicholas munificently.

José waved Gunter over. Gunter, the professional, assessed the power of the currents and their direction again, at the same time, gauging the distant from the starboard side of their boat to the headland of Cabo Girāo, a sheer headland often to be seen protruding through a morning sea mist. Satisfied, Gunter secured the helm. He stepped forward and gratefully accepted an empty glass from José who filled the glass with champagne.

'Thank you, Colonel Milano,' said Gunter courteously.

Nicholas beamed at Gunter for acknowledging his Spanish military rank. 'A toast,' suggested Nicholas to both men.

José turned around and pulled a brown envelope from his bag and waved it with a smile. 'A toast to cash. Lots and lots of cash,' he called, adding, 'and to friendship too.'

The three men raised and clinked their glasses. As they did so, the powerfully built Gunter let his glass drop from his hand and into the sea as he grabbed Nicholas' right forearm. He pulled and turned a startled Nicholas easily to face the Atlantic Ocean and pushed him towards and over the port-side gunwale. Gunter swiftly grabbed Nichols' left trouser leg at the ankle as he released Nichols' right arm, at the same time grasping his right trouser leg in a vice-like grip. He easily heaved Nicholas completely over the gunwale, dangling Nicholas' head and shoulders under the cold turquoise sea. Nicholas struggled violently. He was seized by fear. He chillingly understood what was happening. He had been greedy. He had never shown José the letter only tantalizingly relayed its content, but he had tormented them for far too long and had failed in Bristol after so many promises. Now he was petrified. He had been reckless. He had given them his 'cunning plan'. He had become an expensive liability. Now he was dispensable. In panic-filled desperation he shook his torso violently left to right and right to left in the vain hope of breaking free of Gunter's grip. He twisted and struggled to bend his knees so as to bring his head above the water, but to no avail. Gunter had deliberately not gripped his legs so as to avoid leaving any tell-tell hand marks on the skin but grasped the material of his trouser legs. Nicholas should have tried to undo his trousers and swim free but terror completely filled his mind and confused his thoughts. He thrashed about with both arms. He sought a hand-hold on the boat's smooth hull, but there was none to be found, just green slippery slime. As the slow seconds passed he knew that hope was fading, but, there seemed to be the trace of a smile upon his lips as if, in his final moments, he took some comfort in the knowledge that he had also given her his 'cunning plan'. Then salt sea water entered Nicholas' trachea. Within little more than a minute, there was a loss of consciousness due to hypoxia, followed rapidly by cardiac arrest. Gunter continued to hold Nicholas' inert body in the water for a further few minutes until death was assured.

The name of the near-by Cabo Girāo means 'Cape of the Turning' in recognition of the navigator, Captain João Gonçalves Zarco, who, at this very point turned his galleon for home. But, for Captain Nicholas Milano, alias Obit, he would never again turn for home.

Chapter Eighteen

Wednesday, 21st May.

Bristol, England, the island of Madeira and the British Overseas Territory, Gibraltar.

THERE HAD BEEN A FLURRY OF CALLS during the previous forty-eight hours.

The first had been from Brian Craven to Kay Yin. Burn-phone to burn-phone. It was short. As it needed to be. A simple message. 'Check our local paper.' She did so via the internet.

'Prominent English resident drowned.'

In both the Portuguese *Jornal de Madeira* and the English *Madeira Life*, the story was the same. The body of Nicholas Milano had been washed ashore on the very narrow strip of pebble beach at the foot of the second highest sea cliff in Europe, the Cabo Girão. Recovery of the body had been difficult. The tide had been high and the swell heavy. Now Captain Milano's body lay in one of the refrigerated lockers in the local mortuary awaiting a post-mortem. A police spokesman had said that: 'We must await the outcome of the post-mortem. At this stage the death appears to be as a result of drowning'.

Detective Superintendent Kay Yin immediately informed the ACC (Crime) who informed the Chief Constable and the

Foreign and Commonwealth Office. Kay then informed Mark, who informed the Chief Minister.

By late afternoon today, Faraday had received a comprehensive report, via Julie Levant's address, from Craven. A duplicate report had been received by Kay at their home address, using her mother-in-law's maiden name, and addressed to 'Miss S Marsh BSc'.

In his report, Craven explained that he had kept observation on Nicholas Milano during the 19th and had observed him getting on board a *SeaRay 220* from the Reid's Hotel jetty. In the boat was the man he knew only as José, an estate agent based in Gibraltar. Also in the boat was an unknown male. The three men appeared on very relaxed terms as they cast-off and made their way towards Câmara de Lobos. Craven explained that he was able to observe their friendly drinking and follow their progress by taking the 101 coast road and parking in a lay-by at Ponta da Cruz and later at Câmara de Lobos. But, at this latter point, the road zig-zagged and wound its way inland until skirting the coast again at Estreito de Câmara. By the time Craven had reached this town, the *SeaRay* was nowhere to be seen.

Craven had waited a half-hour hoping that the boat would appear but without success, and so, he retraced the route back towards Reid's Hotel. Again there was no sign of Milano's boat at the hotel's jetty and so Craven drove along the Avanida do Mar towards the marina. There were many hundreds of boats moored in the marina at dozens of pontoons. Craven explained that he pretended to be a prospective purchaser and walked along each pontoon, making a point of photographing the boats that were for sale. He located the *SeaRay* at pontoon number 8 and surreptitiously photographed it. He had hoped that he could have retrieved bottles or glasses for their fingerprints but he could not detect anything of significance in the vessel. Nor was there any trace of Nicholas Milano, José or the other man, either on any of the boats, at the quayside or in any of the cafés and bars.

Chapter Nineteen

Friday, 23rd May.

Bristol, England.

THEY MET DISCREETLY.   In the Divisional Commander's office, Faraday's former office, at the Bristol City Divisional HQ at The Grove, vacated by the temporary commander of the city who was attending a meeting with community leaders in St Pauls. Faraday's secretary provided Assistant Chief Constable Robert Perrin and Detective Superintendent Kay Yin with coffee and privacy. They sat at a small conference table in the corner office with its views across Bathurst Basin towards the church of St Mary Redcliffe.

'Mr Gareth Evans,' said Kay, 'the proprietor of Hay's Antique Emporium, has confirmed that a man purchased a pair of Forehand and Wadsworth *Hammerless* .38s on the 18th March ... '

'A pair?' interrupted Perrin with astonishment.

'Yes, sir. A pair in a rather nice wooden presentation case with a blue velvet lining,' Kay replied, returning her coffee cup to her saucer and removing a catalogue from her brief case. Perrin allowed her to continue. 'This is the proprietor's catalogue and here,' she said as she thumbed through the pages, 'at page 23 is the pair with a full description of the mahogany presentation case, the pistols themselves and their provenance.' She pointed to the colour photograph. 'Importantly, the previous owner, the Viscount Villiers, had "<>" engraved immediately below the chamber on both sides of each pistol.' Kay continued to speak as she removed a SOCO photograph from her case. 'As you can see an identical engraving can be found on the weapon found at the Avon Gorge which we believe was used to murder Victor Jenkins.'

'And who purchased this weapon on the 18th?'

'The male purchaser paid in cash and the receipt was made out to a Ronald Days-Brown of Rochester. Needless to say, the Rochester address does not exist, nor does Mr Ronald Days-Brown. But, Mr Evans was shown a series of photographs, one of which was of Nicholas Milano, and he picked out, although hesitantly, that of Milano.'

'You say hesitantly?' queried Perrin.

'Yes, only because Milano was wearing a high-neck pullover and knitted *beanie*, both of which partly covered his hairline, cheeks and chin, thus making his features appear less distinct.'

'Any CCTV?'

'Yes, we have one piece of footage in the main street of the town which seems to show Milano. There is no CCTV in the car park or roads leading to the town, although there is CCTV in the shop itself. But all these images are unclear due to his clothing. However, the purchaser did walk with what could be interpreted as a military gait,' adding confidently: 'Although the images are not perfect, and we only have a partial print from the receipt, I think we can be ninety percent certain that it was Milano who purchased the weapons.'

'But the CCTV and partial print alone would not be sufficient for a successful conviction?'

'That is absolutely correct.'

'Okay,' he said accepting the conclusion, sipping his coffee before continuing. 'Any thoughts on why Milano should purchase two guns and where is the second?'

'It doesn't make a great deal of sense, unless it was part of a deception plan.'

'A deception plan?' questioned an intrigued Perrin thoughtfully.

'It's only speculation but, in the unlikely event of the police carrying out a routine check with the antique dealer, the purchase of two pistols in a presentation case would not ordinarily arouse suspicion. Killers don't usually purchase a pair of pistols. But this does seem to fit the MO of Milano's planning and preparation: the purchase of a pair of weapons, and the use of a weapon that could easily be passed-off as an antique to an enquiring officer.'

'And we have no idea where the second pistol is?'

'No, we don't,' replied Kay, adding: 'We know the second weapon is not in Milano's apartment in Gib because Mark has searched it. It could be in Madeira, but it would have to be taken through airport security checks. Or it could be back in Gib with the army in a locker on the base.'

'And I think you said that Captain Milano's course finished on the 14th,' recalled Perrin, 'followed by a weeks' leave, then he returned to Gibraltar?'

'Yes, and if he returned to Gib on a military aircraft or his kit was sent on ahead, I can't see Customs doing a thorough search of every soldier's mucky kit after an exercise on the Brecon Beacons,' surmised Kay. 'And it's unlikely that a commissioned officer would be searched that thoroughly, if at all.'

'You are right,' Perrin concluded, 'it could easily be slipped through and be back in Gib.'

'He could have sold it on, of course,' she suggested, 'but it is still of concern that there is this second weapon connected with the case.'

'And now Milano has been washed up?'

Kay selected a three-page report, written on crested Madeiran government paper, containing the outlines of a human body, front and back, on the first page. 'These are copies of the Portuguese post-mortem findings which have concluded that the death of Nicholas Milano was a case of accidental drowning. The PM found no signs of external injuries, other than a few minor bumps and grazes on elbows and knees, heels and toes, and around the cheek bones, but these have been attributed to Milano being buffeted about on the pebble beach below Cabo Girão. There were no signs of head injuries, a struggle or marks around the throat, neck, arms or legs and sea water was found in the lungs.'

'But you are not so sure that death was accidental?'

'What I am sure about is that we cannot be sure,' replied Kay without evasion. 'There appears to be no physical evidence to contradict a finding of accidental drowning and, either way, there are no substantial witnesses. The local papers refer to a waiter in Reid's who recalled a very charming Milano taking afternoon tea. The papers also mention a guest who vaguely remembered "a man" joining "two other men" in a "cabin cruiser" at about the same time, and other hotel guests can't recall anything or had already checked-out or were just passing through for afternoon tea.'

Chapter Twenty

Monday, 26th May.

British Overseas Territory, Gibraltar.

'A SUBJECT HAS ENTERED THE APARTMENT, sir,' said Detective Inspector James Frobisher as he peered around the door of Commissioner Faraday's office. Faraday grabbed a note pad and walked briskly along the corridor followed by Inspector Purchell. Frobisher tapped in the code on the reinforced door of the Special Branch offices. They entered the vestibule and closed the door behind them. Then he tapped in a different code for the second door. They entered. The open-plan office was bright but cool. The monitoring station was window-less and slightly warmer. They crossed to the monitors. Faraday waved the operator to remain in his seat.

The subject was Grace Milano.

Grace Milano carried with her a large hessian shopping bag, the sort that you would use at the supermarket. She had placed this on the floor in the lounge and was now standing quietly in the middle of the lounge, deep in thought.

'How long has she been standing there?' Faraday asked the operator.

He checked the counter on the screen. 'Seven minutes, sir.'

It was a sombre and poignant scene. There was utter silence in the apartment. There was utter silence in the Special Branch monitoring station, broken only by the soft whirl of the computers and air conditioning. Then Grace Milano moved, unhurried and dignified. She removed the key from the Moroccan sandalwood box in the lounge, used it to open the study door, stood silently in the doorway for a little over two minutes, entered and opened the louvres so as to allow the sun to flood into the study. She made no effort to search for anything, simply re-emerging to walk to the kitchen, returning with a red plastic container with cleaning materials: cloths and dusters, furniture polish and cleaning sprays. And she cleaned. Cleaned like a nun obediently cleaning her abbey. Thorough. Committed. Dedicated to her solemn task. Everything was dusted, polished and wiped clean, and replaced in perfect order.

Grace had brought nothing for the apartment, with two exceptions. She removed a large framed photograph of her son from the hessian bag and placed it reverently upon a central coffee table. She stood back. Then adjusted the frame's position. Stood back and adjusted it again. And yet again until satisfied that its position was absolutely perfect.

Grace would take nothing from the apartment, with one exception. She entered her late son's bedroom, the master bedroom, picked up the bedside photograph of Maria Miller and returned to the lounge. She sat on a dining chair and carefully removed the masking tape at the back of the frame so as to lift clear the hardboard backing to reveal the photograph. This photograph she placed on the coffee table, and tried to replace it with the second item she had brought with her – an unframed photograph of her son. But it didn't fit perfectly. From her bag she removed a pair of scissors, picked up the photograph of her son and very precisely trimmed it so as to ensure a perfect fit. Grace had been well prepared. With a roll of masking tape from her bag, she secured the hardboard back in place, then took the frame to the smaller of the two bedrooms and placed it on the bedside table.

Throughout the two hours, twenty-three minutes that Grace Milano was in the apartment she was calm and dignified. The only exception was when she returned to the lounge and picked up the discarded photograph of Maria Miller. She looked at the photograph and began to tremble, then violently tore the photograph into the smallest of pieces. She seemed to be overcome by tiredness and knelt on the floor only to sob. After a few minutes she regained her composure and began to collect the fragments, careful not to leave any behind that would desecrate this sacred place.

Chapter Twenty-One

Thursday, 29th May.

Brussels, Belgium; the island of Madeira and Murder Investigation Room, Police Headquarters, Bristol, England.

DEPUTY CHIEF CONSTABLE Winters rang from her office at police headquarters. It was 2.30pm. It was made as Mrs Miller was about to take her long weekend. Well before her flight time of 4pm from Brussel-Nationaal. The call was quickly routed through. Mrs Maria Miller answered.

'Anita. What a pleasant surprise,' she said but with little true pleasure. 'Can I help you in any way?' asked a perplexed and irritated Mrs Miller.

'Oh, no, Maria, thank you,' replied the DCC. 'I thought I should call and up-date you as to progress, so as to reassure you.'

'That's kind of you, Anita. Is it good news?'

'I always have good news, Maria,' she said in a superior manner. 'The main suspect in the murder of Guy Hernandez,' she continued, 'namely Nicholas Milano, was drowned off the coast of Madeira just over a week ago.'

The thought of the unexpected death of this remarkably attractive and charismatic man, a lover, stunned Maria. For some moments Maria was speechless. She pretended that her phone was faulty by making a noise running a pen along the metal net of a filing tray, so as to gain time to compose herself. 'I'm sorry Anita, there seemed to be gremlins on this line. I do hope it's not President Putin,' she jested. 'Can you hear me clearly now?'

'Yes, perfectly,' replied Miss Winters.

'You said that this man was drowned. Oh, my God. Was he murdered too?'

'No, the local police and coroner have determined that his death was due to accidental drowning.'

The death had not been reported in the British press and Maria was shocked and not inclined to enter into any small talk, but thanked Miss Winters for her kind consideration.

Mrs Maria Miller replaced her phone slowly. She seemed rooted to her desk. She wasn't relaxed.

Miss Anita Winters replaced her phone promptly. She stood up from her desk. She was relaxed.

The DCC smiled. She was pleased that she had phoned Mrs Miller at her EU office, a little before she would be taken to the airport for her flight home at 4pm, and did not make the mistake of calling Mrs Miller at her home by telephone that she knew to be tapped. But it *had* been a mistake. Mrs Miller had been informed that her British Airways flight had been delayed by one hour and ten minutes and so she had remained in her office for a little longer than usual. And Mrs Miller, who knew that her husband had appointments away from his Queen Square offices, took the opportunity to ring Grange Lodge and leave a message on the house answerphone, to be picked up by her husband when he returned home.

***

Brian Craven had spent much of the day in the shaded square of banana and fig trees, trees festooned with electric lights of coloured bulbs. He was seated at a café table with his back to the table that was always reserved for the seven ladies. Today this group, representing the local social élite, were joined by Grace Milano. Grace Milano had been absent for a number of days, in Gibraltar, occupied with discussions with Colonel David Contaldo regarding the military funeral of her son, Captain Nicholas Milano.

Today there had been heart-felt embraces and tears. From the ladies. Not from Brian Craven. He appeared completely absorbed with typing on his laptop surrounded by holiday brochures. As he had been for three of the previous six days.

Mrs Milano, although clearly tired and drawn, was proud to speak of the arrangements that had been approved by the Military Governor himself. She spoke of the Order of Service. The bishop that would be presiding. The ceremonial guard that would parade. The regimental band that would play Elgar's 'Nimrod' from the 'Enigma Variations'. The choir that would sing 'The Armed Man' by

Karl Jenkins and, finally, 'Jerusalem' by Hurbert Parry. There were nods of approval. There were more tears and the timely gentle touching of hands when appropriate. There were kind and understanding words.

But, during those three days that Brian Craven had been at the café, in the absence of Grace Milano, there had not always been kind words, and, some of the words were less than understanding.

Craven had heard those words.

'He was so handsome and charming,' Vera had said with an approving smile.

'Extremely charming,' agreed Deidre. 'Maybe a little too charming,' she continued, her head held at a knowing angle. 'And I can never understand why he remained unmarried.'

'And a hero by all accounts,' remarked Alex provocatively.

'In Afghanistan so they say,' reminded Christine as if privy to all matters regarding the Milano family.

'And Grace,' contributed Alex with an ill-concealed smirk, 'had understood that he had been recommended for an MBE.'

'Yes,' said Christine, adding sceptically, 'but apparently the recommendation had not been written up properly and so the poor man missed out.'

'And what will Grace do now. She so relied upon him?' whimpered Deidre.

'Nicholas was apparently very generous to his mother,' offered Sophia approvingly, 'supplementing her income, so I have heard.'

'He was a steady hand guiding her through difficult times,' agreed Deidre.

'Yes, although I hear that the business has not been in good shape for some while,' Alex suggested mischievously.

'I think that is true, but the hyenas are gathering,' said an all-knowing Christine. 'A number of companies are keen to acquire the Milano name,' adding contemptuously, 'rather like the Germans buying Rolls Royce.' There were mumbles of agreement at this remark.

'And what about the burglary at her home?' questioned Alex, adding, with little conviction, '*so* cruel. Who could be *so* heartless?'

'Strange, I would have thought,' suggested Christine.

'Strange? Strange in what way?' questioned Vera who appeared to have just woken up.

'Nothing was stolen,' remarked Christine with raised eyebrows.

***

ACC Perrin was sat in the SIO's office with Superintendent Yin. 'As you know, sir,' Kay said, 'Craven, our man in Madeira, saw Milano get into a motor launch with two men and sail down the coast and out of sight. When Craven saw the boat again, there were only two occupants. The boat didn't return to Reid's Hotel but eventually docked at the Avanida do Mar marina. Enquiries by Craven confirmed that the boat was hired on a one-day rental basis for cash.'

'And no ID for the other men in the boat?'

'Craven knew one man only as José, an estate agent working in Gibraltar. Special Branch there have now identified him as José Torno. Mark is following this up as we speak, but no ID for the second man. Meanwhile, Craven has picked up rumours that the Milano wine business is not thriving as it once did. Its premier position, occupied for decades, has been overtaken by more dynamic and imaginative companies.'

'But the Milano family is respected, you say.'

'Grace Milano lives in very comfortable style and is the local British Consul.'

'And how does she manage to keep up appearances?' he asked.

'Income from the wine business, an income supplemented by her son.'

Chapter Twenty-Two

Friday, 30th May.

British Overseas Territory, Gibraltar.

GRACE MILANO'S VISIT had not gone unnoticed by Special Branch. They knew she would be at North Front Airport when her son's body returned. Once through Customs and Immigration, she had taken a taxi to her son's apartment, unpacked her case in the smaller of the two bedrooms and returned to the awaiting taxi. Near Casement Square, she had a coffee in one of the cafés as she checked her camera. However, her main attention appeared to be Casement Square itself, seemingly concentrating on its proportions – not a precise square, of course – together with the surrounding buildings and the pattern of shadows cast by the late morning sun.

Her coffee finished, Grace took photographs of the square, from the north-east, from the south, from everywhere. Apparently satisfied, she returned to the café for lunch throughout which she scrutinised the pictures she had taken and earnestly and carefully wrote notes in her little notebook with her gold Mont Blanc pen. After lunch she didn't visit the Cathedral of the Holy Trinity where her son's funeral would take place but, instead, visited the Kings' Chapel, then the Church of the Sacred Heart and the cathedral of St Mary the Crowned. At these churches she studies the text inscribed on the memorials and marble tablets that adorned their walls. Some she ignored, others she photographed, carefully checking that she had clearly recorded the text.

From St Andrews Church, Grace emerged into the sunlight and took a taxi to the Admiral Rooke memorial at the Waterport, the American War Memorial at Line Wall Road and the British War Memorial in John Mackintosh Square, photographing the memorials from various angles and, again, studying the inscriptions with intense care. Finally, she returned to Casement Square and entered the cathedral church of the Holy Trinity, which looked more like a civic hall than a church. Here she sat still and erect in silent contemplation for more than forty minutes. Eventually, her expedition concluded, she returned to Nicholas' apartment where she changed into a beautifully-cut dark blue suit, before returning to the airport to await the repatriation of her son's body.

***

'And what are your conclusions, James?' asked Faraday as they, together with Peter Purchell, sat at the commissioner's conference table.

'The photography could have been her hobby,' he said without conviction, 'or therapeutic. But we don't think so. Peter and I have double-checked the inscriptions on the memorials, the ones she ignored, the ones she didn't. The ones commemorating a priest or a devout wife, a young child or a prominent merchant, she ignored. What she did concentrate upon were those memorials to soldiers and sailors who had fallen in battle during the Great Siege, the Napoleonic Wars and the Great War.'

'And why do you think she was doing that?' asked Faraday with a knowing smile which anticipated their response.

Both inspectors looked at each other, then at Faraday. 'I think we have all arrived at the same conclusion, sir,' said Inspector Purchell.

'Go on,' encouraged Faraday.

'Grace Milano is considering an appropriate memorial to her late son,' replied Peter Purchell.

'You see,' ventured Inspector Frobisher by way of explanation, 'Mrs Milano's first port of call was King's Chapel.'

'You will have to help me here, James, and assume that I have no local knowledge at all – which will be the case.'

'Of course, sir,' replied Frobisher, having not wished to appear patronising by going into too much local detail. 'King's Chapel actually formed part of The Convent, the governor's official residence, and was the principal chapel of the British forces from 1844 until 1990. I suppose it was natural that she should have been drawn to this place of worship, but, what may be telling,' suggested Inspector Frobisher, 'is that Mrs Milano took photographs of the Spanish coat of arms that are still to be found in the courtyard, as well as a statue of a Royal Engineer, but, in particular she seemed to be fascinated by one tomb in particular.'

'And which one?' enquired Faraday, his interest aroused even more so.

'The chapel is the resting place of a number of British governors. It is also the resting place of the wife of a Spanish governor.'

'Interesting isn't it, gentlemen?' observed Faraday after some reflection. 'Maybe she thinks that the Spanish coat of arms and the tomb of the wife of a former Spanish governor somehow legitimises her desire for a memorial for her son.' Faraday leaned back into his chair. He looked around his office thoughtfully in silence, then spoke again. 'I'm sure that you are both correct to conclude that she is considering a memorial to her son, but, what is worrying is that she believes that some sort of heroic inscription would be appropriate, yet, he is supposed to have died by accidental drowning, not fighting an enemy, not dying heroically.' There was silence again before he continued. 'And if such a monument was to be erected, it certainly would not be erected with the blessing of the Chief Minister who knows of his treachery. She must realise that it could only ever be erected by the Spanish authorities.'

'She must be in the same fantasy world as her son,' remarked Frobisher with contempt. 'There is not the slightest intelligence that Spain is contemplating military action. There is the usual bunch of Spanish politicians who predict dire consequences for Gibraltar, whilst most sensible people follow the former king's view that if the Spanish demand sovereignty over Gibraltar, the same argument would be put forward by Morocco over its claims to the Spanish *plazas de soberania*,' said Frobisher, but, seeing Faraday's frown, added, 'that is "places of sovereignty", sir, namely the Spanish enclaves of Ceuta and Melilla on the Moroccan coast.'

Faraday pondered the inspector's remarks for a few moments. 'Maybe it is absurd but, does she have anything else left?' remarked Faraday eventually. 'Her life is empty except for memories and delusions.' He paused for some moments before he finally spoke again: 'And the deluded can be very dangerous, particularly when their delusions are not realised.'

Chapter Twenty-Three

Saturday, 31st May.

British Overseas Territory, Gibraltar.

CAPTAIN NICHOLAS MILANO's body had been solemnly returned to Gibraltar late the previous afternoon. The precision of the military pall bearers, the smartness of the guard of honour and the dignity of the whole affair would have done credit to the Brigade of Guards. Faraday, in full uniform, was there at the airport as was Mrs Grace Milano. Her stoic bearing and demeanour impressed all of those in attendance.

Today, Captain Milano was buried in the military cemetery after a service at the Cathedral of the Holy Trinity. There were large crowds, partly to witness the military parade, partly to show respect – or both. The sun shone brightly in a clear blue sky and a stiff breeze ensured that the Union Jack, the flag of Gibraltar and regimental flag strained proudly at half-mast. The reception in the Officers' Mess, that followed the service and burial, was appropriately dignified and restrained. All seemed satisfied that the funeral arrangements had gone off perfectly and pleased that Grace Milano seemed to be coping well with the pressures of the day.

Most of those present wore cautious smiles of relief, although Faraday thought that the Chief Minister was in danger of allowing, from time to time, a trace of annoyance, or was it contempt, to show in his stony expression. Although a model of courteous towards Mrs Milano, he was one of the first to leave the reception.

The Chief Minister had spent some time talking to Faraday in generalities although, when completely alone, commented icily: 'A fine masquerade wouldn't you say, Commissioner?'

'A necessary one I think, Chief Minister,' replied Faraday diplomatically.

Bite-sized sandwiches, dainty cakes, English Breakfast tea, freshly squeezed orange and chilled wines continued to circulate, with a pleasant rhythm of conversation permeating the Mess. Throughout, Colonel David Coltaldo acted as a discreet, but protective, chaperone to Grace Milano whose dignity impressed all who saw her or spoke with her. At twenty minutes to five, Grace seemed to be everywhere dealing with the perpetual stream of condolences with ease, speaking with her son's colleagues with equal repose. Then she was gone, spirited away by Colonel Coltaldo as pre-arranged. By nine o'clock that evening Grace had returned to her home in Madeira.

Chapter Twenty-Four

Monday, 2nd June.

British Overseas Territory, Gibraltar.

THE PHONE RANG. FARADAY ANSWERED. 'We have a visitor, sir,' said Frobisher. It was a little after 11am.

'I will be there in two minutes, James.'

It was less than two minutes. Frobisher was waiting at the reinforced door as Faraday approached. 'One man,' said Frobisher, 'as you will see, neatly dressed, wearing an Australian-style bush hat and only carrying a briefcase.' Both officers entered the darkened monitoring station and sat in chairs immediately behind the operator. They stared at the screens absorbing what was revealed. The visitor to Nicholas Milano's apartment who had apparently used a key, had gloved-up, removed his hat which he replaced with a forensic-styled cap. As he moved about the apartment, the visitor appeared thorough. There was method in his approach and what he did. He photographed everything, paying particular attention to pictures hung at a slight angle; the placement of cushions; the contents of each drawer; the position of place mats and Moroccan rugs. He felt over the ledges at the top of the kitchen cabinets; in and under drawers; and behind mirrors in the bedrooms and bathroom. He unzipped cushions and searched under the beds, chests of drawers and the bookcase. Every framed picture was taken from the walls and the backs removed to be carefully replaced and re-sealed with masking tape.

Faraday spoke first. 'I think we can assume that he isn't looking for anything that is more than two inches thick.'

'And not too wide or too long for the briefcase.'

'Precisely,' agreed Faraday. 'A key, a document, maybe a CD disc,' he suggested.

'I would have thought so, sir. And he has paid particular attention to the drop files.'

Faraday was intrigued and eager to stay, to relive his days as a young detective, but he was mindful of his own precious time and the possibility of unintentionally undermining DI Frobisher. 'I will leave this with you, James. I will be back in my office. Unless something startling happens, brief me when he leaves, but have him followed, please.'

***

It was just after three when Frobisher entered the Commissioner's office. Before he could speak, Faraday, always mindful of his officers' welfare, asked: 'Have you had any lunch, James?'

'No, sir.'

'I'll arrange for some sandwiches and coffee, sir,' offered Inspector Purchell helpfully.

Purchell left the office and conferred with Julie. They made coffees which he brought into the commissioner's office on a tray. 'I stole a few of your biscuits, sir,' he said with a smile. 'Julie is arranging sandwiches. About ten minutes.'

They sat at the table, adding milk and sugar to their coffees – and eating the Commissioner's favourite shortbread biscuits. 'What are your conclusions, James?'

'He appeared to be very forensically aware,' explained DI Frobisher, 'he was exceptionally careful and extremely thorough. He removed kickboards under kitchen units and the air-conditioning vent covers. He removed full length mirrors from wardrobe doors, the back panel of the TV and searched every book on the shelves. Whatever he was looking for, he didn't find it.'

'Okay,' suggested Faraday, 'although it could mean that his search was satisfactory in the sense that it confirms his view that what he sought was not in the apartment and never had been.'

Frobisher wasn't sure that he accepted that reasoning. 'Maybe,' he replied, adding: 'What is our next step, sir?'

'Before we come to that, did our visitor search for cameras, bugs, that sort of thing?' asked Faraday.

'No. No sweeps, nothing.'

'Well, that's good. That may indicate that he doesn't believe that we are on to him,' concluded Faraday.

There was a tap on the door and Julie entered with a platter of assorted sandwiches, three side plates and napkins.

'Thank you, Julie,' said Faraday delightfully, 'they look delicious.'

'Tuna and mayo, ham and tomato and cheese and cucumber, plus some crisps,' she winked, adding mischievously, 'I can recommend the tuna.'

'Well, I think we should all share James' sandwiches,' Faraday said, 'he would feel uncomfortable if we allowed him to eat alone, don't you agree, Peter?'

'And we couldn't allow that, sir,' warned Peter, 'James might get indigestion.'

They laughed, then they ate, then talked, not initially about Milano but spoke of family and home, cars and cooking, a conversation punctuated by more ripples of laughter. For an outsider looking in, for those who did not know Faraday well, they could consider him to be flippant or irresponsible. In public he always appeared to be calm and in control and possessed the knack of being genuinely relaxed, even when dealing with a crisis or discussing serious issues. Out of the public eye, some of his superiors and peers back in the UK often viewed him as having too casual an attitude towards mistakes made by subordinates and being insufficiently serious. That was far from the case. Behind a persona of a warm, seemingly amused and calm man, Faraday was very serious and extremely disciplined. His view was that retrospective supervision was often negative and counter-productive, and panic and anxiety simply served to smother and overwhelm pragmatic and logical thought. And so it was when the sandwiches had arrived. The inspectors relaxed. They felt free to offer opinions. To disagree with their chief. They joked and laughed. And laughter was good as Faraday eventually sought to summarise their discussion.

'Well, we have to continue our enquiries on the visitor who was followed to the estate agent's office. Your information, James, is that he is José Torno, which may fit with a character by the name of José whom a contact in Madeira has informed me about.' Faraday looked at Frobisher. 'What else do we know about José Torno?'

'He holds a Spanish passport,' replied Frobisher. 'He had not come to our attention before but we now know that he came from an estate agency in Valencia, and enquiries show that he flits between here, Spain, and Madeira and lives locally in rented accommodation.'

'And as an EU national,' interjected Purchell, 'he can flit about as freely as he wishes.'

Faraday nodded in acknowledgement of the inherent dangers and operational realities of these loose arrangements. 'And not known on our PNC?' he asked, referring to the British Police National Computer database.

'Nothing known, sir. If he is connected to Milano, I am reluctant to approach the Spanish police for fear of alerting them to our interest.'

'Okay, that's fine,' conceded Faraday, 'meanwhile, I am minded to search Milano's apartment again.' Frobisher and Purchell exchanged glances. Faraday recognised their scepticism and sought to explain. 'I accept that our visitor was extraordinarily thorough and careful,' continued Faraday. 'One can assume, therefore, that whatever he was seeking was important. If it was important to him, we agree that we can reasonably assume that it would have held a similar significance for Captain Milano. The question is: where would Milano conceal such a significant item? At his mother's home?' he posed rhetorically, 'but we know that her home, which she shared with her son, was searched, apparently without success, otherwise it would have been unlikely that his apartment here would have been visited.' He was silent again as he looked at the far wall deep in thought. 'An assumption, I know, but let me ask you this: Would Milano hide something on the army base in his locker?'

'I doubt it,' suggested Frobisher

'Why not?' tested Faraday.

'Because,' said Purchell, 'he wasn't a regular officer and therefore not always on the base, consequently, whatever it was would not always have been close at hand and readily under his control.'

'Quite so,' agreed Faraday.

'A bank vault maybe? Purchell said.

'Yes,' replied Faraday, 'certainly a possibility. Attractive to him because whether he was in the UK, Gibraltar, Madeira or on deployment, whatever the item was would be secure in a bank ...' He paused as he dabbed his mouth with a napkin. '... but there's a problem with a bank. Banks aren't open 24/7 and I don't think that Milano would have wanted to make an appointment with the bank or to wait in a queue to get hold of something that was so important or vital to him.'

They discussed further options, then Faraday summarised again.

'If we think of Milano, his previous behaviour, his character, then my guess is that whatever it is will be near-by, close and easily accessible. Are those reasonable assumptions?'

'I think so,' said Frobisher.

'I can't think of a better assumption,' Purchell replied.

'Okay, thank you both for that ... oh, and thank you, James, for allowing us to share your sandwiches.'

'It made my day. It was such a tremendous pleasure, sir, as I so hate eating alone,' he said jokingly.

'Anyway,' said Faraday, once the laughter had ceased, 'we will need to search the apartment again.'

'Do you want to search the apartment this evening, sir?' asked Frobisher.

Faraday thought for a short moment, then glanced at the wall clock. 'No. Too late and we might draw attention to our nocturnal activities. Tomorrow, tomorrow I think, just you and I, James. Here in plain clothes, at ten-thirty please?'

Chapter Twenty-Five

Tuesday, 3rd June.

British Overseas Territory, Gibraltar and Bristol, England.

THEY ENTERED THE APARTMENT. 'Let's replicate yesterday's search,' Faraday said.

'Do you mind if I say that I'm not sure I follow, sir,' said DI Frobisher. 'Why replicate it. You have to agree that he was thorough?'

'I don't mind you saying at all,' replied Faraday. 'I agree. He was thorough. But he may have been looking for something that we aren't looking for. We are assuming the item, whatever it may be, will not be too thick, too long or too wide. It could be a document or CD but it could also be something in a DVD case or substitute DVD, for example.'

'Although I think he searched the CDs and DVDs, sir.'

'He opened the cases, James, saw a disc and shut the lid. If the collection is anything like mine, there will be plenty of blank discs.'

Frobisher considered a variety of possibilities. 'You are quite right, sir. It could be that he was looking for a folded document and, not finding it, returned the CD to the shelf.'

'That's another possibility. Or it could be a mobile or iPad or USB stick or even diamonds,' suggested Faraday, making finger gestures like Fagin. 'I jest. I doubt very much if it were to be diamonds but, humour me, unless it's in a bank vault, if it was valuable to Captain Nicholas Milano, I'm sure it would be close to hand, so let's search again.'

They spent more than two hours searching the apartment, during which they made constant reference to Frobisher's laptop containing the down-loads of yesterday's surveillance recording. Eventually, Faraday returned to Milano's study and sat in the high-back swivel chair in complete silence, facing the door, thinking, elbows on the arms of the chair, hands steepled.

Many moments passed. 'Sir?' said Frobisher enquiringly, interrupting Faraday's thoughts.

Faraday turned to face the desk. 'This was his inner sanctum, James,' he said reflectively. 'This is where Milano felt comfortable and secure, confident and at ease. Everything of importance to him is here. Here with his colonel's epaulettes, his heroic award, his heroic ancestor and this,' he said pointing to the brass statuette to the left of the blotter, 'the Norman knight in a heroic pose.'

Faraday picked up the statuette and read the inscription. 'El Cid', he said, 'all very romantic, James. All part of the heroic fantasy.' Faraday replaced the statuette to the left of the blotter and swivelled in the chair to face the inspector, but Frobisher's expression had not gone unnoticed.   'Go on, James, you were going to make a comment.'

'It's not important. I was about to be pernickety.'

'It's okay,' replied Faraday with a smile, 'I like pernickety.'

'It's not Norman, sir. El Cid was a Spanish nobleman.'

'Oh,' said Faraday with surprise. 'I thought El Cid was a fiction, rather like Robin Hood.'

'Oh, no. El Cid was a minor Castilian nobleman, Rodrigo Díaz de Vivar, born in about 1040, so the chain mail, helmet and weapons would have been similar to that worn by the Normans.'

'Was he an important figure?' questioned Faraday, his mind whirling with a dozen thoughts.

'Oh yes. He was famous for driving the Moors out of Spain resulting in the eventual unification of Spain.'

Faraday thought for a long moment and turned the chair to face the desk again. He reached forward and picked up the statuette. It was about eighteen inches high, about the same height as the brass lamp to the right of the desk blotter. It consisted of a fluted pillar with El Cid standing on the top. 'El Cid drove the usurpers out of Spain, you say, and played a part in the unification of Spain,' he reflected, then he lapsed into deep thought, replacing the statuette on the desk.   Many minutes passed before he spoke.

'Everything, James, about Milano is symbolic,' he said as he grasped the brass pillar again, this time testing the fixing of the figure. He held the column at its square base and pulled at the figure. But nothing gave. He continued to hold the column but, this time, twisted the figure. After considerable force, the figure gave. Faraday twisted the figure to its left again and gradually unscrewed the figure from the column. He placed the figure on the desk and peered into the inch-wide hollow opening of the column. He could see nothing. He inverted the column. He shook the column. As he did so a rolled, single piece of paper fell out onto the leather-bound blotter.

Frobisher was about to move forward but he had headed-up Special Branch for three years. Long enough for him to be circumspect. He understood. He stood back. 'I think I will leave this to you, sir.'

Faraday unrolled the paper and smoothed it out on top of the blotter. He read the hand-written words. The words were in English. It was dated 1782. It was addressed to Colonel Henry Bartolomeu Milano. It was signed by General Antonio Barceló y Pont de la Terra.

Faraday read the letter twice. He recognised the significance of the document. He recognised its hugely damaging potential. He gave his instructions purposefully and calmly. 'James, have an unmarked car with two of your officers pick me up please. Both with side arms. In code, if you would.'

'Right, sir,' replied Frobisher without question.

Faraday pulled out his mobile and called his office as Frobisher spoke on his. Julie answered almost immediately. 'Julie, I'm going to my apartment to pack. I will be with you in about twenty minutes, meanwhile, get me on the very next flight to Bristol.'

'All arranged, sir,' said Frobisher as Faraday finished his call. 'And, if I may say so, well done, sir.'

'Police work is always a team effort, James, irrespective of what some senior officers are prone to claim. If you hadn't been bold enough to challenge my lack of knowledge and explain to me about El Cid, I would have simply looked upon the statuette as a rather sad, Walt Disney-type, prop of a deluded crank.'

***

As they left Milano's apartment, they found one Special Branch officer in the foyer, the other standing at the parked, unmarked, police car. Both wore the ubiquitous sunglasses of surveillance officers – useful in the sunlight, of course, but much more useful because suspects are never sure if the officers are watching them. The detectives drove Faraday the short distance to his apartment. The same procedure was followed. One SB officer remained with the car, the other accompanied Faraday. In his apartment, Faraday checked his always prepared go-bag, a carry-on, then returned to the waiting car and the short drive to the police headquarters.

In the quiet of his office Faraday phoned Kay on their burn-phones. He didn't call ACC Perrin on the secure line as he harboured some nagging doubts that the secure line was not as secure as he would have liked, suspecting that there was always the possibility that MI5 or MI6, or both, were in the mix – and experience dictated that it would always be foolish to think otherwise. Faraday was aware that MI5 and 6, together with GCHQ, monitored every country, whether this was in respect of enemies, neutrals or allies. The only countries off-limits were Canada, Australia, New Zealand and the USA. For many years, this monitoring had been extended to include eavesdropping on international negotiations and specific targeting so as to ensure the 'economic well-being' of the UK - and the future of Gibraltar and its relationship with Spain would undoubtedly fall within the last category. And so, Faraday relied upon Kay to understand his cryptic call and for her to simply persuade Robert Perrin of the need for an urgent meeting. He gave her details of his flight and the requirement for 'the same arrangements as for Brandy', referring to one of their previous prisoners, the beautiful assassin Brandy Myers, mention of which he was certain she would interpret as the need for armed officers to meet him when his flight arrived at Bristol International Airport.

***

Commissioner Faraday was guided smoothly through Gibraltar Customs and joined other passengers unobtrusively in Departures. But he wasn't just another passenger. He had with him his carry-on case. In the outside zipped pocket was a padded A5 *Jiffy* bag addressed to the Foreign and Commonwealth Office. In the bottom of the carry-on was another padded A5 *Jiffy* bag. It was unaddressed. The *Jiffy* bag in the outside pocket was empty although the zip was secured by a substantial padlock. The *Jiffy* bag in the base of the bag was not empty. It contained the 1782 letter and the zip to the main compartment of the carry-on was secured by a more modest looking padlock. The hope being, in the unlikely event, that Faraday's carry-on be snatched by the Spanish intelligence services, the thief would be attracted to the more secure external zipped pocket, remove the addressed envelope and discard the carry-on case. One armed SB officer, Detective Constable Penny Drew, discreetly joined Faraday on the aircraft, seated four rows back but with line-of-sight to the overhead locker containing Faraday's carry-on. They didn't acknowledge each other.

Faraday disciplined himself to relax and enjoyed a light in-flight meal, although his thoughts were focused on the Milano/Miller case. Whilst Faraday could recognise the possible motives that led Captain Nicholas Milano to betray his country - simple greed and arrogance, maybe frustration too – but he could not fathom the need to murder Christopher Miller. What would the murder of Christopher Miller achieve? he pondered. Faraday thought of the complex planning that surrounded the murders, the purchase and choice of the Forehand and Wadsworth firearms, the search of Victor Jenkin's flat and his subsequent murder, and the telephone conversations between Maria Miller and Nicholas Milano. What had been their 'plans'? What had been their 'unfinished business'?

***

At Bristol International Airport, Faraday and the SB officer exited along with the other passengers, DC Drew allowing Faraday to pass in front of her in order that she could follow discreetly behind. At Arrivals, both officers had no need to await their luggage from the aircraft's hold, they had none, just their carry-ons, and they passed swiftly through Nothing to Declare. Two plain clothed Severnside officers moved unobtrusively to escort Faraday and DC Drew to the awaiting staff car.

Once seated in the car, Faraday thanked DC Drew as the Jaguar XF staff car moved away from the kerb, an unmarked BMW X5 with four armed officers following close behind. At the junction with the main A38, the driver of the Jaguar activated the blue strobe lights in the radiator grill and turned left. They didn't race but drove, purposely, dominating the road, along the A38 and descended towards Lulsgate Bottom, the road then snaking its way up to the brow of the hill and along the Bridgwater Road, descending as they approached the city's vast reservoirs at Barrow Common. As they did so, an Audi A7 attempted to overtake, but the unmarked BMW four-track moved smoothly to the right and as it did so activated a 'POLICE DO NOT OVERTAKE' sign in the rear window. The Audi complied as they drove along Bedminster Down with a perfect view of the Clifton Suspension Bridge to the distant left, then into Winterstoke Road, onto the Brunel Way fly-over, dropping down onto Hotwell Road and the Portway and the M5 a few miles further on. Soon they were on the Portbury Hundred and onwards to Valley Road and Police

Headquarters. Once through the entrance gates, Faraday's Jaguar turned into the carpark in front of the main entrance to the headquarters' complex, whilst the BMW peeled off to the left and Operations HQ. Faraday thanked DC Drew again who was then driven to a Premier Inn for an overnight stay before her return flight to Gibraltar the following day.

Kay was waiting with Robert Perrin in the ACC's office. Faraday and Perrin shook hand warmly. 'Go on you two,' said Perrin with an encouraging grin, 'give each other a kiss, for heaven's sake, then we can get down to proper police business.' They did – the kiss that is - then proper police business.

They sat around the coffee table as Faraday outlined the details of the search of Captain Milano's apartment by a man who had been followed to an estate agency, and who was clearly forensically aware. Faraday described the subsequent police search of the Milano's apartment and the discovery of the letter. Faraday produced a little key from his pocket, unlocked the smaller padlock and unzipped his carry-on and produced a brown envelope containing photographs of Milano's apartment, his study and the statuette. He then foraged to the bottom of the bag and extracted the *Jiffy* bag and unpeeled the gummed flap. The anticipation was electric.

Faraday placed the letter in front of Robert Perrin.

'Do you know what it says, Kay,' the ACC asked without censure.

'Not at all, sir.'

'Well, get closer and read it with me,' he said as he spread the letter on the table in front of them. They read in stunned silence.

'Oh, Christ,' said Perrin eventually. 'This is dynamite.' He read the contents again slowly, considering as he did so all the ramifications. 'We need an urgent meeting with Sir George.' The ACC hesitated then picked up the phone and pressed one key. 'Silvia, I need to speak with the Chief Constable immediately,' he said to the Chief's personal assistant. Silvia knew that Robert Perrin wasn't an alarmist or a time-waster. There was only a twenty second delay before Emily Woodland was put through.

'Yes. Thank you, ma'am,' he said as the Chief took his call. 'I have Faraday with me. He's just got in from Gib and has with him a document. To say the document is very sensitive would be a complete understatement. I will need to see Sir George Sinclair urgently tomorrow at the FCO. I'm simply keeping you in the loop and, if you agree, I will make the appropriate arrangements.' There was a pause as Perrin listened to the Chief Constable. 'No, ma'am,' he replied reassuringly, 'there's no need for you to be aware of the contents, in fact, it's probably best if you don't. And no, none of this refers to the other matter,' he said alluding to the DCC, 'and does not in any way at all endanger the reputation of our force, in fact, some really first-class work by Faraday and his team.' There was another short pause. 'Thank you, ma'am.'

'Good, we have the green light,' said Perrin as, still holding the handset, he dialled direct. Almost immediately he was put through to Sir George's private secretary, Maurice Underhill. Perrin did not justify the need for a meeting by revealing the existence of a letter or its contents, merely that a meeting the following day was paramount and that it would be prudent to include the Chief Minister who, Faraday had told him, was attending a Commonwealth Conference at Lancaster House. Underhill agreed to a three o'clock.

Robert Perrin returned the letter to the *Jiffy* bag and placed it in his wall safe. 'I don't think I have ever read or handled such a sensitive or important document in my twenty-eight years of police service,' he said as he pressed some keys on the safe's door. 'And I don't really know why I put anything in this safe, I wouldn't be happy to leave my sandwiches in it overnight,' he said with a slightly nervous chuckle, then added, raising his index finger to indicate the seriousness of what he was about to say: 'Kay, you will need to arrange for an armed SB officer to be in this office overnight, in fact, locked in. He or she can use my en-suite and there is ample tea, coffee and biscuits here.'

Chapter Twenty-Six

Wednesday, 4ᵗʰ June.

Police Headquarters, Bristol and the Foreign and Commonwealth Office, London.

THE DOOR BURST OPEN. 'I'm sorry, sir,' said ACC Robert Perrin's flustered personal assistant.

'It's alright, Cilla,' said Perrin as DCC Anita Winters pushed passed his PA into his office.

'Why is Faraday here?' demanded the DCC of Robert Perrin arrogantly ignoring the presence of Chief Constable Emily Woodland.

Nevertheless, the Chief Constable replied. 'Commissioner Faraday is passing through.'

'But why did Cilla attempt to prevent me from entering Robert's office?' she asked in a belligerent tone.

'Because this meeting is a "need to know" meeting, Anita, and there is no need for you to know,' said the Chief Constable.

'Faraday … oh, I'm *so* sorry, I should have said *Commissioner* Faraday … and Yin are here and so should I,' said Miss Winters contemptuously.

'Commissioner Faraday and Miss Yin should be here, and you should not,' said the Chief as she opened the ACC's door. 'Please leave us now and come along and see me at one-thirty.'

'I'm tied-up at one-thirty,' the DCC replied haughtily.

'Un-tie yourself, Anita. One-thirty. And be prompt.' The DCC hesitated, shocked at her rebuff, then stomped out of the office. There was a further pause as the Chief closed the door and gathered herself. 'Let me apologise to all of you. I have been reluctant to speak with Miss Winters about her attitude because I suspect that it would be you, Kay, who would be on the receiving end of any back-lash, but I will speak to her. This can't go on. Anyway, the only reason I popped in Robert, was to thank you, Mark, for the work you are doing. Robert has given me no details at all, other than you are off to the FCO, but he tells me that you have been doing very commendable work.' She walked to the door, opened it and turned. 'Commendable work is never easy or straight-forward and often when politics are involved it's a quagmire, and so, thank you. In fact, thank you too, Kay.'

As the Chief left, Cilla entered again but spoke in a hushed tone. 'They are waiting for you, sir.'

The same Jaguar staff car had been brought to the main entrance together with a black BMW X5, the only difference being that Kay would drive to London and Mark would take the wheel on the return journey. Perrin removed the *Jiffy* bag containing the letter from his safe and handed it to

Faraday who put it into his briefcase together with the photographs and two typed copies of the letter. Then they left the office, walked along the corridor and down two flights of stairs and out through the front entrance foyer to the staff car. Kay and Mark removed their suit jackets and placed them in the boot. Both were 'carrying' – Glock 9mm. Perrin removed his jacket too, although he was unarmed. Both men stepped into the staff car, Mark in the front passenger seat, Robert behind the driver's seat as Kay spoke with Sergeant David Dark in the four-man crewed BMW. Kay and the sergeant confirmed their route, discussed their heads-up on road works and possible congestion points; their speed, contingency plans and vehicle-to-vehicle communication channel.

Then they drove sedately out through the gates of the police headquarters, down Valley Road and along the Portbury Hundred and onto the M5 motorway where Kay activated the blue strobes and entered the outside lane, increasing her speed to ninety miles per hour. At the Almondsbury Interchange they exited the M5 to join the M4 for London. ETA was estimated to be 2.20pm. Although there were road works and 50mph speed restrictions near Membury and Slough, they arrived at the Foreign and Commonwealth Office at 2.17pm. ACC Perrin thanked Sergeant Dark and allowed him and his team to return to Bristol before he, together with Mark and Kay, entered the FCO.

The three officers had only to wait a few minutes past three o'clock before Sir George Sinclair, not his personal secretary, opened the double doors to his grand office.

'Mr Perrin, thank you for coming up so promptly,' he said as he shook hands, 'and good to see you again Commissioner and Miss Yin.' The hand-shakes were warm as was the smiling welcome as he gestured them to enter. They walked into his office as he closed both doors behind them. Sir Clifford Amanda, Gibraltar's Chief Minister, rose from his seat and stepped around the mahogany conference table. He was affable but unsmiling. 'I don't think you have met the Chief Minister before, Mr Perrin?' said Sir George.

'A pleasure to meet you, sir.' They shook hands.

'I've heard a great deal about you from Sir George,' said the Chief Minister, but he wasn't relaxed. There was a tension in his tone.

'And you know Commissioner Faraday, of course, Sir Clifford, but not his wife, Detective Superintendent Yin.'

The Chief Minister shook Mark's hand and then Kay's. 'And likewise, I have had good reports about you too, Superintendent,' he said. For a moment he seemed to relax a little, clearly distracted by her captivating smile and beauty.

Further pleasantries were exchanged as everyone took their seats around the conference table, the two knights one side, the three police officers on the other.

'May I suggest, Sir George,' said Perrin, 'that Commissioner Faraday explains the reason for what we believe to be a very significant development.'

'Of course. Please go ahead, Commissioner, we are eager to hear of the development,' said Sir George, who was certainly eager – and hopeful.

'Thank you, sir.' Faraday opened his brief case and withdrew photographs, A4 sheets of typed paper and the *Jiffy* bag before he spoke. 'On the 2nd June we know that Milano's apartment in Gibraltar was searched by an unknown male, although we now have some intelligence on who he might be. He ... '

'And who do you believe him to be?' interrupted Sir Clifford.

'We believe him to be José Torno, a Spanish national and, we believe, a member of the Spanish intelligence services, sir.' If Sir George and Sir Clifford hadn't been alert before, they were seriously alert now. 'He was clearly forensically aware and thorough, but left empty-handed,' continued Faraday. 'As a consequence, with our own Special Branch inspector, I searched Captain Milano's apartment.' Faraday placed the photograph of Milano's apartment in front of Sir George and Sir Clifford which showed the lounge/diner with the open study door beyond. Both men had clearly anticipated a photograph of more interest. Their examination of this photograph was cursory.

'Of more significance is this photograph of Milano's study,' said Faraday as he produced a second photograph showing the interior of the study from the open door. Their examination of this photograph was not cursory. Faraday allowed a few moments to pass, then produced, without comment, a third photograph showing Milano's desk. Their examination of the third photograph was all-consuming. 'You will note,' said Faraday after a suitable delay, 'the Spanish colonel's epaulettes, the Spanish military award for *"service that involved high personal risk"* and the name plate.' Faraday paused a while to allow both men to closely examine the photograph and noted the concentration etched upon Sir George's face, and anger upon Sir Clifford's. 'To the left of the blotter,' continued Faraday, 'you will see a statuette. It was inside this statuette that I discovered a letter.' As Faraday removed the 1782 letter from the *Jiffy* bag, Sir George had great difficulty in maintaining a placid expression, a 'tell' that did not go unnoticed by Kay.

Faraday placed the letter between both men, giving each a typed copy of the original on a single sheet of white A4 paper. There was silence. Faraday looked at both men. Once Sir George had read the letter, his attention seemed to be on something in the far distance as if his mind was searching to find the right words – it was. And Sir Clifford stared at the letter too, loathing filling his silent thoughts as he digested the contents. Sir George spoke first.

'Remind me, Sir Clifford,' he said as he appeared to study the letter again, 'who is this General Antonio Barceló y Pont de la Terra. I suppose he was the Spanish commander?'

But Sir George knew perfectly well the identity of the Spanish officer and that Sir Clifford would be proud and delighted to respond, for a moment reducing the tension.

'No, Barceló y Pont was in charge of the actual blockade of Gibraltar, but the over-all Spanish commander was the Duc de Crillon,' said Sir Clifford with the slightest of smiles, 'who took Menorca from the British but failed to take Gibraltar from us. He was later created Duc de Mahon.' But his moment of pride and satisfaction was temporary as he added: 'And clearly this Colonel Milano was a traitor.'

'No, he was certainly no traitor, Sir Clifford, far from it,' Sir George explained confidently, touching the Chief Minister's hand gently for a pico-second, but a gesture that did not escape the police officers. 'Colonel Milano was, in fact, a double-agent feeding the enemy with false information. We know that from classified documents held here at the Ministry of Defence. We knew of a Spanish letter, of course, but did not know if it existed and, therefore, we are very grateful indeed for your extraordinary, excellent work, Commissioner.' Sir George swept up the photographs, typed sheets and the old letter. 'Have you photocopied this letter, Mark?' he asked, his old eyes watery but sharp.

'No, sir.'

'And who typed these two copies?' he challenged pointedly.

'I did, sir,' replied Kay.

Sir George relaxed a little. 'And so you have kept this matter "in the family" so to speak?' he said pleased with his attempt at levity. Mark didn't respond otherwise than with a nod and a smile. 'But the local Special Branch officer, he must know of the contents surely?' probed Sir George.

'He witnessed me shake the letter from the statuette but did not read the letter and knows nothing of the content, sir.'

'Good. Excellent. Very prudent, Commissioner,' praised Sir George. 'So, whilst the Spanish believed that Captain Milano possessed something of importance, maybe a letter, the only people who seem to know for certain of the letter's existence and contents are here, sat around this table?' he said, spreading his arms expansively.

'That appears to be the case,' responded Perrin.'

'And that,' said Sir George in a deep gravelly voice, 'is how this unexpected but welcomed development must remain.' He looked at each of the police officers in turn, adding: 'If the existence and contents of this letter were to be known to the Spanish they would have a field day. They would be able to produce an authentic and rather colourful old letter signed by General Antonio Barceló y Pont, in truth a military failure who they would undoubtedly transform into some sort of national hero, and twist the contents of the letter in order to demonstrate the betrayal of the people of Gibraltar by the English. We could, of course, produce documents proving that Colonel Milano had duped the gullible Spanish but the moment would be theirs, not ours.'

Sir George relaxed a little in his chair adding, as if discussing a matter amongst close family. 'I'm sure you are all aware that this would be rather like a highly regarded police officer charged with the beating of a prisoner. It would be a matter that would feature prominently on the ten o'clock news and would be front page headlines, with the officer's subsequent acquittal getting a three-line mention on page seven, if on any page at all. No. No, this must stay within these four walls.' He paused again, glancing at each officer rather like an understanding uncle before continuing. 'That said, I'm sure that the Chief Minister shares with me my admiration for your outstanding and discreet detective work.'

Sir George and Sir Clifford rose from their seats and engaged in congratulatory handshakes, broken only by Sir George pressing one of the keys on his desk telephone bank.

Tea and biscuits arrived almost immediately and convivial conversations ensued, but not before Sir George had placed the precious documents carefully in an extremely large and immensely secure safe, containing the salacious details of the sexual exploits and proclivities of junior FCO ministers and embassy staff, the MI6 personnel accredited to our embassies around the world and suspected moles within MI6 itself.

They discussed the murder enquiry and the coroner's conclusion that Guy Hernandez had been killed by Victor Jenkins, a disturbed former soldier; the necessarily cynical funeral of Captain Milano, and the forthcoming visit to

Gibraltar by the Duke and Duchess of Cambridge. Sir George offered more tea, but Perrin thought, rightly, that he should make polite excuses to leave, referring to anticipated, although in truth non-existent, traffic congestion.

***

Mark drove along the Embankment, Kay at his side, Robert Perrin behind Kay, past the bridges spanning the Thames, taking the elevated Chiswick section of the A4 and onto the M4 motorway. As they passed Windsor Castle to their left and leaving London behind, Perrin spoke.

'I have to admire Sir George for his quick-thinking. There he was burdened down with all his vast responsibilities for foreign affairs, including the continuous bickering with the European Union; a Russian president perpetually flexing his muscles - literally; an unpredictable American president; the problems in the Middle East and East Asia; a lunatic in charge of North Korea; and then there's the Commonwealth – what, consisting of fifty-plus countries and representing more than two billion people with decades of history, yet, Sir George would have us believe that he was able to instantly recall an obscure colonel who was acting as a double-agent in 1782, and knew that there were letters squirrelled away in the MoD confirming this!'

'You don't believe him?' queried Mark.

'I don't believe the pretence that your discovery of the letter was unexpected.'

The traffic began to slow and then ground to a complete halt. After a few minutes the traffic began to edge forward, then gathered speed past a broken-down car and caravan on the hard shoulder.

'Mark, when interviewing witnesses or suspects,' Perrin continued, 'don't we always adhere to the maxim that when it comes to sex and money, we should suspect everyone and trust no-one?'

'Yes, that's true.'

'Well, I think it would be prudent to add to that intoxicating brew of "sex" and "money" one other: "Whitehall".'

Mark and Kay smiled in agreement. 'I'm sure you are right,' said Mark, 'I think Sir George knew all about Colonel Milano and the letter, but Sir Clifford didn't.'

'Sir Clifford was certainly agitated at the beginning of the meeting and I think the letter came as a complete surprise to him,' agreed Perrin.

'Mark and I had been thinking of the last meeting we had with Sir George,' said Kay turning around in her seat.

'Go on.'

'Sir George spoke of the North West Frontier and the hill tribes amongst whom it was inconceivable to consider a cousin to be anything other than an enemy,' said Kay. 'We have wondered whether Sir George put that comment out there to encourage us to look at Christopher Miller's cousin.'

'Which had the potential to lead us to the letter?' suggested Perrin.

'We think so,' Kay said, adding: 'Maybe MI6, which is answerable to the FCO, had some knowledge of a letter but they, and Sir George, didn't know if it still existed or where it was. He could, I suppose, have asked Commissioner Thornton to investigate, but I am sure that Mr Thornton would have felt duty-bound to inform the Chief Minister. He could have asked MI6 but there was always the danger that their presence would have not gone unnoticed in such a relatively small community. It was reasonable for Sir George to conclude that our enquiries into the murder of Hernandez could lead to a cousin and the letter.'

'You think that Captain Milano was Miller's cousin?' the ACC asked.

'They could certainly be related,' Kay said.

'Okay, what are you suggesting?'

'We are all agreed that it is reasonable for us to assume that Victor Jenkins intended to murder Christopher Miller, but why?' she asked.

'We believe that he was acting on behalf of Nicholas Milano,' replied the ACC.

'If that was the case, what was his motive?' posed Kay.

'To marry the *merry widow*,' Perrin replied humorously referring to Maria Miller.

'But from his phone call to Mrs Miller, he didn't appear to know that she had married,' suggested Mark. Perrin nodded in agreement, recalling the conversation. 'If they were cousins,' continued Faraday, 'even distant cousins, is it possible that Nicholas Milano believed that he could have inherited a £8.7 million fortune in the event of Christopher Miller's death?'

'It seems that the question of any inheritance would rest upon whether Miller and Milano were actually related,' said Perrin.

'That's right,' agreed Kay.

'And how do you propose to find out if they are related?'

'Our man in Madeira,' she replied.

Chapter Twenty-Seven

Tuesday, 24th June.

Bournemouth, England.

CHRISTINA ALVEAR HAD MET HARRY HOLT on the previous Saturday, in the four-star Hotel Miramar, once the weekend home of a European ambassador to Britain. Harry was a guest at the hotel and Christina worked there as a waitress. He had registered as Douglas Tovey. He knew which tables Christina served in the hotel's restaurant and had eaten a late lunch ensuring that she would be his waitress. He had taken the opportunity to compliment her on the service she had provided and her command of the English language. He appeared to be kind. He was amusing. He showed an interest in her family home in Alcalali and her aspirations for the future. She had been flattered.

She wasn't beautiful in the traditional sense but there was a vivaciousness about her, and her appearance was always pristine and neat, and, when not working her appearance was also pristine, invariably wearing white trousers and bright blouses, yellow, red or candy-striped. As an employee she was hard-working, smiling and capable. She had been working in the UK for eleven months and was content. She enjoyed her work. The hours were long and, as with most hotel work, tiring. But the pay was better than back home in Spain and many of her fellow waitresses were Greek, Polish or Spanish. As a result a bond developed between them and they mixed well. They liked

Bournemouth with its six miles of beautiful sandy beach and there was a lively night-life too. In her spare moments, Christina liked to sit on the benches along East Cliff which gave spectacular views across the English Channel from Hengistbury Head in the east and Sandbanks to the west.

Today, she was not smiling, nor was she content. She sat near the Red Arrows' Memorial. Not her normal place but the place that Harry Holt had dictated. At 4.30pm he slid alongside her. She shivered. She didn't look at him. She stared blankly out to sea. Normally she would admire the pretty sail boats, the larger ships on the horizon and be enthralled by the skill of the hand-gliders. But not today.

'I'm glad you came, Christina,' said Harry smoothly, but there was a tinge of menace in his tone as he added: 'That was wise.' He let the words sink in as he shaded the sun from his eyes with his hand, pretending to search the horizon. 'I'm sorry to hear about your brother,' he continued, only to pause again for effect. 'His injuries are not serious I am told but, for all prisoners, there are always dangers as they continue to serve their sentence.'

Christina thought of her brother, Garcia. So young. So vulnerable. And still another three years to serve in the Valdemoro prison for possession of cocaine. But Harry Holt had offered her hope, hope of a reduced sentence and Harry knew, from personal experience, how attractive that would sound. But, Harry wanted a favour in return. Of course he did.

'You told me that in your early days as a waitress you accidently dropped some plates?'

'Yes, that I do,' she replied with a confused frown, unsure of the significance of what Harry had asked. Soon the meaning would become abundantly clear.

'You have visited the Russell-Cotes museum as I asked?'

'Yes, I go.'

'And you saw the beautiful lady?'

'The "*Perfection on the Rocks*". Yes, I find her.'

'That is good,' he said as he returned the smile of a passing elderly lady with a walking stick. 'You have a computer, a lap-top?' he continued as he looked out to sea.

'I have the lap-top as you say.'

'And you brought pen and paper as I asked?'

'I have them.'

'Write what I tell you,' he instructed ensuring that he touched no paper nor wrote any words. Christina delved into her fawn, canvas shoulder bag and withdrew a small floral note pad and neat little green-coloured pen. 'You will use your lap-top to look up the name of "Nick Flynn". That is F-L-Y-N-N.' Harry lowered his hand from his eyes and waited patiently as Christina pedantically wrote the name.

He glanced down surreptitiously and, when he saw that she had finished, he instructed her again. 'And the "Fitzwilliam Museum". That is F-I-T-Z-W-I-L-L-I-A-M.' He waited as she again carefully recorded the name in her little note book. 'An incident occurred at this museum in 2006. I want you, Christina, to read of this incident on your lap-top.' Harry shielded his eyes against the sun as he looked out towards the sail boats. 'Thursday is your day off,' he said firmly. 'You will visit the Russell-Cotes museum again and we will meet here on Friday at the same time.'

Chapter Twenty-Eight

Thursday, 26ᵗʰ June.

Bournemouth, England.

SIR MERTON RUSSELL-COTES had East Cliff Hall, now named the Russell-Cotes Museum, built for his beloved wife, Anne, as a birthday present. Sir Merton was a multi-millionaire hotelier and the owner of the Royal Bath Hotel, the 'royal' title being added as the result of a visit by the Prince of Wales in 1856. Sir Merton was mayor of Bournemouth in 1894 and endowed the town with two libraries and two schools. Both he and his wife were inseparable. They loved to travel and travelled the world together, amassing a vast collection of remarkable works of art and fascinating curios.

Christina visited the Russell-Cotes Museum as she had been instructed. From the café she entered the Main Hall, then climbed the staircase to the galleried Balcony. Wherever she looked, Christina was surrounded by a stunning and remarkable collection of art, including beautiful paintings by Rossetti and Moore, an equestrian masterpiece by the royal artist Munnings; the Peacock Mural in the Dining Room; and artefacts such as Napoleon's magnificent wine cooler brought from his island prison of St Helena. There were also marble busts and statuettes; porcelain and antique vases. Some were free-standing, others could be discovered in alcoves and yet others were on pedestals; whilst some formed part of a floral or water feature.

'*Perfection on the Rocks*' was there. At the foot of the stairs. On a pedestal in the Main Hall. Christina walked about the building nervously. She assessed furtively how the soles of her shoes gripped the carpet of the stairs and the wooden floor of the Main Hall, particularly near a water feature where the floor was a little damp.

She returned to the first floor and the rest rooms. She entered a cubicle, locked the door and sat down on the toilet. She sobbed silently. She thought of her brother, Garcia. She thought of what she had been asked to do. She stared at a hard copy print of '*Perfection on the Rocks*' from New York's Metropolitan Museum of Art catalogue. And she made her decision.

Chapter Twenty-Nine

Friday, 27th June.

Bournemouth and Bristol, England.

JOSÉ TORNO HAD BEEN UNDER SURVEILLANCE ever since he left Captain Milano's apartment and had been tailed to the estate agency. The previous Friday, he had been allowed to board the flight from Gibraltar to Bournemouth, using his British passport in the name of Harry Holt. Special Branch officers immediately alerted DI James Frobisher of his departure who, in turn, informed Commissioner Faraday. Mark called Kay. Kay spoke with Robert Perrin who liaised with the ACC (Crime) in Dorset and the Chief Constable of Dorset Police spoke with Sir George Sinclair.

Within two hours, and before Harry Holt's aircraft had landed at Bournemouth International Airport at Hurn, it had been agreed that the surveillance upon Harry Holt would continue and be a joint operation with Detective Superintendent Kay Yin taking the lead.

On Saturday, the 21st, Detective Sergeant Pippa Blanchard and Detective Constable Jennifer Elston of Special Branch had booked, separately, into the Hotel Miramar. If these officers met in the hotel's dining room or Ocean Bar, or on the hotel's sun terrace or in the town, they never acknowledged each other. They never spoke, other than a natural 'excuse me' or a casual 'good morning', unless in either of their bedrooms.   Nor did they acknowledge Harry Holt. But they were getting to know him quite well.

***

Kay had driven along Gervis Road the previous evening, the 26th, and pulled into the kerb alongside Christina Alvear. Kay had wound down the front passenger window.

'Hi, excuse me,' she called.   Christina, a kind and helpful young lady, stopped walking and peered into Kay's Golf GTi. 'Can you tell me where the Hotel Miramar is please?' Kay enquired.

'The hotel, it is not this way you go.   You go the more round, you go back and go the right. It is there you find it,' she said pointing back along the road, 'at the sea,' her forearm on the door, her helpful, smiling face through the open window.

'Christina,' said Kay, producing her warrant card with its glistening silver badge. 'I am a police officer,' adding in a no-nonsense tone. 'Do *not* walk away from me Christina. Please open the door and sit in the car.'

'I not understand,' she said utterly alarmed, 'I am good person.'

'I believe you are a good person, but the man you have been seeing at the memorial is a bad person.'   Christina hesitated, her face filled with fear. 'You know he is a bad person,' continued Kay, 'but you are not a bad person, Christina. Step into the car ... *please.*'

Christina looked up and down the road fearfully before opening the door and quickly occupying the seat, lowering herself as much as she could as if she was now safe, her thoughts full of a mixture of relief and anxiety.

'You are not in trouble with the police but you are with the man you have been meeting,' said Kay as she drove towards St Peter's Roundabout. 'I am now driving to Christchurch police station and we will talk.'

'You not go the station at Bournemouth?'

'No. I don't want there to be any possibility of you being seen with me. Do you know the name of the man you have been meeting?'

'He only tell me the name Douglas Tovey.'

'And why are you meeting with Mr Tovey?'

Christina does not answer but bursts into tears. Kay continued to drive as Christina continued to sob and gradually composed herself. They arrived at the police station on Barrack Road, Christchurch, one now not open to the public but still in use as a police base. Kay used the intercom to gain entrance, although the uniformed sergeant seemed unsure of this unknown, but beautiful, Chinese detective superintendent. He examined Kay's ID carefully.

'This young lady is not a prisoner, Sergeant, but a witness and I need to speak with her in some privacy. Do you have a room I could use?' The sergeant hesitated as if not sure as to what he should do. 'If you have any doubts, Sergeant, please contact your ACC (Crime) who will be aware of my presence in your force area.'

'No. That's alright, ma'am,' he replied, reluctant to disturb his ACC at home. 'We have a room here, ma'am. Used to be the inspector's office.'

'That would be perfect, thank you. And your name is?'

'Button, ma'am. Sergeant Button.'

'Thank you, Sergeant Button.'

The sergeant led them down a narrow corridor to an office on the right. He pushed open the door and switched on the ceiling lights which flickered, then glowed brightly, as Kay looked around the office that was musty and gloomy. It was claustrophobic with some tall grey lockers in a corner and pea-green blinds that had been lowered and so she pulled these up with a clatter and allowed some street light to enter. The sergeant removed two old mugs from the desk and arranged two chairs. Christina was offered a padded wooden chair with arms and sat down, Kay occupying a similar worn chair behind the dusty, but bare, wooden desk.

'If I could just have the young lady's name, ma'am, just for the records. You know what it's like,' he said apologetically.

'Of course, Sergeant. This is Miss Christina Alvear, and she's from the Hotel Miramar in Bournemouth.'

'And very nice too, ma'am. Thank you,' said the sergeant, pleased that he had covered his back. 'And can I get you both a coffee or water or something?'

'Would you like a coffee, Christina?'

'Please. The white coffee,' she replied with a sheepish smile.

'Two white coffees would be good, Sergeant, thank you.'

As the sergeant left the office, Christina spoke. 'You take my work permit? You make me go home?'

'You are welcome here in the UK, Christina. You have nothing to fear from the police, but you have a lot to fear from Mr Tovey. He is a bad man.' Christina began to sob again.

'No more crying, Christina,' said Kay firmly. 'Just tell me why are you meeting with him?'

Christina didn't answer immediately but foraged about in her shoulder bag and retrieved an A4 picture of *'Perfection on the Rocks'* which she unfolded and handed to Kay. 'He tell me to write down the name, many name, and go to museum and to have the accident and break it to the floor.' She searched in her bag again and pulls out another piece of paper, 'like this man.'

Kay read the computer print-out detailing the incident that occurred in 2006 involving Nick Flynn. 'And the museum, you mean the Russell-Cotes museum?'

'Yes.'

'That is all he has asked you to do, Christina, to break *'Perfection on the Rocks'* like Nick Flynn broke the Chinese vase?'

'Yes, only this, the much breaking.'

'Did he tell you why he wanted you to do this?'

'He say he help the friend more.'

'A friend. Did the friend have a name?'

'He a Mr Christopher Miller.'

The mention of Christopher Miller's name was unexpected but Kay concealed her concern, asking: 'And why would Mr Miller want *'Perfection on the Rocks'* damaged, do you know?'

'So the Mr Miller can make much more the money.'

'And how will this make Mr Miller money?' asked Kay, although she had now reasoned why.

'Mr Miller, he has same,' she explained. 'If I break this one, his worth more the money.'

'I understand, Christina, but you seem to be a good person, why are you doing this?'

'My brother, he in the prison in Spain. He has been the much the beaten.' Tears flooded over her cheeks. She wiped the tears away with a tissue and stifled another sob as the sergeant entered the office with two mugs of coffee and a handful of sugar sachets and one spoon.

'Hope you don't mind mugs, ma'am, we don't have any cups and saucers,' he said without the slightest hint of disrespect or sarcasm.

'Mugs are good, Sergeant, thank you,' she said as she offered him a two-pound coin. 'For your tea kitty.'

'No, ma'am, but thank you,' he replied, adding as he left the office, 'it's not the best coffee in the world.'

As the door closed, Kay continued her questioning. 'Did Mr Tovey promise to help your brother?'

She nodded, the sad nod of someone who knew she had been foolish. 'Mr Tovey say he can have my brother the … how you say … reduce sentence if I make the accident happens.'

'You said that Mr Tovey asked you to write down names. What names?'

Christina pulled her little note book from her bag. 'These the name,' she said as she handed the book to Kay, opened at the third page.

'He asked you to write these names down?' she said as she read the neat writing.

'Yes. The much difficult name he spell.'

Kay read an address under a man's name, then asked: 'Queens Park Avenue is an address in this town. Do you know who lives there, Christina?'

'The other name,' she answered, pointing to the name immediately above the address, 'the next line higher, Mr HughThornton. He live there.'

'Mr Tovey told you this?'

'Yes and tell me to write.'

'And you have written here "Jigsaw". What is that, do you know?

'It the hospital big building Mr Thornton visit.'

'And did Mr Tovey tell you why Mr Thornton is visiting a hospital?

'No, he not tell.'

Kay thought this very likely. Harry Holt would not have wished to alarm Christina and reveal that Thornton was a police chief. He had also, no doubt, assessed Christina as a kind and sensitive young woman, who could easily have endangered his plan by becoming sympathetic to Hugh Thornton's illness and, therefore, reluctant to act as he wanted.

'When do you have to meet Mr Tovey again?'

'Tomorrow.'

'At what time?'

'Thirty minutes past the four.'

'And at the same place?'

'Yes, the place the same.'

***

Christina Alvear sat on the three-seat park bench looking out to sea. She was dressed in her white trousers and a bright yellow blouse. She nervously checked her watch. There was no need. Harry Holt was punctual. On time. Four-thirty. Christina was seated on the left and had placed her bag at her right side as Harry had instructed. Now she moved the bag as he approached and he sat on the bench.

'You visited the museum yesterday?' he asked.

Christina nodded.

'There, that wasn't difficult, was it? That is good.'

But it wasn't good for Harry Holt. Harry had taken no notice of the young lovers, hand-in-hand, taking a selfie. The pair also casually took evidential photographs of Christina Alvear and Harry Holt seated together, then innocently photographed the sail boats out to sea before they resumed their walk along East Overcliff Drive. As the young couple approached the bench, one of them, the female, broke away and sat next to Harry as the other took up a position immediately in front of the bench. Kay siting on the bench next to Harry Holt was the signal for other officers to act. A police siren sounded. Now it was time for Harry to be nervous. And he had every reason to be nervous.

'Hullo, Mr Tovey,' said Kay. 'I'm Detective Superintendent Yin and this is my colleague, Inspector Purchell.' Harry Holt looked behind towards the road and at the police car that had pulled into the kerb. 'Ah, you've noticed. More of my colleagues have just arrived and, yes, Mr Tovey, you are under arrest.'

'There must be some mistake,' said Harry Holt as he looked about for any escape route. But there was none.

'No mistake, Mr Tovey, other than the mistakes you have already made. Stand up and place your hands behind your back.'

For a moment, Harry considered his options for escape. The Chinese officer seemed confident and competent, he thought. Inspector Purchell looked alert and fit. The two uniformed officers who had just arrived looked eager as they stepped from their unmarked police car.

'Mistakes, what mistakes have I made?' he asked as if completely shocked.

'You have conspired, Mr Tovey, with this young lady to commit criminal damage at the museum.'

A little smirk creased his lips. Only criminal damage and there is no proof, he thought, and he was being addressed as 'Mr Tovey'.

'As I say, this is a mistake,' he said as Kay cautioned him and he was placed, handcuffed, into the back of a second unmarked car.

***

Kay Yin and Peter Purchell entered the interview room at Bournemouth Police Station and sat at the grey metal table opposite Harry Holt. Harry was dressed casually but smartly. Kay and Peter had rid themselves of the shorts and t-shirts of young lovers and both were now dressed in dark-grey business suits. The officers explained the interview preliminaries and pressed the record button.   Harry appeared unfazed. He exuded a false confidence.

'When you arrived here you gave the custody sergeant your name as Douglas Tovey and your home address as Gibraltar?' stated Kay.

'That is correct,' replied Harry with a crooked smile.

'And what is the nature of your visit to the UK, Mr Tovey?'

Harry Holt was relieved that the police didn't question the veracity of the name he had given. 'I'm an estate agent and we hope to expand here, selling Spanish properties to British pensioners,' he replied, then attempted to control the interview and glean as much information as he could, he asked: 'A bit over the top isn't it, a detective superintendent investigating an allegation of criminal damage?'

'Not if the item is worth £2 million,' responded Kay.

'Wow. And what item was that?' he asked as if amazed.

'I believe you know, Mr Tovey,' she said calmly.

'I don't know what you are talking about?' he said, opening his arms wide, a gesture of complete innocence.

'I think you do, Mr Tovey. You see, you told Christina Alvear to go to the Russell-Cotes museum, and locate a fine piece of porcelain entitled 'Perfection on the Rocks'.

'Russell-Cotes museum, you say. Never heard of it,' he said, although she knew he had already visited the museum but didn't want Harry to know that he had been constantly under surveillance since his arrival. 'But how intriguing,' continued Harry, '"*Perfection on the Rocks*". I'm fascinated to know what that can be. Can you tell me?' he asked leaning forward as if genuinely curious.

Inspector Purchell removed a paper print from his file and placed it in front of Harry on the grey interview table. Harry studied the picture for a few moments. 'It is certainly perfection but I don't understand how this has any connection with me,' he said as he pushed the paper back across the table, full of conviction.

Kay continued her interview strategy. She wanted Harry Holt to believe, for the present, that her sole concern was the conspiracy to destroy *'Perfection on the Rocks'*, so as to allow him to become even more arrogant and potentially to drop his guard. The prime objective of the interview, however, was to place Harry Holt in Captain Milano's apartment as she knew that the video of the intruder was not clear enough evidentially, nor was there any fingerprint evidence to connect him with the apartment. 'I will tell you what I think,' she said. 'You are just a cheap conman who took advantage of a susceptible young woman, Christina Alvear, and sought to persuade her that you were in a position to help her brother who was in prison, although I doubt whether you would be in a position to help an old lady cross the road.'

Harry bridled at the insinuation that he was a nobody. That was good, thought Kay. He controlled his anger – or at least tried to – but a twitch to his crooked smile gave away his anxiety. 'I would have thought that this ridiculous and unfounded allegation could have been quickly investigated by a sergeant, not a superintendent,' he countered, his twitch giving way to a smirk, 'if that is what you are.'

Kay was deliberately silent for a moment as if hurt by the slight, allowing her prisoner to believe that he had scored a little victory, before asking evenly: 'You are not denying the allegation?'

'Christina is not an unattractive woman I suppose, if you like that type of girl. But my politeness and courtesy to a waitress was misinterpreted by her. She followed me about. I wasn't interested in such a *plain Jane* and now she has clearly made up this ridiculous tale because I showed no romantic inclination towards her,' he explained so very plausibly.

'Mr Tovey,' asked Kay reasonably, 'is it really conceivable that a young lady from Spain, who has only been in the UK for a matter of months, would know anything about Nick Flynn?'

'Nick Flynn? Who is he?' he asked as if bewildered.

'You know nothing about Nick Flynn?'

'No,' he replied, adding unnecessarily, 'firstly it's "*Perfection on the Rocks*" and now a Mr Nick Flynn. Maybe you would tell me who this Nick Flynn is?'

Kay judged that Harry was now comfortable with his performance, and was more relaxed. Less alert. Less prepared. Now was Kay's moment. 'And I suppose, Harry, that you know nothing about breaking into and searching the apartment of Captain Nicholas Milano?'

Harry was caught completely off-guard by this sudden change of tact and the use of his true name. He cleared his throat nervously. 'You have me mistaken, officer. My name is Douglas Tovey.'

'No, Harry, I'm not mistaken,' affirmed Kay. 'You are Harry Holt and you broke into the apartment of Captain Nicholas Milano, didn't you?'

Harry's first instinct was to spontaneously lie. Always a mistake. 'Captain Milano. Who is Captain Milano?' It was a silly but impulsive response of a liar and he realised, too late, that it was. Harry's heart rate began to increase.

'Harry, you were living in Gibraltar at the time of Captain Milano's very splendid military funeral. It was in all the papers. *You* knew all about Captain Milano, didn't you?'

Harry Holt's heart rate increased again. He didn't like the emphasis that this Chinese officer had placed upon the word 'you'. He began to wonder if his beating heart was an internal combustion engine, the engine would probably blow a gasket. 'I recall something, now you mention it,' he answered. 'Yes, a military funeral, something like that.'

'So you are Harry Holt and not Douglas Tovey?'

'Okay, it's no big deal,' he replied, his words so likely. 'I very often use a different name when I travel and I'm interested in getting laid. I'm sure *you* understand,' he added in the hope of disconcerting her, but Detective Superintendent Yin was not disconcerted at all. Far from it. In fact, Harry should have been applying his full concentration upon what Kay Yin was saying, not trying to be clever and point score. And so, Harry was moments away from falling into a trap.

'And you don't recall breaking into his apartment?'

'I'm an estate agent, not a burglar.'

'But that's precisely what you are, Harry, a burglar.' Kay pressed a key on the computer and turned the screen towards Harry who eyed her warily. As he did so she continued. 'I am now showing the prisoner a clip of video, Exhibit JF14.' The screen illuminated to show a male entering Milano's apartment, closing the door and removing his bush hat. Kay froze the screen. And Harry froze too, not knowing that the remainder of the video footage equally lacked clarity. 'Harry,' continued Kay with absolute confidence, 'you seem to be so much more acquainted with Captain Milano and his apartment than you say. Do you want to offer an explanation as to why you were in his apartment?'

'Okay. Okay,' he replied reasonably as if chatting to his mates, 'everyone had read about Captain Milano's drowning and the military funeral, all pomp and ceremony, you know the thing. His address had been given in the papers and I reasoned that his apartment would be unoccupied. It presented me with an opportunity.'

Kay's face was expressionless, although she was more than pleased at Harry's confession that it was he who had entered the apartment. 'An opportunity for what, Harry?' she asked.

'He was a gambler and the rumour was that he had come into the possession of some rare stamps. I thought I might find them,' he lied.

'What stamps?'

Harry Holt responded quickly, deploying his ready-made and well-rehearsed explanation – all of which was totally untrue. 'Milano had apparently acquired a Registered Mail letter sent from Malta dated 1879, valued at about £750; a 1901 half-penny proof Edward VII, thought to be worth about £3,500; a 1901 penny Edward VII purported to be valued at £11,000 and, I think, yes, there was a 1902 one penny at £5,000. But I couldn't find them in the apartment.'

Harry had now further confirmed that it was he who had entered the apartment, but Kay continued as if the admission was of little relevance. 'But you had a good look?' she suggested.

'Yes, I did, but without success.'

'Well, Harry, I have to tell you that we've been having much more success than you. We have been having a good look, that is, at *your* apartment, Harry, with a great deal of success.'

For a moment Harry Holt was silent, his crooked smile replaced by an uneasy grin. He had anticipated that one day the police might search his home and, if they did, they would quickly locate his wall safe - a decoy, a distraction - placed in his wardrobe with the bundles of bank notes inside. £4,000. $7,500. €6,000. They would also find two International Driver's Licences in the names of Donald Haines and Leslie Owen – he'd found these and didn't have a clue who the two men were - and three gold watches. He hoped that if his apartment was searched, the police would be satisfied with such a find and be preoccupied with determining the ownership of the money and watches and waste their time attempting to trace Donald Haines and Leslie Owen. But DI James Frobisher had not been satisfied nor distracted. He discovered Harry's other hiding place under the gas-fired, imitation log fire grate.

'What do you mean?' asked Harry, his voice now strangely strained.

'A search warrant was executed on your Gibraltar apartment, Harry, and we have uncovered very clear evidence that you have been engaged in espionage on behalf of the Spanish with, let me see,' she said reading the sheet of paper handed to her with perfect timing by Inspector Purchell. 'Oh yes. Sergeant Dan Hinge, the colonel's clerk; Sofia Manaras, a cleaner employed at the barracks with particular responsibilities for the officers' quarters, and Mercedez Kemos, a typist in the Chief Minister's office.'

Harry knew the accuracy of what the superintendent was saying. It was damning. Now he decided to play his 'get me out of jail free' card. 'You have forgotten another?' he said with supreme smugness.

Kay looked at Peter Purchell as if confused, then spoke to Holt. 'Another, Harry? Is there another we have overlooked?'

'Oh, yes,' he answered with a smirk, his confidence restored, his heart rate lowered, 'there *is* a fourth.'

'A fourth? And can you tell us who that fourth person might be?'

'There's no *might* about it, Superintendent,' he mocked, pausing for affect, 'the fourth person was Captain Nicholas Milano.'

Kay turned to the inspector in feigned astonishment. 'Peter, was any evidence found to suggest that Captain Milano was spying on behalf the Spanish?'

Purchell made a pretence of looking through his file of papers, some of which he studied more closely than others or re-read a page. Apparently satisfied he said as if bemused: 'No, ma'am, no reference at all to Captain Milano.'

'You bastard,' responded Harry angrily, pointing at Peter Purchell, 'you bloody well removed it.'

Purchell remained poker faced and calm. 'Harry,' he said factually, 'the warrant was executed this morning at 5am and I flew in here on the 22nd.'

'And I have been here for ever, Harry,' contributed Kay with a smile.

Harry Holt, liar, bully, drug smuggler, killer and traitor, sat back and tried to make himself appear as comfortable as he could in his uncomfortable chair. He reviewed his options. It didn't take long. There were no options. Then Detective Superintendent Kay Yin spoke again.

'Let me tell you what is going to happen to you, Harry. Or is it José Torno? You will appear before the local magistrates tomorrow and then flown back to Gibraltar, courtesy of the RAF, where you will stand trial for espionage and burglary.' She stood up and collected her papers together. She looked towards Peter Purchell. 'This interview is concluded,' she said, '17:24.'

Inspector Purchell switched off the recording machine with a click, which was followed by a heavy silence, only broken when Kay spoke again. 'Before you are flown back to Gibraltar, Harry, some of our friends from the intelligence services will want to speak with you, although my judgement is that they won't find any use for you, and, as your forthcoming trial will be held in camera, no one will be taking any notice of your claim regarding Captain Milano. That said, I have not the slightest doubt that you will be found guilty and receive a very long sentence, maybe twenty years, which, I understand, you will very likely serve at Her Majesty's Prison, Dartmoor, here in the UK.'

Kay put her papers into her case and then continued. 'I've visited that prison twice, Harry. Quite a depressing experience, even for a visitor. It is very old and was built of local granite for Napoleonic prisoners of war in the early eighteen-hundreds. It is a forbidding place. The walls are grey and cliff-like. It is wet and cold and is often shrouded in mist … rather like the morning sea mist that can be found at the foot of Cabo Girāo.' She paused and fixed Harry Holt with her unnerving, penetrating dark eyes, which were met by a stare as if hypnotised. 'I believe you may be familiar with the waters around Cabo Girāo.'

At that moment, Harry Holt knew for certain. His future was sealed. The authorities would not be able to convict him of the murder of Captain Milano, but his conviction for espionage was an absolute certainty.

***

The phone on his desk rang. 'I'm sorry to interrupt you, sir,' said Miss Withers, 'Mrs Miller in on the line and is wondering if you have a moment for her.'

'Of course, put her through.' There was a quiet buzz then Maria was put through. 'Hullo, darling, how are things in Brussels?'

'The bureaucracy elegantly but frustratingly rolls on,' she replied, before getting to the crux of her call. 'Sorry to trouble you, but I've had that bloody woman on the phone again.'

'I guess you mean Anita Winters?'

'She rings me to talk about Italian cooking! I think she must have a cook book on her desk. She keeps telling me how disappointed she is when she visits Italian restaurants and wishes she could sample authentic, well-cooked food. I know what it is,' she said full of exasperation, 'she wants me to invite her here for dinner.'

'Look, I don't mind,' he said in a consolatory voice adding, jokingly: 'Why don't you invite her over and prepare a meal that is tasteless and really awful.'

'I can't do that, Christopher,' she said without humour as if her husband was unsympathetic to her plight.

'Of course you can't. I was joking,' he said. 'Just invite her. I can put up with her provided there's plenty of wine.'

'And you know what you are like after a few glasses of wine, you will nod off to sleep,' she said with mild censure born of past experience.

'Probably,' he admitted without concern.

'I don't seem to be able to shake her off, Christopher, and I don't want any unpleasantness when we are both so heavily involved with the Lord Mayor's charities.'

'It's okay,' he replied reassuringly. 'I understand.'

'Thank you. I'll find a date that suits.'

Chapter Thirty

Monday, 30th June.

Police Headquarters, Bristol, England.

DETECTIVE SUPERINTENDENT KAY YIN sat at the coffee table in Assistant Chief Constable Robert Perrin's office. She was up-dating him on events in Bournemouth.

'I think that we can assume that the museum plan was Nicholas Milano's idea.'

'How come?' he asked.

'Mark seized Milano's computer when he searched his apartment. The computer contained images of "*Perfection on the Rocks*" and details of the Russell-Cotes museum and Nick Flynn, very similar to those that Christina Alvear had with her.'

'And Nick Flynn did what?'

'Nick Flynn was a clumsy visitor to the Fitzwilliam Museum in Cambridge some time during early 2006. He stumbled down some stairs and knocked over a seventeen-century Qing Dynasty vase, which was completely shattered.'

'And what would be gained by Holt if Miss Alvear "stumbled" into "*Perfection on the Rocks*" and smashed it?'

'Even if an apparent accident, Christina would have been arrested for criminal damage until enquiries exonerated her. But she would never have been exonerated. She would have been found in possession of pictures of *"Perfection on the Rocks"*. She would have details of Nick Flynn on her laptop. Her note book would contain her written details of Commissioner Thornton and his Bournemouth address, and she would tell the court that she had been acting on behalf of Christopher Miller.'

'Destroying the porcelain would, I assume, increase the value of Miller's piece?'

'I've spoken to Christopher Miller,' replied Kay. 'He has been offered £2 million and estimates that if one of the remaining four should be broken then his would rise in value to between £5 and £7 million.'

'That much! exclaimed Robert Perrin, adding thoughtfully: 'And the Spanish press would, as Sir George put it, "twist the contents" to implicate Christopher Miller in a cheap scam, involving an innocent Spanish dupe to increase the value of his *"Perfection on the Rocks"*, along with his corrupt police friend, Huge Thornton, who would be conveniently in Bournemouth. All very neat.'

'Precisely. This could easily be portrayed in the Spanish press as a conspiracy between a corrupt Miller and a corrupt Thornton, who had become aware of *"Perfection on the Rocks"* whilst cynically enjoying all the benefits of the National Health Service in Bournemouth and the generous hospitality of the Dorset Police, a conspiracy involving their equally corrupt friend, the Chief Minister.'

Perrin nodded in agreement to the perceptive analysis. 'And you have prepared a draft report that I can send off to Sir George?'

'I have it here,' she said handing a copy across the table. 'I would suggest that Mark sends an identical report to the Chief Minister. Once you have approved the draft, I can send a copy to Mark, if you wish?'

'Okay,' he said, but acknowledging the protocols, added: 'although I think I should ask Mark to also approve the draft first. But thank you, Kay. And you say there is one, if not two skeletons, in the Milano cupboard?'

'Certainly one.'

'Go on, you know how I like to hear about family intrigues.'

'Captain Nicholas Milano's grandparents were both born in Gibraltar, the grandmother, Catherine, in 1914. Catherine married Charles Milano in 1934.'

'Who was Charles? What was his occupation?'

'He was in the wine trade.'

'Sorry, Kay. I'm interrupted you.'

'It's okay, sir.   There's intrigue and rumour, facts and innuendo at every turn.'

'Go on, Kay. I will try my best to keep quiet,' he said with little confidence.

'In 1936, Charles and Catherine had a son, David, who was Captain Milano's grandfather. During 1940 the family were evacuated from Gibraltar to Madeira. There were a number of options for evacuees at that time, namely, Madeira, Jamaica or England. For the Milanos, Madeira was an obvious choice as their uncle, Philip, lived there and was already extremely successfully involved in wine production on the island. At the time, that is 1940, there was a good deal of confusion in Madeira with the influx of evacuees; British men who had lived on the island for years returning to the UK to join up, leaving their wives and children behind; as well as unaccompanied mothers with children arriving on the island, and so, when in 1941, the Milanos appeared with a second child, a boy, Henry, no one seemed to take too much notice of this addition to the family.'

'Are there any official records confirming who Henry's parents were?'

'Oh, yes. A birth certificate shows that Catherine and Charles were the parents of Henry, but the rumour was that Charles had had an affair with a much younger woman, Cisca, his foreman's daughter, and that Henry was the product of this extra-marital relationship.'

'And Henry was simply adopted by the Milano family?'

'No, there was no need to formally adopt. Henry became an acknowledged member of the family, absorbed into the local community, and accepted by neighbours and friends.'

'But he was not accepted by Catherine?'

'No, he didn't appear to be. By one account, Catherine bitterly resented the child.'

'But the family kept together?'

'Yes, although Charles and Catherine often lived separate lives. This was not seen as indicative of a family rift,' she explained, 'more an understandable necessity because of his business commitments. As a result, Charles spent more and more time in Gibraltar, where he may have fathered another child. When the war ended in '45, Charles Anglicised his name to Miller. In 1959, Henry moved permanently to Gibraltar. He was fascinated by the tunnels created by the Royal Engineers and studied engineering at university. He later married and had one son, Christopher.'

'So Nicholas Milano and Christopher Miller were distant cousins?'

'It seems so.'

'You mentioned bitterness, any idea how that manifested itself?'

'Catherine resented Henry, which was probably understandable, but, as a result, directed her love and affection towards her son, David, who became the subject of her adoration. David married Grace. Grace and Catherine were very similar personalities and soon Catherine was able to contaminate Grace with her bitterness, particularly when David died early. Grace seems to have, in turn, directed her obsessive behaviour towards her own son, Nicholas, which became even more obsessive as she learned that Christopher was doing so well at school. Nicholas went to university as did Christopher, but Nicholas dropped out after a year, partly because Grace was possessive and encouraged him to return to run the family business.'

'And where she could control and dominate him, no doubt?' suggested Perrin.

'It seems so,' confirmed Kay. 'She completely doted on him. She spoilt him.'

'And the business, did that prosper?'

'It survived but the company lost its premier position on the island, mainly because Nicholas could easily become bored and he wasn't a businessman. Meanwhile, Christopher became a successful property entrepreneur and lawyer and tipped to be a future Chief Minister.'

'All fertile ground for the seeds of bitterness to flourish. Like crops in the field,' reflected Perrin, 'all that is needed is careful cultivation and encouragement, plus a few triggers, a political event, maybe, or the success of a competitor here or a financial crisis there.' Perrin sipped his coffee in deep thought. 'If Nicholas Milano planned to have Christopher Miller murdered, do you think that Grace was the driving force behind the plan?'

'I'm not sure that she was the driving force, but she might have wittingly or unwittingly encouraged her son.'

'And Grace Milano is back in Madeira?'

'Yes, although, interestingly, her behaviour is becoming more bizarre. You will recall that she was taking lots of photographs of memorials and statues in Gib. She has been doing the same in Madeira, but much more extreme.'

'Extreme. In what way?' inquired Perrin.

'Craven followed her to … ,' replied Kay who paused to check a report, ' … Nossa Senhora do Monte Church. It is where Charles, the last Emperor of Austro-Hungary is buried. Craven also followed her to the Santa Catarina Park where Grace was seen studying and photographing the memorial to the beautiful Empress Elizabeth of Austria who had been stabbed to death by an anarchist.'

'Not satisfied with studying local dignitaries in Gibraltar,' observed Perrin, 'she's now studying royalty in Madeira! Is this indicative of anything?'

'Craven has reported that Grace had often referred to Nicholas as being "like a saint", and Pope John Paul II did actually make Emperor Charles a saint.'

'Unbelievable! And does Grace Milano still meets with her normal, *earthly* friends in the café?

'Yes, although Craven thinks that her manner seems to have become strangely calmer and more aloof of late.'

'Maybe she has become even more deluded or has just accepted her son's death and her position.'

'I wonder which one, sir?'

Chapter Thirty-One

Saturday, 12th July.

Bristol, England.

THE HALLWAY TABLE HAD BEEN CLEARED of its flower arrangement consisting of Lisianthus, Cornflower, Alstromeria and Zinnia. The table was completely bare. Bare and inviting. They now had to wait for the front door bell of Grange Lodge to ring.

***

She arrived by taxi and stood, for a few short moments, at the front door. She steeled herself for the task ahead. Composed. Determined. Now she rang the doorbell as Christopher and Maria Miller were preparing the dinner of *bistecca di agnello* for their unwelcomed guest.

The bell sounded and the maid walked slowly along the hall and opened the bevelled glass front door.

'Good evening, madam,' Kay said to Grace Milano. 'Shall I take your coat?'

Mrs Milano had not anticipated the presence of a maid. But it wasn't important to her, she concluded, her eyes bright with intent. The police would believe that a burglar had killed all three. 'Of course,' she said with a distained expression as if the question was completely unnecessary and foolish. She didn't bother to look at a mere maid but quickly confirmed her knowledge, gleaned from *Country Life*, of the configuration of the hall, lounge and dining room beyond. She had planned and knew what she would do. Grace Milano would enter the dining room and confront Christopher and Maria Miller, the two people whose forefathers, she considered, had ruined her life and had been ultimately responsible for taking the life of her beloved son.

Grace placed her handbag on the bare hallway table and turned to face the front door so as to allow Kay to remove her coat from her shoulders.

'I understand, ma'am, that the main course is *bistecca di agnello*, a very pleasant lamb dish,' said Kay pronouncing the Italian words with a very liberal English interpretation.

Grace was minded not to reply, but felt the need to remind the maid of her position. 'I am fully aware of what *bistecca di agnello* is,' replied Grace in a contemptuous tone, pronouncing the dish's name perfectly. Grace waited for a few moments longer and could not understand why this silly maid had not taken her coat. Grace turned with an annoyed expression. As she did so, her expression changed from annoyance to sudden and uncontrolled rage.

'Oops,' said Kay as she held up the Forehand and Wadsworth revolver she had removed from Grace Milano's handbag and made safe.

As Superintendent Kay Yin lowered the weapon to her side, Inspector John Harding and Constable Fay Dunning emerged from the cloakroom to Kay's right and grabbed Grace's arms. But they had not seen the terrible anger in Grace Milano's eyes - eyes as hard as pebbles. And the officers were decent people, conscious that Grace Milano was seventy-one years of age, and so they failed to take hold of their prisoner firmly enough. An enraged Grace Milano broke free from the officers and burst through the open double-doors that led into the lounge, her rage giving her additional strength. PC Dunning was taken aback, stumbled at the lounge doors and fell to the floor as Kay sprang over the fallen officer, sprinting across the lounge between the Portland stone fireplace and the coffee table with its beautiful arrangement of flowers. As Grace reached the open double-doors of the dining room, Kay leapt onto Grace's back, fixing her left arm around the taller and older woman's neck, at the same time swinging both of her legs in the air so as to give her slight body weight some additional traction and brought Grace to the floor.

Grace Milano let out an animal-like, hysterical roar that seemed to wash over Christopher and Maria Miller and the three police officers as she desperately attempted to crawl and claw her way forward along the carpet. She managed to raise her left hand towards the dining room table and, for just a moment, yanked at the table cloth. Knives, forks and spoons clattered onto the carpet; dinner and side plates crashed into each other; wine glasses tumbled everywhere as *'Perfection on the Rocks'* was drawn towards the edge of the table, but the older woman had been winded and the physical effort became too much for her.

The two other officers quickly joined their superintendent and restrained and handcuffed their prisoner, a prisoner still shuddering with a terrible anger. They pulled Grace to her feet, an undignified spectacle, her beautiful dark hair disarranged, the exquisite pearls of her necklace scattered on the floor and one high-heeled black court shoe discarded.

Then Grace Milano looked down at *'Perfection on the Rocks'* as if this beautiful object of perpetual enchantment epitomised all that she despised. Grace's shoulders slumped as she recognised that her personal comfort and social status amongst the élite of Madeira and, the memorial she had hoped to have built in Gibraltar to commemorate her beloved son, were lost for ever.

But the jealousy and hatred still lingered. Grace Milano's knees seemed to buckle, and the officers had to support her as she sobbed hysterically.

Then she screamed haltingly at Christopher Miller: 'You … you ruined everything. You deserved to die. Did you know that? Die … along with your Italian whore. Why?' she raved as she leant forward and leered, 'because you are nothing … ' But her voice became strained, then lost, at the exertion.

Two uniformed officers arrived and Grace Milano was taken away, through the luxury of the lounge and hallway of Grange Lodge, to the awaiting police van with its bleak grilled windows and steel rear door. Once inside the vehicle, Grace stared out through the grill in the inner door, a bewildered stare of empty eyes, as the outer door was slammed shut on her last day of freedom.

Kay closed the front door of Grange Lodge, the scene of the cruel murder of an innocent, Guy Hernandez, and returned to the dining room and helped Maria collect up the pearls from the carpet. They moved *'Dirty Nell'* carefully away from the edge and repositioned her in the centre of the table, where she belonged, the beauty of the contours of her satin-bronzed body enhanced by the bright lights of the glistening chandelier above. Both Kay and Maria looked at this inanimate object of serenity and beauty which seemed to engender a strange calm, a calm that began to return to the house as if an unpleasant episode was ending for ever. But it would never really end. There would always be memories and reminders. And questions remained.

They went into the kitchen and Maria turned off the hobs and closed down the oven. Maria and Christopher would have little appetite for food. There was no triumph or congratulations, just subdued silence as they sat at the English farmhouse table until Maria spoke.

'Why the hatred?' she asked of neither of them in particular. 'Grace was still beautiful and so elegant. She was still financially comfortable. She had a highly respected name in Madeira and was a member of one of Gibraltar's most distinguished families. All of that has gone. Lost. And why?'

Christopher nor Kay answered. But Maria persisted searching, like many people do, for a rational explanation for irrational behaviour.   'You must have come across this sort of thing before, Kay?' she ventured.

'Yes.   Yes I have,' she replied, adding gently, 'but not so extreme.'

'And so, why?' she asked.

'I suspect that we will never know for certain,' replied Kay, not wishing to speculate and to be drawn into what was now essentially a family matter.

Maybe Maria Miller wanted Kay to exonerate her completely from any fault, and persisted.   'But you have a more complete understanding of this case than Christopher and I. Your perspective may help us understand.'

Kay thought that Maria probably didn't mean 'help us understand', more 'help me out'. There was no purpose in mentioning Maria's pre-marriage association with Nicholas Milano that later served to fan the flames of bitterness. Instead, Kay gave the explanation that she would give to young detectives to help them better understand motive.

'From what I can gather, it was bitterness without any real foundation.' She reflected for a moment on human nature. 'Grace Milano's family members appeared to possess the usual human frailties of most families, but these were exacerbated by the uncertainties of wine growing and the trauma of divorces and unfaithfulness. We all compensate for our inadequacies,' she said charitably, 'mostly in harmless ways, but it seemed that Grace and Nicholas compensated for theirs with arrogance and unjustified superiority, enflamed over the years by Grace's mother, resulting in murder.'

'But, as you say, we all have inadequacies.' Christopher remarked.

'Yes, that is very true, but most of us cope with those understandable failings by recognising realistic expectations, by refocusing, by hard work or even engaging in extreme sports - something like that anyway. But not murder.'

There was a sombre stillness in the kitchen, with Christopher and Maria thoughtful, thinking of their lives, the events of the last weeks – years even.

'How did you know that Grace was so involved?' asked a grateful Maria eventually, breaking the silence.

'It wasn't that difficult,' she replied modestly. 'Nicholas Milano was on a Special Branch "watch list" and when Grace Milano flew into Bristol on the 9th July, her surname was immediately red flagged. We knew that her son had visited Whiteladies Road on the 8th April and we had some bank CCTV footage. When Grace left the airport she was followed by a Special Branch team and yesterday she visited the same bank in Whiteladies Road. When she left the bank she was seen to be carrying a small box, a box that appeared to be of the dimensions of a presentation case that had contained two Forehand and Wadsworth pistols purchased by Nicholas from an antique shop in Hay-on-

Wye. We had already recovered one of these pistols from the Avon Gorge after the murders of Guy Hernandez and Victor Jenkins. When the recovered pistol was examined by forensics, no fingerprints or DNA were found, but, around the heads of two of the screws was found traces of Soya-Ceramide SPF 15 by L'Oréal. It's L'Oréal's *"age perfect skin care"* product,' she explained. 'Your skin is flawless, Maria.' Maria Miller smiled at the compliment. 'You certainly wouldn't use this cream but Grace Milano would very likely do so and, in the guest bedroom of her son's apartment in Gibraltar, Mark had found a jar of the product. We were certain that she had handled both weapons. We had Grace under surveillance in Madeira and Gibraltar for some time and her conduct sounded warning bells. We had to assume that her eagerness to be invited to your home for supper tonight was not motivated by friendship.'

'All this bitterness,' murmured Maria, a sadness in her voice.

'A bitter inheritance,' Christopher Miller answered reflectively, 'of perceived betrayals, a failing family business and diminishing status.'

'But also a deadly inheritance of hatred, don't you think?' observed Kay.

****

Epilogue

One year on.

CHIEF SUPERINTENDENT MARK FARADAY MBE returned to the Severnside Police and resumed command of the Bristol City Division. He received an illuminated Certificate of Appreciation from the Chief Minister of Gibraltar.

DETECTIVE SUPERINTENDENT KAY YIN continued her duties as part of HQ Major Crime Division.

SIR GEORGE SINCLAIR KCMG retired from the Foreign and Commonwealth Office and now lives in Allington, Wiltshire with his wife, Lady Ann, and their three chickens: Mabel, Alison and Claire.

CHIEF CONSTABLE EMILY WOODLAND CBE QPM retired from the Force and is now enjoying her retirement near Hayle in Cornwall with her two faithful Border Collies: Bonnie and Clyde.

DEPUTY CHIEF CONSTABLE ANITA WINTERS applied for the post of Chief Constable. She was not short-listed. She retired prematurely, somewhere, embittered.

ASSISTANT CHIEF CONSTABLE ROBERT PERRIN QPM was encouraged by the Chief Constable to apply for the post of DCC. He declined and continues to enjoy his role as ACC (Crime).

COMMISSIONER HUGH THORNTON CPM returned to Gibraltar and resumed his duties as head of the Force. His chemotherapy and stem cell transplant were successful and he is now in remission.

SIR CLIFFORD AMANDA continues as Gibraltar's Chief Minister.

CHISTOPHER MILLER was appointed Chair of the Economic Development Board. He has retained Grange Lodge in Bristol but now lives in Gibraltar and is tipped to be a future Chief Minister.

MARIA MILLER resigned from her EU post and now lives in Gibraltar with her husband. They are expecting their first child in two months' time.

HARRY HOLT aka JOSÉ TORNO aka DOUGLAS TOVEY was considered by MI6 to be too unpredictable and unreliable for 'turning'. He was found guilty of espionage and burglary and is currently serving a sentence of eighteen years' imprisonment at Her Majesty's Prison, Dartmoor, England.

CHRISTINA ALVEAR was not charged with any offences and has since been appointed Head Waitress at the Hotel Miramar.

GARCIA ALVEAR had never been assaulted whilst serving his sentence in Valdemoro Prison. An exemplary prisoner, he is likely to be released early next year.

GRACE MILANO was charged with Conspiracy to Murder and Unlawful Possession of a Part One Firearm, but found unfit to enter a plea. She never stood trial and is currently detained at Rampton Secure Hospital under the provisions of Part III of the Mental Health Act 1983 as a result of her 'dangerous, violent or criminal propensities'.

Author's Notes

'Dirty Nell' (aka 'Perfection on the Rocks'): *fact (although not exhibited in the Metropolitan Museum of Art, New York or the Russell-Cotes Museum, Bournemouth. However, the author has one, but valued at only £1,000, unfortunately not £2,000,000!).*

SS 'Mobile': *fact (including details of her captain and passengers).*

Herbert and Isaac Smith: *fact (the author's great-grandfather and great-uncle).*

Grange Lodge: *fiction.*

Young and Son: *fiction.*

Stockley, Kray and Burgess: *fiction.*

Fraser Security: *fiction.*

Avon Gorge Hotel: *fact (staff: fiction).*

Forearm and Wadsworth *Hammerless* .38 revolver: *fact.*

Patterson's Circus: *fiction.*

Society of Merchant Venturers: *fact.*

Greaves, Scutt and Pinnock: *fiction.*

Clifton Suspension Bridge: *fact.*

Liquid Metal Coating: *fact.*

Fairbairne-Sykes Fighting Knife: *fact.*

'Heaven on Earth': *fiction.*

'Glover of Clifton': *fiction.*

Queen's Chambers: *fiction.*

'Waiting for the Verdict': *fact (but the property of The Tate, London).*

Gibraltar – World War Two Evacuation: *fact.*

Great Siege of Gibraltar 1779-1783: *fact.*

General Antonio Barceló y Pont de la Terra: *fact.*

4th Duc de Crillon: *fact.*

General Sir George Eliott, 1st Baron Heathfield (Military Governor of Gibraltar)**:** *fact.*

Colonel Henry Bartolomeu Milano: *fiction.*

Certificate of Lunacy: *fact (the author has this one hanging in his study!).*

SS 'Ulster Monarch': *fact.*

Speedwell Deep Pit: *fact.*

Police Staff College: *fact (although now known as The College of Policing).*
Bristol Constabulary: *fact.*
Severnside Police: *fiction.*
Fire Brigade Rocks Rescue Recovery Unit: *fact.*
Foreign and Commonwealth Office (King Charles Street, Westminster): *fact.*
Special Branch: *the unit responsible, within UK police forces, for gathering intelligence and mounting operations in respect of the protection of the State.*
MI5: *the UK's domestic counter-intelligence Security Service.*
MI6: *the UK's foreign Secret Intelligence Service.*
'tell': *a person's unconscious change in behaviour or demeanour.*
Royal Gibraltar Regiment: *fact.*
Pushtu language: *fact.*
Spanish colonel's rank insignia: *fact.*
Spanish Cross of Military Merit: *fact.*
'obit': *fact.*
Major Herbert Rowse Armstrong: *fact.*
Reid's (aka Belmond Reid's Palace Hotel): *fact.*
Ouzzazate: *fact.*
Sercicio de Vigilancia Aduarera: *the Spanish Customs Surveillance Service, particularly responsible for the prevention and investigation of drug smuggling and money laundering.*
Centro de Inteligencia de las Fuerzas: *the joint intelligence department of Spain's army, navy and air force.*
Cabo Girão: *fact.*
Captain João Gonçalves Zarco: *fact.*
Casino da Madeira: *fact (staff: fiction).*
Hay's Antique Emporium: *fiction.*
Plazas de soberandid: *fact.*
El Cid: *fact.*
King's Chapel, Gibraltar: *fact.*
Hotel Miramar: *fact (fiction: staff).*
Nick Flynn: *fact.*
Fitzwilliam Museum: *fact.*
Sir Merton Russell-Cotes: *fact.*

Russell-Cotes Museum: *fact.*
Royal Bath Hotel: *fact.*
Jigsaw Building: *fact.*
HM Prison, Dartmoor: *fact.*
Valdemoro: *Spanish civil prison, Madrid.*
Centre Penitenciari de Mallorca: *Spanish civil prison, Palma, Mallorca.*
Soya-Ceramide SPF15: *fact.*
Charles I, Emperor of Austro-Hungary: *fact.*
Empress Elizabeth of Austria: *fact.*
Rampton Secure Hospital: *fact.*

The first *Mark Faraday Collection* crime novel

International intrigue and brutal murder

DIRTY Business

by Richard Allen

IN THE ABSENCE OF HIS SUPERINTENDENT, Chief Inspector Mark Faraday takes command of the Bristol Central District just as MI6 move in to conduct a covert and unauthorised surveillance operation on his District. To make matters worse, Faraday is required to share his office with the beautiful Helen Cave of MI5.

But when one of Faraday's best young officers is murdered an intricately woven plot is uncovered involving secret bank accounts and a dissident Irish terrorist group.

From County Wicklow and the rarefied atmosphere of an exclusive London club to Salisbury Plain and the streets of Bristol, and against a background of brutal murder and international intrigue, a deadly clock is ticking as Mark Faraday and Helen Cave race against time to prevent the nuclear devastation that threatens the West Country.

Available as eBook or paperback direct from
www.amazon.com or www.amazon.co.uk

The second *Mark Faraday Collection* crime novel

Heartless murder and ruthless self-interest

DIE Back

by Richard Allen

WHEN SUPERINTENDENT MARK FARADAY defies orders and begins to investigate the disappearance of a local lorry driver, a top secret US and UK intelligence operation, designed to destroy the poppy fields of Afghanistan, is unwittingly undermined.

As Faraday is drawn deeper in to the secret world of intelligence, he confronts his own senior officers and law enforcement agencies, cynical self-interest and murder.

From the splendour of the House of Lords and the beauty of the Venetian palazzos to the vastness of the deserts of Western Australia, Mark Faraday relentlessly pursues his investigation, haunted by the murder of one colleague and mesmerised by the beauty of another.

Available as eBook or paperback direct from
www.amazon.com or www.amazon.co.uk

The third *Mark Faraday Collection* crime novel

Treachery casts a long and deadly shadow

Darker than DEATH

by Richard Allen

THE DEATH OF A RESPECTED BRISTOL ARTIST is written-off as the unfortunate consequences of an apparently bungled burglary by an unknown opportunist. But at Police Headquarters, Superintendent Mark Faraday is not so easily convinced.

As Faraday, with DCI Kay Yin, investigate the death, he begins to uncover a web of betrayal and dishonesty that stretches from the battlefields of the Great War and an abattoir in the small Belgian village of Boesinghe in November 1914, to the very heart of present-day British government and the headquarters of the United Nations in New York, oblivious to the betrayal and dishonesty that stalks him in his own headquarters, where loyalty by many is fleeting and deceit by some corrupting.

Available as eBook or paperback direct from
www.amazon.com or www.amazon.co.uk

The fourth **Mark Faraday Collection** crime novel

Espionage, treason and callous murder

In the DARKEST of Shadows

by Richard Allen

WHEN DETECTIVE CHIEF INSPECTOR KAY YIN attends the scene of a fatal car accident, she finds one body with two identities.

At the mortuary, Kay, together with Detective Superintendent Mark Faraday of Special Branch, discover more anomalies about the Ministry of Defence researcher. Who is this man? Why the double identity? What had been his role? What had he been doing? Where had he been? Where was he going and why?

The officers pursue their enquiries which take the reader from Bristol to The Pentagon in Washington, from Rome to the US Embassy in London, from Gibraltar to Bonavista, and from the savage shores of the Costa da Morte to the tranquillity of England's south coast, where they will encounter murder and a callous assassin, treason and double-dealing.

But, Mark Faraday and Kay Yin's dogged search for answers will be concealed in the darkest of shadows by Britain's MI5 and GCHQ, America's National Security Agency and the Office of Naval Intelligence, where deception and duplicity are common place and truth an inconvenience and an illusion.

Available as eBook or paperback direct from
www.amazon.com or www.amazon.co.uk

Printed in Poland
by Amazon Fulfillment
Poland Sp. z o.o., Wrocław